WRESTLING WITH PIGS

Roy W. Frusha

Dancing Fox Publishing

ENDORSEMENTS OF WRESTLING WITH PIGS

"Roy Frusha pens an exciting tale of narcotics agents that is covered with craziness and humor. It is an artfully written work of fiction from an author who has lived the life."

Dr. Gary Copes
Former Chief of Police
Lafayette, LA

"Region II Narcotics took the war on drugs to the streets of Acadiana removing major drug dealers and millions of dollars worth of illegal drugs off the streets. They risked their lives every day."

Phil Haney
District Attorney for the 16th Judicial District
St. Marinville, LA

"LSP Narcotics was the greatest time I had in 30 years of law enforcement. Long hours and hard work were rewarded with a sense of pride and accomplishment. We were the thin blue line."

Sheriff "Bud" Torres
Point Coupee Parish (LSP Ret.)

"They were a special breed of dedicated and productive police officers. As an original member of the LSP 'Dirty Dozen' I salute Captain Roy Frusha for continuing the job. Wrestling with Pigs is a book some former troopers did not want written."

Sheriff Louis Ackal
Iberia, Parish (LSP Ret.)

"Captain Frusha was an excellent Marine, deputy and trooper."

Chief Toby Hebert
LSP Ret. (First commander of LSP Narcotics)

"The life of a narcotics agent is always that he is 'ready to go.' It is difficult on family life and a danger to the officer. However, as challenging as it is, it is also very rewarding to know that your work and efforts are contributing in making our community safer. A good narcotics team must trust each other and know their colleagues are knowledgeable and diligent in their work. In working alongside Roy for a number of years, Roy was always diligent, a quick learner, and very assertive. He could also be stubborn at times. However, we could always count on Roy to get the job done. He was an asset to our team. His literary contribution proves compelling through firsthand experiences."

Sheriff Ronny Theriot
St. Martin Parish (LSP Ret.)

"A narc is not a hero, and his job is not for glamour or fame, which describes Roy Frusha."

Sheriff Mike Couvillion
Vermilion Parish

WRESTLING WITH PIGS

ISBN: 978-0-9830429-3-8

Printed in the United States.

ACKNOWLEDGEMENTS

Wrestling with Pigs is respectfully dedicated to our young men and women in the military. Your job is similar to police work in that you know what it is to experience debilitating periods of boredom followed by abrupt intervals of pure adrenaline. You are our hope for a better America. Thank you for your service, and "Semper Fi."

Thanks to Carlene Domingue for helping with grammar and French. Also to local writer Chere Coen for advice. The cover picture is compliments of Russell Ancelet (LSP retired), a former supervisor in the narcotics section. The group pic is by Daily Advertiser photographer Peter Piazza, when we were all having a lot more fun than we do now. The back cover pic is by Brooke Beduze.

My special thanks to the men and women who shared the narc life with me, and for the anecdotes they produced.

"Think where man's glory most begins and ends....my glory was that I had such friends." William Butler Yeats

When I retired from law enforcement my wife asked me what I was going to do. I replied that I might write a book. "Oh my God," she said. "Will I have to move from Lafayette?" I hope the book isn't quite that embarrassing for her, and that she understands that it is fiction. Teresa Meaders Frusha has been with me for thirty years now, and I realize that it was sometimes tense living with a spouse whose occupation was law enforcement.

Last, thanks to Captain Gabriel Austin Frusha, honor graduate of the Louisiana School for Math, Science and the Arts, merit scholar, United States Air Force Academy graduate and exemplary pilot. You made old dad proud. It's never easy being the son of a Marine.

PROLOGUE

The tug and barge pushed quietly up the Four-Mile Cutoff Canal under a rising half moon, headed north from the rolling swells of the Gulf of Mexico into the idle, marshy flat bayous of South Louisiana. It was seven o'clock at night when they passed the faded, deteriorating fishing boats docked at Intracoastal City. The sun had not fully set and heat could be seen rising off the bayou like steam from a tea kettle. A few lights shined from the unpainted cypress camps with rusty tin roofs scattered along the canal. The tug captain's face was cheerless and worn from too much time in the sun. He watched Brown Pelicans flying close above the water looking for mullet and other fish that may venture too close to the top.

The tug captain, a large man with rural Slavic features, was from the Florida Keys. He wore a faded straw hat and khaki work clothes. He had a gruff and gregarious appearance, but was educated in the ways of the world. He observed his lone deck hand walking about the barge, checking coiled ropes. The deck hand, known only as Pete, wore a thin, black mustache that curved at the ends. His arms and shoulders were lean and brown from a lifetime of working outdoors.

The captain smiled and said, "You look like an old fucking elf."

Neither man knew exactly what the barge contained, nor did they care to know. They were paid in cash, half in advance, and knew, for their own personal safety, not to ask questions.

They passed several abandoned oil wells and waved at derrick hands on nearby drilling rigs working high above the Gulf waters. In the distance, crows cawed from dead cypress limbs. Except for the crows the only sounds were the soft hum of the tug's engine and the gentle ripple of the brackish water as they moved toward Vermilion Bayou. The captain checked his watch, noting that he was on schedule.

Egrets and herons hovered nearby as he stopped the barge for registration at the Freshwater Bayou Locks near the Louisiana coast. It was the only way to get the barge into the Intracoastal Canal. The captain did as he had been ordered, and listed the tug as the "Bulldog," and the barge as the "Lion." It was mid-June, 1983, and there was nothing suspicious about either vessel. It was just one of many barges having come from the Intracoastal Canal, traveling north, delivering supplies to inland oil rigs that were common along the marshy coastal waters of Southwestern Louisiana.

The captain was experienced with tugs, but it would be his first time attempting to navigate the narrow canals and bayous of South Louisiana. He checked his compass and maps once more as he slowly pushed his way across the Vermilion Bay and into the mouth of Vermilion Bayou. The further north he pushed the tighter the curves and the more narrow the bayou became. The sun was setting. Blue-black clouds moved in, and the heat turned into a light mist, rising and enveloping the dark bayou. To the west lightning made a crisscross pattern among the thunderheads.

The river banks were lined with four hundred-year-old swamp cypress trees that were giving way to forests of chicken trees which seemed to monopolize the area. Chicken trees were known to survive shade, full sunlight, flooding, or drought, and in some cases, fire. It was hot and there was little wind to cool the captain or his deck hand. On a nearby bank, a lone red fox lifted his head and watched the barge go by as he ate a swamp rat.

"The only value to this cheerless, humid oven is oil and gas," the captain said to the elf, as many sets of eyes blinked at them from the river bank.

"I suppose that most of the white eyes are frogs and such," said the elf, "but I'm not sure about the orange ones."

"Those are gators," answered the captain. "Look at the fuckers swimming toward us. They have a brain the size of a pea, but they somehow know they are at the top of the food chain in this part of the world."

"Do you think they have giant snakes here?" asked the elf, shivering.

"No doubt they have some badass snakes in these parts. When the oil field is dead, there is nothing here except ancient creatures that have crawled upon the earth for centuries," the captain answered.

The captain returned his attention to the bayou and straightened the tug and barge. He passed occasional signs identifying names of canals feeding into the bayou. He noted that the signs were filled with bullet holes. A lone Cajun fisherman could be seen at the far end of a canal in a cypress pirogue hunting for bass, goggle-eye and mud cat, where no one else could, or would, venture to fish.

He slowed the tug and strained his eyes to see the mud-covered banks. A half moon had been sufficient, but now dark grey clouds were forming over the rising air currents. He knew instinctively the clouds were cumulus, and that if they moved to a higher level it would bring rain.

The old tug, which would soon be abandoned, was not air conditioned and mosquitoes entered the cabin in droves, so thick they resembled a cloud. "When God was making the world, on the seventh day He must have gotten tired and just dumped the leftovers here." The captain's khaki shirt was wet with sweat and stuck to his back. Horse flies bit him through the thick cotton.

Then the rain came. "This is no Presbyterian rain either," he said to the elf. "Like my mother used to say, this is a by-God Baptist cleansing."

The captain and the elf stood together in the tug and watched small frogs jumping on the deck of the barge, giving it the appearance of raining frogs.

The captain slowed the tug almost to a stop and strained to see the river banks. The air was putrid with the odor of decaying plants. "Everything here smells like rotting fish," the elf said.

"What you smell is mostly sulfur escaping from the brackish water."

"It's really getting dark out there," the elf said.

"I'm not afraid of the dark," responded the captain. "It's what lives in the dark I'm scared of."

As the night descended, hordes of mosquitoes attacked, beginning with the flesh around the ankles, working their way up

3

their trousers. The captain decided to move the barge closer to the bank and wait out the rain when the tug developed clutch problems. He knew he could no longer negotiate the tight curves of the bayou.

"Now what?" he said to the elf, as he stopped the engines and used his walkie talkie to contact the man he had met briefly in Florida.

"Boss," the captain said, "we have engine problems and I can't get the barge to Banker unless I can get a mechanic to work on the tug. I'm shutting it down."

"Are you okay?" Leigh Ray Starwood asked, sensing the fear in his voice.

"I'm surrounded by cottonmouths, alligators, and mosquitoes big as black birds. My deck hand is so nervous you couldn't drive an eight penny nail up his ass. He's shaking like a dog trying to pass a peach seed, and you want to know if I'm okay?"

"Don't panic," replied Starwood. "I have a backup plan. I always have a contingency plan. Stand by where you are."

The captain relaxed some, and thought about his old job of chartering fishing boats for rich people in Key West. He had been paid fifty thousand up front for this trip, and would be paid another fifty thousand upon its conclusion. With that kind of money he could buy his own boat, relax for a few years, drink beer at the Green Parrot in Key West, and chase the young Russian girls who flocked there by the dozens.

Starwood was stationary at the Lafayette Regional Airport, about thirty miles north of the tug. As always, he had a backup plan. He looked at a map of Vermilion Bayou, called Broussard Brothers Oil Field Service Company, and requested a tug to tow the Lion and Bulldog the rest of the way to its final destination, which was Fontenot's Shipyard, near a backwoods abandoned crossroads known as Banker. The conversation with the tug captain had not lasted more than five minutes. Within another five minutes, he had someone en route to Broussard Brothers with a cash payment.

The sun was just rising over the marsh when the Bulldog and Lion arrived at Fontenot's Shipyard. They were hastily tied to the docks, and the Broussard Brothers tug departed. Almost immediately fifty husky men descended upon the barge and began utilizing the waiting cherry pickers to offload its contents into ten

4

tractor-trailer rigs, each capable of carrying eighty thousand pounds.

Men with guns and hand held radios in small aluminum bateaus moved into position on the river north and south of the dock in case a fisherman or crabber stumbled upon the operation. Other than the river, there was only one entrance into the shipyard, and it was a long shell driveway, at the end of which was a locked and guarded gate.

Starwood and his beautiful, leggy female pilot had taken off from the Lafayette airport and were now circling the shipyard in a twin engine Aero Commander. The operation was back on track and only slightly behind schedule. It was early Saturday morning, and they had to be finished by Sunday night. As with all of Starwood's operations, it was detail-oriented and well-organized. He had structured an organization that was part military and part corporate business; it could have been designed by an MIT business professor. He had learned from the best; he did not waste his years in Army Intelligence in South America.

"This is a worth a lot more than the lousy two hundred and fifty thousand a year I was making selling drugs in Houston," Starwood said to Sherry Cox, his young and talented pilot. Cox, who was sitting in the left seat of the cockpit, was five feet six inches tall, had long straight blondish hair that hung over tan shoulders. She wore short cut-off denim jean shorts and a white tee shirt that did little to hide her smallish breasts. Five years later, a fuel truck driver at the Lafayette Regional Airport would be able to identify her in a photo lineup saying, "She looked like a James Bond girl."

"How lucrative will this one be?" Sherry asked.

"My share will be fifty million, more or less," Starwood said, as they circled the shipyard and observed the cherry pickers unloading the barge and placing the bales on rollers. "Vince will get the same amount."

"What are you going to do with all that money?"

"The first item will be to purchase a Lear jet. Can you fly it?"

"I can learn," she replied, smiling. "We have an auto pilot on the Aero Commander, want to join the mile high club?" She removed her flimsy tee shirt, unbuckled her seat belt and harness, leaned over the console and unzipped Starwood's trousers.

CHAPTER 1
The Dopers

Leigh Ray Starwood was eight years old when his father left him and his mother to fend for themselves in a run down South Houston trailer park. The neighborhood was primarily Hispanic, but there were African Americans and a few Asians in the area. Black teenagers sold drugs out of empty trailers, or used them to pimp out women. Many of the trailers had broken windows that were patched with duct tape. Leigh and his mother lived in a two-bedroom, one-bath dwelling at the edge of the park that could hardly be called a mobile home. His mother kept plastic buckets scattered about the trailer to catch the water that dripped through the ceiling when it rained. There was no air conditioning and very little furniture.

Leigh knew little about his father, other than he had been a Merchant Marine, and was gone more than he was home. Then one day, he just never came back. Leigh's mother found a job as a cashier in a nearby convenience store, and eight-year-old Leigh had gone to work cleaning floors and equipment at one of the many pawn shops that occupied every other block in South Houston. When other kids went to play after school, Leigh grabbed a quick snack from his trailer fridge and walked to the pawn shop where he worked until six p.m.. On weekends, he worked eight hour days.

He knew he was different from the other students at the local primary school. He was tall, had light skin with a reddish tint, thick sand-colored hair and large blue eyes. Most of his classmates were black or Hispanic. All of the workers and most of the patrons at the pawn shop were Mexicans. By the time Leigh was ten years old, he was fluent in Spanish. He walked the short distance to the school, never missing a day, even when he was sick. He understood that an education was a path out of the trailer park. Good grades came easy for him and he absorbed every course of instruction with enthusiasm. At the pawn shop he immersed himself in people and personalities, and found he could get along with all types, especially the adults.

By the time he was twelve, Leigh became impatient to make more money. His language skills were invaluable at the shop. He learned how to repair equipment, bargain with customers, conduct sales, collect money, make bank statements and keep accurate records. He knew that most of the goods that the Mexicans brought in were stolen, but he didn't care. It was all about making money.

There were always drugs present in the park. Marijuana, cocaine, methamphetamine and heroin were plentiful. Overweight women and broken-down old men were regulars at pain clinics and doctor's offices all over Houston. They obtained pain killers by the hundreds that were paid for by the government and turned them over for twenty-five dollars a pill, except for the ones they washed down with cheap whiskey. Money and drugs traded hands twenty-four seven in the park.

At thirteen, Leigh began purchasing small amounts of marijuana and cocaine from the Mexicans that hung around the shop. He sold it to older kids at his school and to customers he had developed at the shop. He never stole a piece of equipment or a nickel from the register, but selling drugs was a way of life, and there was good money in it.

Leigh turned seventeen and began his senior year in high school. On weekends, he transported trunk loads of marijuana across the border from Mexico. He had purchased a small home in a decent neighborhood and an automobile for his mother. He was impatient to move on, and though near the top of his class, he quit school, obtained a GED and got his mother to sign for him to join the Army. He could have had numerous scholarships to college, but he did not want to be a scholar. He wanted to be rich.

The Army provided a whole new level of education for Leigh. He excelled in boot camp and scored high on a battery of standardized tests. He learned to stand ramrod straight and carry himself with a new level of confidence. He emulated the officers and developed social skills. He was respectful of his superiors and got along well with co-workers. He became engrossed in the Army as he had in the pawn shop. He developed a reputation that he knew would get him promoted and into a meaningful job that he could use to his advantage. The Army taught Leigh that his body and mind were capable of much more than he had ever realized. It was a free education in learning how to organize, manipulate, and control people and events. He knew he was capable of conceptual thought, and the Army would provide all the training necessary.

Leigh was barely nineteen when the Army promoted him to buck sergeant and transferred him to INSCOM (Army Intelligence and Security Command) as a communications specialist at Fort Sam Houston in San Antonio. After four months in Texas, the section commander walked into Leigh's office and informed him he was being transferred for the good of the Army.

"Where am I going?"

"Sergeant Starwood," said the commander, "you speak Spanish fluently and you have demonstrated tremendous organizational and administrative skills. The Army needs you in its CDB Unit down in Colombia."

"No problem, sir," said Leigh, standing erect before the commander. "If you don't mind me asking, what is CDB?"

"CDB is the Army's Counter Drug Brigade. Your MOS, master occupational specialty, is technically that of a communications specialist, but your job down south will be to assist in analyzing data concerning Columbian drug cartels, developing sources of information and forecasting intentions and events concerning those cartels."

"Sounds interesting," said Leigh, squirming slightly, barely containing his excitement at the prospect of learning how international drug smuggling organizations worked.

"It's a very important assignment," said the colonel, "but you've earned it, and we feel you are the best person for the job."

Except for the humidity, Leigh thought the weather in Bogota, Colombia may have been the same as San Diego, California. Magnolia and cashew trees provided shade for the various orchids that surrounded the buildings that had been rented by the Army. They worked side by side with Colombian intelligence analysts translating stacks of reports for the officers. He routinely read reports and inserted information into intelligence systems for dissemination to other government agencies such as DEA, FBI and CIA.

As always Leigh immersed himself in his work, studying local newspapers, watching Colombian television, and listening to local radio stations. During the day, he learned how the major Colombian drug networks were sending illicit narcotics to the United States via civilian shipping containers and commercial air carriers. In the evenings, he ventured into town, watching small-time drug dealers pushing their products openly on the streets. He soon learned that only a small portion of drugs scheduled for the states were intercepted.

Six months after beginning his new assignment, Leigh was again promoted, this time to staff sergeant. He was given a new position as a full-time assistant to the Army's Intelligence Officers at the Counter Drug Brigade. The position included top secret clearance and a place at the table when intelligence briefings were given. It was in these briefings that Leigh learned which cultures were friendly or hostile, what political assignments were made by the United States in South America, and what a country's military capabilities may be. He learned about adversary intent, but more importantly, he learned about smuggling networks. His group assisted in tracking illegal armed groups that participated in the drug trade, which organizations were less violent and which organizations seldom got caught. He intently studied the organizational structure of all of them.

It was during this assignment that Leigh learned about Panamanian President Manuel Noriega. Noriega was one of the many recipients of the daily intelligence reports that Leigh disseminated, but Leigh also noted that Noriega was the subject of other reports, naming him as being associated with major drug cartels.

"Captain," Leigh asked one day, "can you tell me why we are sending intelligence reports to the President of Panama?"

"No problem," answered the captain. "You have top level clearance, and you are a valuable member of our team. As such, you should know how things work. Some years back, in 1967 to be exact, the U.S. Army trained Noriega in intelligence and counter intelligence techniques at Fort Gulick in the Panama Canal Zone. We also trained him in psychological operations at Fort Bragg, North Carolina."

"Why?"

"Well, I realize it is somewhat of an enigma. The army knows Noriega is a double agent. We think he is giving information to Taiwan, Israel, and maybe even to Communist Cuba, but the United States is willing to turn a blind eye to his corruption and drug dealing because he is our double agent. The CIA uses him, though we are not privy as to how they use him. I guess they have their reasons."

Leigh thought about the information and would put it to good use within five years, after he was out of the military and after meeting a future associate called Vince.

Michael Vincent Vargo, known to family and friends as "Vince," was born in Detroit to a devoutly Catholic mother in an upper middle class neighborhood. He was a throw-back to his Russian heritage. Vince's head was overly large for his body. He was short and husky, a raw-boned kid with a hoarse voice and a pug nose. Even at an early age, with broad shoulders and short, muscular legs, he looked like a prize fighter. His dark brown hair was so thick there was little space between his eyebrows and hairline. When people looked at him, he made it a point to never blink first.

Vince's mother doted over him, sending him to the best Catholic schools in Detroit. Vince was smart, but he was also stubborn, lazy, and mean. He resented teachers telling him what to do, and he resented classmates who were attentive and wanted to learn. He was often angry, and he took his anger out on his classmates. By the time he entered the ninth grade, he weighed almost two hundred pounds and had the features of a much older person. He had also been expelled from three schools for fighting, disrespect toward teachers, and possession of drugs.

The best Catholic schools meant that most of the parents, and subsequently the kids, had money. Vince was twelve when he started dealing marijuana to upper class students. When he was seventeen he was making enough money to purchase expensive clothes and a motorcycle and have plenty of cash to spend on girls, who as a rule did not care for his rough appearance and demanding attitude. Vince had become a conspicuous and flashy school yard bully with the look and attitude of a mafia boss. He relished in his reputation.

His flamboyant lifestyle was not lost on his parents. His father was afraid of him, and his mother covered for Vince, defending him, constantly begging him to be a good boy.

"Every decision you make leads to consequences and eventually to yet more consequences," his priest counseled. "Poor decisions lead to more poor decisions, and the cycle will start over again."

"I'm making my own decisions," Vince informed the priest and his mother. "I have been for a long time, and right now it's my decision to make the most money I can, the fastest way possible."

Vince was kicked out of so many schools he did not graduate until he was nineteen. He despised school, and everything about it, but it had not occurred to him what he might do after graduation. He was certain about one thing, a job was not an option. It never had been. Punching a clock for someone else was for fools. An Army recruiter had visited him and Vince laughed in his face.

"If you've read the papers lately or watched the news, maybe you noticed there's a war going on, and I don't want any part of it."

There was only one option for Vince, and that was to get into a college. Not just any college, but a good one, where there were a lot of rich kids. He needed new contacts, ones with money so he could enhance his drug sales and make some real money.

For the first time in his life, Vince actually did some academic research. He knew he needed a large liberal school, one that was open minded about drug use, but not too far away from his current sources of cocaine and marijuana. He checked all area colleges and universities thoroughly and finally settled on the University of Michigan at Ann Arbor. It was historically liberal, anti-military, anti-establishment, and had a student body in excess of fifty thousand kids.

Vince's mother was so elated she called in favors from her friends in Catholic circles to assist with entry requirements, and she paid his first year's tuition. He enrolled in August, and in October, he joined the largest, richest fraternity on campus.

Vince appreciated the opportunities that frat life offered. There were lots of parties, and parties meant drugs and girls. If he had learned anything in school, it was that girls are attracted to boys who have money. He was fond of saying, "It's the lump in the back pocket that counts, not the front pocket."

It was in the fraternity that Vince met Clint "Shine" Armstrong. If it were possible, Shine liked school even less than Vince, and like Vince, he was a drug dealer. Shine was studying to become a polygraphist.

"It will give me the flexibility I want, and if the IRS ever looks at my salary and expenditures, it's a way I can wash the money I make from drug sales." Shine informed Vince.

"I see it on a different level," responded Vince. "Listen, I have contacts and suppliers for large amounts of drugs. Until recently, I was dealing to rich high school kids. At this school, I can bring it up to one hundred thousand per year, maybe more. Give me a few months, and I can make us rich."

"Where do I fit in?"

"You will work for me. Stay with the polygraph classes at least long enough to learn how to use the equipment. We'll test our major suppliers and dealers. It will be a professional organization. I just have one problem right now."

"What's that?"

"I need more supply, but I'm working on it," he said, grinning like a Cheshire cat.

Before the end of Vince's first year in college, he was the largest drug dealer in Ann Arbor. He developed and used mostly fraternity guys, but he also had a smattering of other people he had met around town. In all, Vince managed forty street dealers. He spent lavishly on clothes and paid cash for a new BMW. He lived at the frat house, which he considered a great cover, and it was a great source for parties and women. Vince Vargo was having the time of his life.

Six months into his second year at Michigan, Vince had over one hundred dealers, and his territory moved from Ann Arbor to encompass Detroit as well as parts of New York, New Jersey, Pennsylvania and North Carolina.

"My issue," he told a fraternity brother, "is that I can't score enough weed and coke. I need bigger suppliers."

It was at a fraternity party that someone introduced him to Sherry Cox. Sherry was five-foot-six, almost skinny, with strawberry blond hair that flowed comfortably over freckled shoulders. She was wearing a black mini skirt that accentuated long, muscular legs. Vince could see the shape of her pencil eraser nipples through a white linen blouse. When she walked across the room she demanded the attention of every man in the room. Sherry Cox was nothing short of spectacular, and she knew it.

"I've heard of you," she said to Vince.

"It's nice to meet you," Vince replied, searching for words, trying to think of something clever to say. Words were never his strong suit, and they failed him now, when he needed them most.

"Uh, what are you majoring in?" he stumbled.

"That is a trite question, Vince," said a nearby frat brother, "but nice try. By the way, you're drooling on her shoes."

"I'm majoring in aeronautical engineering," stated the obviously intelligent beauty queen, but school is part time for me. I'm also a twin-engine-rated pilot, and I'm on call for different companies, so I'm gone a lot."

"The reason I'm introducing you to Sherry," said the frat brother, "is because she is flying a hop for some clients tomorrow, and she needs to score a little coke for them."

Now it was Vince's turn to smile.

"How much toot do you want?"

"An ounce ought to do. It's just for the weekend."

"Done," said Vince. "This one is on me; maybe we can have lunch when you get back."

CHAPTER 2
The Narcs

Curious tourists watched anxiously from the grounds of the Briers antebellum home, where eighteen year old Varina Howell had married Jefferson Davis, as the narcotics agents gathered on the banks of the Mississippi River just down the hill from the old Best Western Inn Motel in Natchez, Mississippi. It was almost dark and the day's flying was over. The narcs had an ice chest filled with beer and were shooting their handguns at turtles and any other debris that might be floating by. They knew someone would likely call the local police, but they were not worried, as the local police were participants.

Natchez, founded in 1716, and named for the mound building Natchez Indians, was the oldest city in Mississippi and was the location of choice for the annual marijuana eradication convention and beer bash between agents in the Louisiana State Police and agents from the Mississippi Bureau of Narcotics. It was an opportunity to make new friendships and renew old ones. It was also a seven day drunk, held at the expense of the taxpayers, but no one felt guilty over it. The bigger reason for the event was to establish relationships and a comfort zone between agencies in order to seamlessly facilitate investigations across state lines. It also made for good training to spot marijuana patches hidden in the thick undergrowth bordering the river north and south of Natchez. Several marijuana patches had been located, and the plants had been pulled.

"I think it's time we went back up the hill," said Bugger Red, one of the pilots from the Louisiana State Police. "If we don't hurry, we might be late for happy hour, and I hate paying full price."

The agents and pilots began the long walk up the hill toward the motel. They were an unkempt bunch. The narcs, mostly with long hair and beards, wore denim jeans and tee shirts, and had their service revolvers strapped to their hips. The pilots were clean shaven and had neatly trimmed hair. They wore the typical green, heat resistant nomex flight suits. Occasionally, a motel guest would look and point, but no one said anything to the group.

It had been a tiring day. They were probably still legally drunk, with a BAC (blood alcohol level) of .10 or better, when they had taken off just after sunrise. The pilots handled it better than the agents, as several agents had puked on their helicopters before their flight was over.

Lt. Miles "Mac" McCullough was the team leader for the Louisiana agents. The pungent fumes from the helicopters reminded him of Vietnam, where CH-46 helicopters had brought Marines places they didn't want to go, and left them to walk back. Mac noted that the thick foliage on each side of the Mississippi River was similar to the elephant grass and "wait a minute" vines they dealt with in I Corps along the border of North Vietnam. That was seventeen years ago. This was 1983, and the war was just a blurred memory.

Bugger Red Ware and Mac walked the two hundred yards or so from the river toward the parking lot where they routinely locked their service weapons, typically a model nineteen Smith and Wesson with a two and one half inch barrel, in the trunks of their units. Bugger Red, whose real name was Michael James Ware, had been recruited into the state police for his experience as a Huey pilot and former warrant officer with the Army. Bugger Red was short and thin, weighing no more than one hundred thirty pounds. He had steel blue eyes and thick blond hair that he kept closely cropped. It was little more than a crew cut.

Bugger Red, like Mac, was a Vietnam vet and had won a bronze star for bravery when he flew into a hot LZ (landing zone) to retrieve three army rangers under heavy fire from Charlie. He was also nominated for a purple heart but refused it. He had been shooting in the general direction of Charlie with a .45 pistol while flying the Huey and had shot the landing skid. The bullet ricocheted off the skid and hit Bugger Red in the butt.

"I will not accept a medal for shooting myself in the ass," Bugger Red had told his colonel and squadron commander.

Bugger Red was originally from Homer, Louisiana, which was a farming community close to the Arkansas border. Bugger often said there are more Wares in that part of the state than fleas on a coon dog. Bugger's southern drawl was thick and very similar to the agents from northern Mississippi. There were times, especially in the motel bar, when Bugger had to interpret for the Cajun agents, most of whom were from a twenty-two parish area known as Acadiana. The narcs were noticeably different from standard issue police officers. They avoided the normal practice of calling each other by rank, preferring undercover names, or nicknames they had picked up along the way. They dressed the role they often played in order to purchase drugs in undercover situation, and several sported beards, tattoos, and earrings.

After securing their guns, Mac and Bugger Red met the other agents in the motel lounge. It was a large room with a curved bar and roped off area where a band played late evenings. On the far side of the lounge there was a sliding glass door that opened to a patio area overlooking the banks of the Mississippi. There was also a good jukebox, with mostly classic rock and roll music. All in all, it was a good watering hole, frequented by the locals as one of the better establishments in Natchez.

The agents were disappointed that they had not located larger marijuana fields, and they discussed the possibility of better results if they flew more inland. They were drinking cocktails and telling war stories when Bugger Red had wondered off to the corner of the bar to try his luck with a young woman wearing a low cut dress revealing ample breasts. The woman, who was ten years younger than Bugger Red, and four inches taller than him, was not impressed. She ordered a margarita and ignored Bugger Red.

"I'm a pilot and an American hero," he said. "What is your problem, don't you love your country?"

"I don't like your jumpsuit or your attitude," she replied. "Now please leave me alone."

"Come on now, sugar," Bugger continued, in his north Louisiana drawl. "Give me a chance."

"You have about one chance in a million," she said.

"Then you admit I have a chance," said Bugger Red.

The woman approached the narc table and said, "If y'all don't get this redheaded Howdy Doody looking asshole away from me, I'm going to call my boyfriend to put a can of whoopass on somebody."

"Ask her what type of sexual harassment she prefers," Bugger Red said to Mac.

"Usually there is a chance with margarita drinkers," Mac told Bugger Red, "but she is not there yet. Timing is everything; wait a little while."

"That little home wrecker just called me Howdy Doody. I think my self-esteem has been damaged."

Mac paid the tab, grabbed Bugger Red, and walked him to his room. Several agents brought ice chests to the room and the narcs continued the grab ass session, drinking beer and making plans for the following day's flights.

The next morning heat came upon them with a vengeance. Before noon, the temperature rocketed to over one hundred degrees with a heat index of one hundred seven. The clouds turned a deep bluish, and thunderstorms rolled in often and unannounced. Heat could be seen rising off the river and nearby lakes. There was only an occasional gust of wind to cool the sweating, hungover agents. They flew in low circles, constantly staring at the ground. Several of the agents puked, but no one requested to return to base.

It was not really difficult to find marijuana patches once you got the hang of it. Most dopers would dig a tunnel through thick undergrowth and clear a spot in the middle for their plants. They tended to leave implements, such as water buckets, hoes, and shovels lying around. Often, there would be fences around the smaller plants to keep rabbits and deer from eating the fresh growth. When flying at a few hundred feet off the ground, the terrain looks thick with varying colors of green. A clearing with isolated green plants in the middle was easy to spot.

Most of the Louisiana narcotics agents were from the Lafayette area, which was in close proximity to the Atchafalaya Basin. The basin was hot, humid, fertile and isolated, making it an ideal area for growing marijuana. As a result, the Cajun narcs were some of the most experienced at finding the fields.

Bugger Red found a patch with about seventy-five plants, all over eight feet in height, a mile north of Ferriday, Louisiana, famous for being the home town of cousins Jerry Lee Lewis, Jimmy Lee Swaggart and Mickey Gilley.

The marijuana patch, about forty feet across, was cleared of brush, but it was surrounded by thick undergrowth of briars, scrub oaks, chicken trees, and poison ivy. Bugger Red landed his

Bell helicopter a good fifty yards away and dropped Mac and Hungry Harv Gaspard on the ground with machetes and rope. The undergrowth was so thick that Mac could not find the marijuana and Bugger Red had to direct him using state issued Motorola two-way radios. Mac and Hungry Harv slashed their way to the plants, cut them at the roots, and tied them into bundles. The bundles were then secured to the landing skids of the copter and flown back to the Natchez-Adams County Airport, where they were moved to a MBN truck and tagged, photographed, weighed, measured, and then burned.

Agents Darrell "Bubba" Green and Grady "Rooster" Milam were riding with a Mississippi pilot looking for marijuana near Lake St. John, north of Waterproof, Louisiana. Bubba, who had a master's degree in history, and a good memory for southern trivia, said, "Did you know that Waterproof is over ninety percent African American, and that in 1935 a local resident drowned in a flood, and the Tensas Parish Gazette ran a headline that said 'Waterproof Nigger Drowns?'" Rooster was not sure whether he should laugh at the irony. He just looked at Bubba.

They were just inside the Louisiana border when Rooster spotted a large marijuana field, which he estimated had over one hundred plants.

The pilot hovered a few feet over the field, "They appear to be five to six feet in height, but they are almost that wide. I'm going to drop you off as close as I can and call for another copter and some help to bag and tag those plants. It's too many for my bird. The whole area is infested with Kudzu vines. Y'all will have to cut your way to the field."

"Kudzu was introduced into the United States in the late 1800's from Japan," said Bubba. "It was originally thought that it would help prevent soil erosion, but they did not research it properly. It will take over one hundred fifty thousand acres per year and will kill every growing thing in its way."

"All I know," said the pilot, as he dropped Rooster and Bubba off near the field, "is that Kudzu vines and democrats are taking over Mississippi."

After lunch, the agents and pilots flew north again. Mac, Hungry Harv, and Bugger Red were flying over Lake Bruin, when Bugger Red spotted a small patch of marijuana plants in the middle of a cornfield that covered a good four hundred acres. He commented to Mac that it was a good place to hide the plants, but they would have to be harvested before the corn was cut. Hungry Harv understood rice, not corn, and had trouble understanding Bugger Red's drawl.

"Hungry Harv," said Bugger Red, "I'm going to drop you outside the cornfield, and talk you into the patch."

"How big is the patch?" Hungry asked.

"Small," said Bugger Red.

Hungry Harv just looked at Bugger Red, not unlike a monkey would look at a wristwatch, thought Mac. Then Hungry Harv smiled as large as he could.

Finally, Mac said, "Hungry, Bugger Red said 'small, not smile.'"

"Oh," Hungry Harv said, looking at Bugger Red. "You Yankees need to learn how to talk."

All of the agents had returned to the Best Western by four p.m., tired, dirty and thirsty. It had been a long day. Mac estimated that over two hundred plants had been seized on the Louisiana side of the river, and at least that many had been bagged and tagged on the Mississippi side, and there were three days of the convention left.

There was a message on the phone in Mac's room to call the Troop I commander in Lafayette.

"Captain, this is Lieutenant McCullough," Mac said into the phone. "What can I do for you?"

"There is a report of a tug and barge at a shipyard just south of Abbeville, in Vermilion Parish. No one at the shipyard seems to know why it is there. It was called in to Customs for them to handle, but somehow Colonel Kazan in Baton Rouge learned about it and instructed me to have you check it out."

"No problem," said Mac, "I'll get Hungry Harv, and we will head that way." Mac set the phone in its cradle and wondered why Customs was not checking out a tug and barge, and why Colonel Kazan, known to the agents as Simple Eddie, would have learned about it.

Mac called Agent Anthony "Hollywood" Bordelle and Hungry Harv and asked them to meet to meet him in the lounge.

"Hollywood," Mac said, "Hungry Harv and I have a mission down in Vermilion Parish. You stay with the rest of the agents and coordinate the activities for the Louisiana narcs. Don't let your cousin search any Mexicans inside the state of Mississippi, or for that matter, throw any Mexicans into the Mississippi River. He could set relations back fifty years."

"Find some marijuana plants," said Mac, smiling, "and get some MBN contact numbers, but above all, have fun."

"Ten-four, Mac, see you in Lafayette."

They crossed the Mississippi River and headed west on Highway 84 toward Jonesville, following pulp wood trucks toward Catahoula Lake. The return trip to Region II Headquarters in Lafayette brought them from the most rural parts of Louisiana to the heart of Cajun country. The trip was slow by trooper standards, but it allowed Mac and Hungry Harv to rest and joke about their time working together in the narcotics section.

Though he was not from the Lafayette area, Lieutenant Miles "Mac" McCullough had graduated from the University of Southwestern Louisiana and had quickly adapted to the lifestyles of the area's French speaking people. After a four year stint in the Marines, with one tour in Vietnam, he returned to Lafayette and joined the state police. He worked patrol at Troop I, detectives in New Orleans, and finally in the narcotics section, where he was promoted to section supervisor.

"How is it going with Marcelle?" Hungry Harv asked. "I haven't seen y'all together in a while." Hungry Harv was smiling because he knew the story.

Mac had met Marcelle Stevens while working as a road trooper. The relationship had brought Mac some attention, though not in the way he would have wanted. Troopers were always visiting hospital emergency rooms to check on accident victims, and as a result, several troopers became friendly with the nurses. They worked the same shifts, and in many cases, dealt with the same people. It was not unusual for a trooper to marry a nurse, and Mac became attracted to one nurse in particular.

Marcelle Stevens was not particularly tall at five-foot-three. She had curly blond hair, muscular legs, and large breasts. She was friendly and flirtatious. Most of all, Mac liked her because she could laugh. Mac had just finished interviewing an accident victim when he decided to test the water.

"Marcelle, this is my weekend off, would you like to go to dinner?"

Marcelle thought about it for a few seconds, like she was not quite sure if she had other plans. Finally, she agreed. Mac was elated.

The next day Mac picked Marcelle up at her townhouse off College Drive in an old, worn out Corvette, he liked to call "vintage."

"Nice looking, but a little hard to get into," said Marcelle.

Mac drove down South College, headed toward La Fonda's, Lafayette's favorite Mexican restaurant, where the food was cheap and the margaritas lethal.

"Your car is stiff and bumpy," she told Mac.

"The salesman promised me it would make women's clothes fall off."

"Har Har," she said, looking at the console and bucket seats. "It looks like it was designed by Planned Parenthood."

Mac couldn't think of a good reply, but made a mental note to level the playing field by loading her up with margaritas.

After dinner, Mac brought Marcelle to his residence, only a few blocks away. She was slightly tipsy and Mac felt good about his chances of pulling out his seven iron and hitting the long ball. Marcelle had different ideas. She noticed Mac's dirt bike in the garage.

"I love motorcycles," she said. "Let's go for a ride."

"It's a dirt bike, Marcelle, not legal for riding on public highways," answered Mac, trying desperately to get Marcelle into his house before the tequila wore off. Timing was everything.

"Come on, the night is still young," Marcelle said, as she lifted her already short skirt, revealing the edges of black lace underwear, as she prepared to mount the bike.

It took Mac about three seconds to crank the bike, and off they went, barhopping down Johnston Street. It seemed inappropriate to wear helmets, since the bike had no lights, license plate, registration, or insurance. They drank beer and shot pool with area oil field workers in the bars until two o'clock in the morning.

They closed the last bar and departed for Mac's house.

It was now two-thirty in the morning and Mac was running out of energy. He put the bike in the garage and half expected Marcelle to get into Mac's car for the return trip to her townhouse. He had pretty much given up on the prospect of getting Marcelle into his rack.

"Where is the ladies room?" Marcelle asked.

"It's a small house" replied Mac, while opening the door for her. "There is only one bathroom, and it's between the two bedrooms."

"What are the chances of the toilet bowl being clean?"

"It's very clean," said Mac. "I always sit to pee."

"Why would you sit to pee?" Marcelle was looking at Mac for an answer.

"I hurt my back, and the doctor told me not to lift anything heavy."

Marcelle laughed and entered the bathroom. Mac was leaning against the kitchen counter when she walked into the room in black lace panties and matching bra that strained to hold it contents. She kissed Mac, unzipped his pants, and led him into the bedroom by his putter, which she commented, "was not all that heavy."

"Is it true that men name their penises?" Marcelle asked.

"Did you hear that, Godzilla?" Mac asked, looking down.

Marcelle laughed heartedly, and Mac felt he was losing the moment. It was late, and he was tired and nervous. Marcelle and Godzilla would have to wait until morning.

Mac brought Marcelle back to her townhouse after lunch the next day. He inquired about her schedule and learned that she was on the day shift, working from six o'clock in the morning until six o'clock in the evening. Mac was working nights, and Marcelle suggested that he come over for coffee before he went home from his shift. A wreck occurred late in the shift, and Mac could not make it to the townhouse before Marcelle's shift started.

Two days later, Mac being aware of Marcelle's hours, stopped at a local pastry shop and purchased two dozen donuts and various pastries for Marcelle to bring to the hospital emergency room for her coworkers. The sun was just rising when he knocked on Marcelle's townhouse door at in the blue uniform of the Louisiana State Police.

After a couple of minutes, a man in his briefs answered the door. He had curly, shoulder length, unkempt dark brown hair, tattoos on both arms, and the look of someone who worked with his hands to make a living.

"Is there a problem in the complex, officer?"

"Uh," stammered Mac, being caught off guard, and feeling rather stupid, especially since he had a degree in English.

"Officer," continued the almost naked man, "is there a problem in the neighborhood? Are you sure you are at the right location? No one here called the police."

"Uh," was all he could muster.

Mac stood his ground, dumbfounded and embarrassed, and he could see that the man was clearly getting suspicious. Finally, Mac simply said, "Here, I brought y'all some donuts." It was not a very intelligent plan of action, but the man took the bag, and Mac walked away as quickly as possible.

As Mac walked back to his unit, he thought to himself, "You dumb shit, why didn't you just say, 'excuse me sir, I seem to be at the wrong damn apartment?'"

Mac later learned that the man pondered the situation for a few moments, after which he walked upstairs to the bedroom, where Marcelle had observed the situation through her window, and said, "Guess what, Marcelle, the fucking state police is delivering donuts these days. Isn't that fucking courteous of them?" Then he hit Marcelle with the bag.

Mac later learned that Marcelle had been married, and the man who answered the door was her husband. He had been working on a rig for the past two weeks when Mac was making a run at his wife.

"Why didn't you tell me the rules?" Mac asked Marcelle at the hospital emergency room the next day. "I don't have a problem with dating a married woman, but I need to know what my schedule is."

"It doesn't matter, and I did not tell you about him, because we were going to get divorced anyway."

"Oh, well, in that case, I have annual leave on the books. Would you like to ride up to Colorado and do some barhopping through the mountains?" Mac asked.

"When do we leave?" Marcelle said.

It was then that Mac heard some of the emergency room nurses whispering and pointing, and talking about donuts.

The next day, a Troop I desk sergeant called Mac on the air and requested he bring a bag of donuts for the troop personnel. Mac soon transferred to the narcotics section.

"The relationship with Marcelle is off and on," Mac said to Hungry Harv, as they continued west following tractor-trailer rigs filled with freshly picked cotton.

"Working narcotics is hard on a relationship," he said absent-mindedly. He was thinking about the suspicious barge in Hungry Harv's home area of Vermilion Parish, where Cajuns had established small villages and towns along the Louisiana bayous, and for the next two and a half centuries mixed with Spanish, Indians, Africans and Americans, until they had formed their own unique culture. Most of the Region II narcotics agents were of Cajun ancestry, and they rarely left the area unless it was on assignment or the occasional family vacation to the beaches of the Florida panhandle. Even Mac had a little distant Lejeune blood in him, though he and Bubba were considered rednecks.

Hungry Harvey Gaspard was a sergeant in Region II Narcotics, and had been in the business for over ten years. Mac considered Hungry Harv a perfect example of the typical Cajun. Cajun French was his primary language. His mother spoke no English and his father very little. Hungry Harv did not learn to speak English until attending grade school. On his first day at school, a Catholic Nun scolded him for speaking French, so after the first week at school he would dutifully walk to the school bus stop, wait until his mother was no longer looking, then run home and hide in the barn until the bus returned in the afternoon. After several days of hiding, the school reported him missing and he was punished at home and at school. As a result, Hungry Harv never cared for formal schooling, never joined the military, or attended college. Hungry Harv was not prone to complexities. He preferred to keep things as simple as possible.

Hungry Harv's hometown was not much more than a village. His father was a tenant rice farmer, working for a percentage of the monies his crops yielded. He had four brothers and three sisters, and there never seemed to be enough to eat. It was not uncommon for Harvey's father to kill blackbirds, which barely had enough meat to make gravy for the rice they ate at every meal. It seemed that Hungry Harv was always wanting something to eat, and once he started he could not stop. After graduating high school, he got a job in the oil field and, for the first time in his life, he could have all the food he wanted. It was on the rigs that Harvey Gaspard became known as Hungry Harv.

As an adult, Hungry Harv had become a large man, well over six-feet-two inches and weighing two-hundred-thirty pounds. He had a square head, deep set brown eyes with bushy, thick eye brows, and weathered, wrinkled skin from too many days in the blistering Louisiana sun. He did not mind the physical labor of the oil patch, and he considered the money good, but he needed something more challenging.

Like most Cajuns, Hungry Harv never considered living outside the comfort zone of the marshes and bayous of his native Kaplan. Becoming a police officer, working the areas around his hometown seemed the logical thing to do.

At age twenty-three, Hungry Harv left the oil patch and applied for the state police. After two years as a uniformed trooper, he joined the narcotics section and found a life that would become his passion. Hungry Harv absolutely loved being a cop, and, in particular, a narcotics agent. He was never really comfortable working undercover, as was the specialty of some agents, but he developed in-depth interviewing and interrogation skills. Other agents could purchase drugs in an undercover capacity, and Hungry Harv could almost always talk the suspect into giving up his source, into "trading up," as he called it.

Hungry Harv had gotten married soon after joining the state police. His wife, the former Ruby Rae Melancon, was also a Kaplan native, and was somewhat of a legend in the area as a supervisor of the Department of Motor Vehicle Offices in Southwest Louisiana. If you had problems with driver's license issues, she was the "go to" person. Since high school, Ruby Rae maintained short, reddish colored hair that never seemed to be out of place. She was tall, with broader shoulders than most women. She was fit, stern, and authoritative. Ruby Rae could also be obstinate and possessive. All in all, she was a good catch for Hungry Harv, except that she did not care much for cooking.

Ruby Rae thought the change from road trooper to narcotics agent would be more conducive to a happy home life with regular working hours. She could not have been more wrong.

26

Women were never Hungry Harv's area of expertise. He could talk a male suspect into giving up his mother, but in almost every instance of interviewing a female suspect, Hungry Harv got a severe ass-chewing.

Hungry Harv had dated only two women in his adult life. Unfortunately for him, he dated both at the same time. Betsy Daigle was from the nearby community of Nunez. Hungry Harv had stopped her for speeding, but after talking to her for some time on the side of the highway, he thought it wiser to get her phone number than to give her a citation.

Betsy had attended the Aveda Training Institute in Lafayette to study cosmetology, and had opened Betsy's Beauty Shop in Kaplan. She made good money, by Kaplan standards, was easy to look at, but, more importantly to Hungry Harv, Betsy, like most Cajun women, could cook.

For several months, Hungry Harv had the best of both worlds. He jockeyed his schedule and made excuses, managing to make each woman feel as if she were the only person in his life. Hungry Harv did not require much from either woman, but a woman that was an expert cook definitely had the inside track.

Hungry Harv would have been happy with either of the women in his life; he just didn't know which one was the best choice for a long-term relationship, or more importantly, how to break up with the one he did not choose. Hungry Harv was afraid of no man, but he was timid around women.

During his dating years, Hungry Harv lived in a trailer at the end of a narrow gravel road about two miles out of Kaplan. It backed up to a rice field and had small levees covered with chicken trees on each side of the trailer. It was perfect for Hungry Harv, who loved his privacy.

One night, when Ruby Rae was thought to be visiting her folks, Betsy was at Hungry Harv's trailer, making a duck and andouille gumbo, one of Hungry's favorite dishes. Betsy was cooking and humming to herself when Hungry Harv heard the familiar sound of Ruby Rae's Volkswagen bug coming down the shell driveway. There was no way to get Betsy out of the trailer, and no place to hide her.

Ruby Rae knocked on the door.

"It's Ruby, sweetheart, open the door."

Hungry Harv did not know what to do, so he did nothing.

"Who is in there with you, Harvey?" She was getting louder and more authoritative with her voice. Hungry Harv said nothing and was beginning to shake. In all his life, Hungry Harv feared only two things, snakes and Ruby Rae.

"Open this fucking door, you asshole." Ruby Rae was screaming now.

Ruby Rae began kicking the door. Hungry Harv did the only thing he could think of. He locked himself in the bathroom.

Ruby Rae kicked the door so hard the lock broke, and she walked into the trailer. Hungry Harv could hear two women screaming, chairs being thrown, tables being knocked over, and dishes being broken. He later said of the fight, "Mais, Ruby Rae used more nasty words than George Carlin."

When the noise subsided, Hungry Harv could hear Betsy's car leaving the trailer, departing down the long drive to the highway, but he would not leave his bunker.

"You can come out of the bathroom now, sweetie." Ruby Rae was at the bathroom door, trying to sound reasonable.

"Where is Betsy?" asked Hungry Harv.

"Your former girlfriend left, honey bunch," said Ruby Rae doing her best to be ladylike.

Hungry Harv opened the bathroom door and stared at Ruby Rae, waiting for her response.

"Your playboy days are over, do you understand that Harvey!" It was a statement, not a question. "The next time you have a lounge lizard over for beer and gumbo, or boudin, or chitlins, or whatever that bitch was cooking, I'm going to kick your ass up through your shoulders. Do you understand me, Harvey?"

"Yes, honey," Hungry Harvey replied, meekly. They were married six months later. Mac attended the wedding and said to some of the other narcs, "Kaplan is a town where the men are men, and so are the women."

CHAPTER 3
The Shipyard

Mac and Hungry Harv continued the drive back to Lafayette from Natchez. They rolled past the old plantation called Frogmore, which had been built and worked by slaves. As they passed through Buckeye, Mac recalled when he was in the academy and had met a former sheriff's deputy from Shreveport who was attending the Louisiana State Police Academy. The deputy always carried a large acorn with a place to rub your thumb.

"Why do you carry an acorn in your pocket?" Mac asked.

"It's not an acorn," the deputy said. "It's a buckeye ball, it's for good luck. Mac later learned that many of the North Louisiana troopers in the 1960s and 1970s carried buckeye balls. They were near Catahoula Lake when Mac asked Hungry Harv about the shipyards south of Abbeville.

"There are at least two," said Hungry Harv. "There is Broussard Brothers, along the Vermilion Bayou, and there is Fontenot's, also on the Vermilion, near a crossroad community the locals call Banker. It's not really a town, or even a village; it's just a rural farming area in South Vermilion Parish."

"Both shipyards are secluded," he continued. "Broussard Brothers is the larger of the two, but both companies stay busy during oilfield booms."

"How do you get to Banker?" Mac asked.

"It's just a few miles south of Abbeville, near Henry, off Highway 330. It's real close to the Gulf. Not much there except marsh."

"Tell me more about the area. I worked Vermilion Parish a few times as a road trooper, but never really learned much about the people. They are close knit, and don't care for outsiders too much."

29

Hungry Harv thought about his home parish. "The Vermilion is wide and deep, surrounded mostly by marsh," he said. "There is only one road going into Fontenot's shipyard, and that is a narrow shell road that floods when there is a big rain. I remember there being a good boat ramp into the bayou that area fishermen use, but mostly it's for oil field workers who load up supply boats and crew boats for transport to offshore rigs. There is a large shell parking lot and a couple of big tin buildings, and not much else."

"There are more cows than cars on the roads near Banker, and they say the mosquitoes there are on steroids," continued Hungry Harv. "People from Henry say the mosquitoes are so big they can stand flat footed and fuck a goose."

They were driving into Alexandria and would soon be on the interstate that would get them to Lafayette in little more than an hour. Mac tried to recall the area between Abbeville and the Gulf of Mexico.

"The few times I worked Vermilion Parish as a uniformed trooper I tried to stay north of Abbeville, where there was more activity. I wish I had learned more about the area and people south of Abbeville." Mac said. "I remember seeing communities like Banker, Boston, and Henry, but I never learned much about them. I once dated a school teacher from Henry who brought cows to school for show and tell."

"There's not much in the area except for a few scattered farms, cattle ranches, and Catholic Churches." Hungry Harv explained. "It's mostly marshland. The brackish water is home to cattails, bulrushes, and all kinds of water lilies and duckweed. The rotting plants make it stink year round, but it provides a perfect habitat for ducks, geese, deer and swamp rabbits. I like the fishing and hunting the marsh provides."

"Who owns the shipyard in Banker?" Mac asked, changing the subject.

"Man by the name of Lawless Fontenot," answered Hungry Harv. "I don't know him personally, but I've heard he is a big shot around Abbeville, owns a lot of property, on the board of directors at the bank, stuff like that. There are a lot of Catholic Masons in the area. Come to think of it, Lawless is the number one Mason in the state, and that carries a lot of weight in this area. It means he has political stroke."

"Does he have family in the operation?"

"He has a couple of boys, grown now: James and Jude Fontenot, maybe twenty-five to thirty years old. I never dealt with them personally, but rumors are that they live on the fringe. They've been arrested by the locals for marijuana possession, DWI, bar room fights, and disturbing the peace. Nothing major like robbery or assault, that I know of. They say their daddy is very protective of them and has contacts in the District Attorney's Office. I doubt that there is a record of their arrests."

The route to Banker took them through the poorest section of Abbeville, passing in front of the Chez Paris lounge, a known whorehouse where hookers service oil field hands, local businessmen, and the occasional Lafayette college student. It was well-known that protection was supplied by the Vermilion Parish Sheriff's Office. "Everybody has to make a living," said Hungry Harv.

A torrid June sun was setting, and the sweltering heat was lifting from the asphalt highway when they reached Banker and pulled onto the long shell driveway leading to Fontenot's shipyard. Cypress stumps, chicken trees and swishy cane lined the narrow road. Reflections of the marsh water in the man-made canal glanced off the windshield as they approached the shipyard. The yard, like the driveway, contained dirty white shell. It had a large tin building for storage of fishing and oil rig supplies, and another, smaller tin building that served as an office. The parking lot around the buildings extended about five hundred yards along Vermilion Bayou, which appeared to be fifty to sixty yards wide in the curve.

Mac and Hungry Harv parked the cruiser and stepped onto the parking lot. The yard was surrounded by a chain link fence, further surrounded by the smelly and dangerous marsh with its rotting plant life. It was a place where a person did not venture after dark. Alligators and snakes ruled with absolute authority.

"Old Cajuns say the 'Loup-garou' lives in this area," Hungry Harv said to Mac as they looked across the fence at the swamp.

"What the hell is a 'Loup-garou'?"

"It's a swamp werewolf," explained Hungry Harv. "People say they can hear him sometimes at night."

Roy W. Frusha

Mac turned his attention back to the yard and noted there were no crew boats or supply boats docked at the wooden pier which extended along the bayou for several hundred yards. The only vessels present were an ocean-going tugboat and barge. There was also the absence of any fishermen or dock hands that would be considered the norm for a working shipyard. In fact, Mac thought, no one seemed to be here. Then he heard a voice coming from the tin office.

"Good evening, officers. I've been expecting y'all; I'm Lawless Fontenot, owner of the yard." Fontenot walked toward the officers. Mac judged him to be around seventy, and slightly less than six feet tall. Fontenot's face was brown and wrinkled and had the appearance of a man who made his living outside. Grey hair was combed over the tops of his large ears, protruding from his head, on which sat an unwashed, gritty Stetson cowboy hat. He wore a generous amount of cheap aftershave, the kind that stung your nose and burned your eyes. He extended his right arm, which seemed too long for his body, toward Mac.

Fontenot looked like a man who came up hard, stepping on anyone who got between him and success. Mac's immediate impression was that he was uneducated trailer trash without a reason to be proud, thinking that monetary achievement was all a person needed to become an elitist within a new southern aristocracy. Mac ignored the gesture to shake hands.

"I'm Lieutenant McCullough and this is Sergeant Gaspard," said Mac, walking toward the tin office building and leaving it up to Fontenot to follow him. "I was asked by the Troop I commander to respond to your request. What seems to be the problem?"

"Well," said Fontenot, "there is not much to tell. Friday, when we closed the yard, the dock was empty. Monday, when we returned to work, this tug and barge had been abandoned here," said Fontenot, as he pointed to the vessels, which were tied with large ropes to the dock.

"Mr. Fontenot, why did you request state police narcotics agents rather than the sheriff's office or Customs?" Mac asked.

Lawless Fontenot ignored the question.

"Mr. Fontenot," continued Mac, "I assume you have some valuable equipment here that is used to load and off-load crew boats and supply boats, maybe some forklifts, cranes, cherry

32

pickers and such. Are you telling me you routinely leave this kind of equipment unguarded on weekends? Don't you regularly have security personnel to watch your yard at night seven days a week?"

"I guess it depends on the workload. Sometimes we may have people in the yard, sometimes we don't."

Fontenot was fidgeting and avoided direct eye contact, thought Mac, which is not behavior you would expect from a successful oil field executive who had developed his own company managing roughnecks, drunks, transients, and other trash that normally moved in and out of the business, many of whom were dangerous men with extensive arrest records and outstanding arrest warrants. Fontenot was not a man to be intimidated. It was evident that Fontenot was financially successful, but not educated. He had the appearance and demeanor of a schoolyard bully. Fontenot was the type of individual who made up for a lack of education and social skills by intimidating people smaller than him, but the badges made him scared shitless.

"Mr. Fontenot, what type of activity do you normally have in your shipyard?"

"Lieutenant, I don't know what your questions have to do with this tug and barge," said Fontenot, who raised himself to his full height and bristled at Mac's rudeness, "but I'll answer your question. Almost everything we do is related to the oil field. Crew boats dock here and take hands to and from offshore rigs. Supply boats pick up tools and other equipment and various supplies and take them to the rigs. If the oil field is booming, we are exceptionally busy, but it's been slow lately. So I don't have as many employees, and we don't always work nights and weekends."

"Have you been on the tug or barge?" Mac inquired.

"I have not been on either one. I thought it suspicious that they were abandoned here, so I called the state police. The only reason I am here now is because you are here. I have a foreman and two sons who manage the yard for me now. I mostly stay on my farm and look after my cattle."

Mac and Hungry Harv just looked at each other; neither believed Fontenot. Any owner or manager of a shipyard would have been on the tug looking for clues as to why it was there and who owned it. Mac was sure Fontenot had searched the tug, unless he had something to hide. Fontenot was lying, but Mac was not sure why.

"Who is your foreman?"

"Clement Thibodeaux," answered Fontenot. "He's gone for the evening, but will be here first thing tomorrow morning."

"Mr. Fontenot, since you mostly look after your cattle, how did you learn the tug and barge were left in your yard?"

"Clement came by the yard at daybreak today. He called me as soon as he saw the boats."

"Do you know if Mr. Thibodeaux went on the tug?"

"I don't know if he checked them out, but I think he would have told me if he had." Fontenot lied again.

"Okay, Mr. Fontenot," Mac was tiring of the conversation. He wiped the sweat off his forehead with a handkerchief and motioned toward the dock. "Let's have a look at the boats."

As they walked toward the tug, Mac sensed that Fontenot was uncomfortable, but it did not seem to have the stressful look of a guilty person so much as it was the appearance of a person who knew things were not as they should be. His temples throbbed with frustration and loathing for the smartass lieutenant.

This wasn't even a basic interview, much less an interrogation. Mac made a mental note to call Fontenot, and have him drive to Lafayette, where he could push him with more in-depth questions. For the time being he felt the best approach was to continue questions in a friendlier manner hoping for better cooperation.

"Mr. Fontenot," Mac said, as they neared the barge, "is there a chance that one of your sons was at the yard over the weekend, and forgot to tell you? I mean, is it possible that maybe one of them was here to receive a shipment?"

"No, I already checked with them, and they said they were in Lafayette Saturday and Sunday," Fontenot said sternly, carefully avoiding eye contact with Mac.

"Is the gate to the yard normally locked, and if so, who has the keys?" Hungry Harv interjected.

"It is my policy to keep the gate locked when no one is here. Clement has a set of keys, and my sons have a set. I don't know if there are other keys out."

They reached the tug first and Hungry Harv, who had spent time on tugboats, led the way.

"Mac, this is a typical ocean-going tugboat, though somewhat old, I'd say between sixty-five and seventy feet long with a flat bow," explained Hungry Harv. "This type of boat is routinely used to push industrial barges up and down the river, or move large ships in and out of their berths."

Hungry Harv opened a drawer on the tug. "Look at this, the tug is flying the American flag, but here are two more flags. Why would a tug have the flags of three countries?"

"I recognize one as Panamanian, but I don't recognize the other," Mac said.

Lawless Fontenot observed the agents with interest, but offered no response or input.

"Mr. Fontenot," said Mac, "is this the first time a strange boat has been left in your yard?"

"Sometimes a local fisherman will leave a boat overnight, but nothing as large as a tug has ever been left here," answered Fontenot, who clearly did not like the continued questioning, or circumstances. He looked south toward the curve in the river, wanting to disconnect from the officers and said, "It will be getting dark soon."

"Okay, let's have a look at the barge before it's completely dark." Mac responded.

Fontenot was silent and showed no emotion as Hungry Harv stepped onto the barge under a rising moon. He walked around slowly, looking intently at the hatches, all of which were welded shut. He stopped at a coiled roped covering an area about twenty feet around.

"Mac," said Hungry Harv, "I've been around barges and deck hands all of my life. I worked in the oil field five years, and I never saw a hand take the time to coil up a rope in a perfect circle."

Hungry Harv began moving the rope, under which appeared a large hatch which opened into the barge. He took a flashlight out of his pocket and descended on rusty iron steps toward the bottom. He was gone less than five minutes when he climbed the stairs and stood, wiping sweat from his brow, again on the deck.

"Mac, I judge this barge to be about two hundred feet long. It's wet and oily in the hold, but there's enough Columbian 'feel good' in this boat to light up all of Louisiana for a year."

"Tell me you are shitting me," said Mac, who didn't particularly want this problem.

"Nope, we've both seen bales of weed before; it's not that different from a bale of hay. I'm guessing the bales weigh eighty pounds or so each, and it's wall to wall, may be fifteen to twenty tons of the stuff is down there."

Hungry Harv looked directly at Mac and said, hesitated, and continued, "The marijuana in this barge is no good. It's been soaked in seawater and oil. The good marijuana was on top, but it's gone."

"How many pounds will this barge carry?"

"Roughly three hundred thousand to five hundred thousand pounds," answered Hungry Harv.

Mac thought briefly about the people, equipment, time, and effort it would take to off-load hundreds of thousands of pounds of marijuana from the bowels of a hot, humid, stinking barge under a sweltering Louisiana sun in June. He turned toward Lawless Fontenot, walked into his space, and looked directly into his eyes.

"A lot of people and equipment were very busy for two or three days and nights in this shipyard, and you expect me to believe you, your foreman, and your two angel sons knew nothing about it." Spittle was hitting the face of Lawless Fontenot.

Fontenot's skin was damp with sweat and he was visibly shaking. He turned from Mac, backed up a step, and regained his composure. "Lieutenant, you have a bad attitude. I was not here this weekend. I don't know where the tug and barge came from, or how they got here, or what they were carrying. And I'm not answering any more of your questions without talking to my lawyer first."

Mac looked at Hungry Harv and said, "Well, I guess we know the origin of the other flag; my guess is that it's Columbian."

"What a fucking mess," Mac said as they walked back to their unit to call for assistance.

CHAPTER 4
Lieutenant Colonel Edward "Simple Eddie" Kazan

Before leaving Fontenot's shipyard, Mac called the Vermilion Parish Sheriff's Office to secure the yard until further notice. He also called Troop I and requested that they contact the Region II narcotics agents, still in Natchez, and order them back to Lafayette.

At daylight the following day, the Acadiana Crime Lab came over from New Iberia and took pictures of the tug and barge and its contents, dusted for prints, looked for clues, and took samples of the marijuana for further testing at the lab. The Vermilion Parish Sheriff's Office provided security for the scene and inmate labor to off-load the rotting, stinking bales of marijuana. When they were finished, sample bales were weighed, after which the bales were counted. Mac estimated that there was roughly fourteen tons of marijuana left behind in the barge.

After the marijuana was weighed and counted, and the crime lab personnel completed their search, the sheriff's office transported the marijuana to a vacant bean field, soaked it in diesel fuel, and burned it. It would take a week for the smoke to subside. Inmates from the sheriff's office readily offered their services to take hoes and bust up the smoldering bales so it would burn quicker. The local sheriff said, "It was the biggest high inmates had ever received from a police agency."

That afternoon, Mac contacted state police headquarters in Baton Rouge, and requested to speak directly with Lt. Col. Edward Kazan, the commander of all state police investigative divisions. The interview time was set, and Mac departed Lafayette for Baton Rouge. As he drove across the basin bridge, lightning flashed in distant thunderheads. When the rain came, it blew sideways to his unit. "I hate Baton Rouge," Mac said aloud to no one in particular.

Edward Etienne Kazan was born and raised in Mamou, Louisiana, a small town of about three thousand people in the middle of Evangeline Parish. It is considered the heart of Cajun country. Some people say that the name "Mamou" came from a local Indian Chief, but it is more likely that, like everything else in Evangeline Parish, it came from France.

Before the Civil War, cotton was the main industry. After the war, rice became the primary source of income for the community.

Mamou is famous for its Mardi Gras and its music, especially Steve Riley and the Mamou Playboys. It is also famous for Fred's Lounge, which has live music every Saturday night. On Sundays, it is a family tradition for the locals to go to morning Mass at the Catholic Church, after which they casually walk to Fred's to get drunk and dance to Cajun music.

Mamou is also famous for the Kazan Hotel, where a person can rent a room for the night, or by the hour if he prefers. Colonel Kazan was a direct descendent of the Kazan family and grew up working at the family hotel.

When he was in high school, he worked in the hotel and at the nearby Fred's Lounge, where a person could purchase a beer, regardless of age, as long as he had a quarter. Both establishments were favorite watering holes for local politicians. It was a preparatory course in Louisiana politics. Kazan listened as rich landowners discussed who would be mayor, sheriff of the parish, city police chief, judge, or state representative. He often witnessed politicians take orders from the rice barons around Mamou. It was a lesson he would not forget.

By the time Kazan was eighteen, he was six feet tall with dark brown hair which he kept trim and neat. He had a square jaw, white teeth and a friendly smile. He did not have many clothes, but he kept what he had clean and starched. He graduated from Mamou High School near the bottom of his class. Aware that he did not have the scores necessary, he did not apply to any area colleges, nor did he have an interest in higher learning. He had enough foresight to realize Mamou held no future for him, so he joined the Army.

Kazan served four years at Fort Polk, near Leesville, never leaving the state. It was at Fort Polk that he watched the officers and learned how to dress. He lost the thick Cajun accent so prominent in Mamou, and developed people skills that would help him get into the Louisiana State Police. It also helped that the state representative from Mamou called the governor's office and requested a slot in the state police for Kazan.

Kazan spent his first two month's salary on clothes. He purchased two pinstriped suits, white cotton shirts, a handful of ties, and a pair of black Florsheim shoes, which he kept spit-shined. He also purchased a leather briefcase, which he carried around empty. He was Willie Loman, going through life on a smile and a shoeshine.

Kazan's first duty station was Troop A in Baton Rouge, but he had been there less than a year when he volunteered to work with the security service at the Governor's Mansion. He also never missed a chance to volunteer his services at the legislature when they were in session. His clothes and manners were immaculate as he worked both sides of the aisle at the state capitol, offering his services to every state senator and legislator he met. He would bring them coffee, take their clothes to the cleaners, drive them to parties given by lobbyists, and drive them to and from their homes all over the state when on weekend breaks. Kazan was tireless at sucking up to politicians. It was a smart move for the ambitious Kazan.

In the late 1950s Louisiana State Police, it was said that you had to be a white male at least six feet tall in order to qualify for a position. Appointments to the training academy were generally distributed from the governor's office to state legislators. They were formed out according to political value. Senators were routinely given more slots than was a representative. Promotions were also generally controlled by politicians, which made donations to political campaign funds of paramount importance. In the Lafayette area, a sergeant's position could be had for as little as five hundred dollars. A lieutenant's position could go as high as fifteen hundred to two thousand dollars. It was not a system befitting of a professional law enforcement agency, but it was what it was, and Edward Kazan innately knew how to work the system.

In Kazan's early career, the state police promotional system was governed by the Civil Service Administration, which handled promotional testing. A board of three supervisors would hold an oral interview for the top three scores for any position up to captain. The superintendent of the state police would determine who was to be made captain, major, or lieutenant colonel. It was a common saying that sergeant was the hardest rank to make in the organization. Kazan used to brag, saying, "I'm the only person in the Louisiana State Police to go from trooper to lieutenant colonel without ever taking a test."

Kazan used his political connections to obtain sergeant and lieutenant promotions at Troop A in Baton Rouge, then captain at headquarters, and finally lieutenant colonel and supervisor of the State Police Criminal Investigation Bureau. The bureau was essentially divided into three divisions: detectives, narcotics, and gaming. Edward Etienne Kazan was a very powerful man, answering only to Colonel Russell "Buck" Carter, Superintendent of the Louisiana State Police.

In terms of personnel, the gaming division was the largest section, overseeing the activities of riverboat casinos, Indian casinos, land-based casinos, racetracks, truck stops and hundreds of mom and pop lounges with video poker machines. They governed the activities of just about every sport, including cock fighting, dog fighting and little old ladies who ran bouree games in the back of hole in the wall bars all over coastal Louisiana. It was ironic that it was against the Louisiana Constitution to have organized gambling in state, so the legislature called it "gaming" therefore making it legal. A large portion of the budget for the Criminal Investigation Division went to the gaming division in an effort to regulate all of the activities necessary. Second in priority was state police detectives. The narcotics section got the left-overs.

Kazan had never worked a day in gaming, detectives or narcotics. Additionally, it was commonly said among troopers, that his wheelbarrow was a few bricks shy of a load. Yet, he understood the value of catering to Louisiana legislators and establishing favors that could later be exchanged or returned.

Agent Bubba Green was heard to have said that Kazan was "so damn lucky, he could shit in a swinging coke bottle."

When confronted by subordinates about investigative matters, Colonel Kazan had the habit of saying, "Do the right thing," or sometimes, "Do what is right according to the law and to state police policy and procedure." He rarely ever knew what advice to give on a controversial investigation, but he always followed up with the expression, "It's just that simple," thus Colonel Kazan became known to his subordinates all over the state as "Simple Eddie."

The drive to Baton Rouge on Interstate 10 routinely took just over an hour. As Mac drove through the rain on the twenty-three mile expanse of the Atchafalaya Basin, he thought about the massive effort and organizational planning it took to bring a barge load of marijuana into the bayous of Louisiana. People had to be used for scouts, guards, and truck drivers. It would have taken fifty or sixty stout men just to off-load the bales onto cranes. He knew they would eventually find out who was involved, but he did not relish the work it would take. It was obviously organized by outsiders, and LSP Headquarters was notoriously famous for not wanting investigators to travel and work outside of their areas. It was a control issue.

"Hundreds of thousands of pounds was too much weed for one state," Mac thought to himself. The weed was probably going all over the damn country. The feds would have to become involved in order to carry the investigation across state lines. Mac had worked with federal agencies before. There were too many restrictions, and they did little of the work, but managed all of the news releases and took all of the credit. Customs did not have the expertise and DEA did not have a Lafayette Field Office. It was likely that the FBI would take over the case. Mac wished that the FBI would take over the investigation and let Region II Narcotics handle the work load they already had, but he knew that would not happen. The FBI would want several state and local agents to do the investigative legwork of an FBI-led federal task force.

Mac walked into the massive LSP Headquarters building in downtown Baton Rouge to Simple Eddie's office on the sixth floor, a large corner office filled with expensive furniture. Simple Eddie's desk was oak, with a matching oak and leather chair. Lamps were on end tables and there were two leather sofas along the walls. Mac wondered how they justified having such opulence in their offices when troopers were driving cars with over one hundred thousand hard miles on them.

Simple Eddie did not offer Mac coffee or a soft drink, both of which were available.

41

Roy W. Frusha

"Sit down, Mac," Simple Eddie said from his leather chair. "Tell me what you think about the mess down in Vermilion Parish."

Mac briefed him about the search, the sheriff's office assistance, the meeting with Lawless Fontenot, and the weight, pictures, and final destruction of the marijuana, except for the samples taken by the crime lab personnel.

"Any ideas about suspects?" Simple Eddie said, looking away, seemingly bored with the conversation.

"Someone at the shipyard is obviously involved, but it is not Lawless Fontenot. He is an old oilfield hand who made a lot of money in the business, but I doubt he knows the difference between marijuana and duckweed. Still, someone in a position of authority in the shipyard is involved. Someone had to make sure the yard was vacant for over two days. It could be his yard foreman, but, more likely, it is one, or both, of his sons."

"What are you going to do?" Simple Eddie asked.

Mac looked at Simple Eddie and thought about a political whore being in charge of over two hundred investigators. He briefly wondered if it was the same with other state police agencies.

"A lot of people were involved, and a lot of money changed hands in order to pull off an importation of this magnitude. It took massive amounts of labor to off-load a few hundred thousand pounds of marijuana, and possibly a few thousand pounds of cocaine, from the hold of a hot, humid steel barge. The dope had to go somewhere, so there were a lot of large trucks and drivers involved. It will take a little time and effort, and we still have our domestic, ongoing investigations in the Lafayette area to handle. Regardless, we will find out who is responsible."

"I want you to personally handle it, and I want to be apprised of what you find out in a timely fashion. You have a habit of giving news releases on your investigations, and I learn about them from the media, and I don't like it."

"Yes sir," replied Mac.

Simple Eddie was standing now, looking out of his window. "Do you think smuggling is prevalent in Louisiana? It wouldn't look good for the governor or the colonel if our citizens thought we did not have a grip on the drug trade in our state."

Mac understood where Simple Eddie was going; if no drugs were seized and no arrests were made, the problem didn't exist. Simple Eddie was not the first politician to take this approach to crime issues.

"Smuggling in South Louisiana is not new. The Bulldog is the largest I've seen, but not the only one."

"We have about fifty thousand bayous and rivers along the Cajun coast, not to mention hundreds of grass landing strips on rice farms and bean fields scattered all over Acadiana. Smugglers regularly use the bayous to bring in loads of marijuana and cocaine."

"What is the standard mode of operation?" Simple Eddie turned to look at Mac, who was still sitting in front of the massive desk.

"Well, in basic terms," answered Mac, "a mother ship, which is usually nothing more than a fifty or sixty-foot fishing boat, will bring a few thousand pounds of weed or a few hundred pounds of coke, and anchor in the Gulf of Mexico. The local smuggler will rent a sport fishing boat or small oil field crew boat and rendezvous with the mother ship under the cover of darkness. They bring partial loads up through the Vermilion Pass to locations south of Lafayette where it can be off-loaded onto waiting trucks at any number of landings. It is invariably at night, and often in bad weather, if the smuggler has his choice," continued Mac. "They know their chances are better when there is less traffic on the bayou. I had one smuggler tell me he always brought in his loads during the first week of January because he knew cops would be watching football games."

Simple Eddie seemed preoccupied for a few moments, and then said, "Preliminary calculations indicate that this could be the largest importation of marijuana in the history of the United States."

It occurred to Mac that Simple Eddie was right, which was surprising, because he knew Simple Eddie was dumber than a piece of wood when it came to investigative matters. Mac was uncomfortable and not sure why. He looked at Simple Eddie, searching for some expression or for some gesture or emotion that would indicate that he may have more information than he was displaying. Mac tried to remember what behavioral systems he

43

should look for. He thought about posture, gestures, attitude, and eye contact.

"What makes you think it was the largest load in the history of smuggling in the country?" inquired Mac, waiting.

Mac was looking at Simple Eddie for some sign of nervousness that might give some credibility to the assumption that Simple Eddie had inside information.

"Oh, I don't know. You said it was a big boat, and I'm just guessing." Simple Eddie was now being overly polite and moving toward the office door. Mac thought his words were without conviction.

"Look," he said, "Acadiana is your area. You are the case agent. Find out who brought the marijuana into Louisiana and where it went from here. Contact Customs and work closely with them." Simple Eddie was setting his jaw and looking directly at Mac.

"In particular," Simple Eddie said, "I want you to work with Agent William O'Donnell. O'Donnell works mostly in Baton Rouge, but he can be in Lafayette as often as necessary. Customs has tremendous assets and contacts. They are our resident experts in the area of smuggling. Make damn sure you keep him apprised of all your progress."

Mac was incredulous. All the Region II agents knew O'Donnell well. He was only one of several federal agents who regularly came to the Region II office on every occasion that the narcotics section or Criminal Patrol Unit made a large seizure or significant arrest. Customs, DEA, and FBI (those "famous but incompetent" people) were all regulars at the office, and most were good people, but Mac wondered about Simple Eddie stressing O'Donnell in particular. "Why not DEA or FBI," he thought.

Mac was thinking about the process as he stood and moved toward the door. Seizures usually came two ways. One, narcotics agents investigated area drug activities and made seizures and arrests, or two, the Troop I Criminal Patrol Unit made traffic stops on Interstate 10 and intercepted drugs coming from Mexico though Houston and Lafayette to the east coast.

Whenever significant seizures and/or arrests were made, Mac notified local media outlets. As soon as Customs, DEA, and FBI heard about the case, as Agent Hollywood Bourdelle once said, "They are quicker than stink on shit to get to our office."

Mac thought about the feds copying LSP case reports and then writing their own reports claiming they assisted, and in some instances, supervised the case. On one occasion, Mac had questioned O'Donnell.

"Bill, why do you want copies of our reports?"

O'Donnell ignored the insult, and said, "More seizures means more funding and more personnel for our field offices, which means we can better support state police."

"Not to mention a better chance for you to get promoted," said Mac, continuing the insult.

"Listen, Bill," continued Mac. "Every local police agency involved in a seizure sends reports to the federal authorities, who keeps a national data base of personnel arrested and seizures made. Local Police Departments, area sheriff's offices, DEA, LSP, FBI, and Customs all claim the seizures. When it is all added up in the national database, the drug seizures are multiplied by six, resulting in Louisiana looking like a drug haven. Do you see a problem here?"

"Can't be helped," said O'Donnell. "That's the way the system works."

All of the agents in the Region II Field Office had become somewhat suspect of O'Donnell. He often seemed to know more than he should about a state police case, and it had been rumored that he and Simple Eddie socialized together in the Baton Rouge bar scene.

Mac thought about some similarities between Simple Eddie and O'Donnell as he was walking through the door into the secretary's office. They both preferred starched white shirts under three-piece pinstriped suits, which they kept immaculate. They both carried black leather briefcases. O'Donnell had somewhat more delicate features, and his self-indulgences included having his fingernails done with clear polish. For these reasons, Region II agents avoided O'Donnell as much as possible.

"One more thing," said Simple Eddie. "Colonel Carter wants to talk to you before you leave Headquarters."

Roy W. Frusha

CHAPTER 5
The S.H.I.T. Detail

Colonel Russell "Buck" Carter was superintendent of the state police for a little over two years, having been appointed by the governor soon after taking office. He was known for his intelligence and high level of education. Carter had a master's degree, whereas very few prior superintendents had any education further than high school. He was well liked in the ranks because of his regular visits to the troops, and his sense of humor when addressing them. It was also common knowledge that Carter, like most other high-ranking state police, had gone from trooper to colonel without ever having felt the flesh of a criminal. Carter was a Vietnam veteran, and had been in the Army Reserves for over twenty years. He had attended some excellent military schools along the way and was considered a capable leader.

Unfortunately, it had been commonplace in the Louisiana State Police for a sitting governor to promote his driver or bodyguard from the lowest ranks to captain or even colonel. It was well known that a particular governor, known for gambling and chasing young women, had promoted his wife's bodyguard to superintendent because she threatened him with a nasty and expensive divorce if he didn't. When the governor informed the captain that he was promoting him to colonel, he said, "It's the least I can do for you, considering that servicing my wife can be hazardous and beyond the call of duty."

It was a poor promotional system, so the rank and file considered itself lucky to have someone with Carter's background. It could have been worse. Carter had simply avoided the rigors of working twelve-hour shifts, weekends, and holidays because he had been smart enough to use his contacts and work the system to his benefit. He was not the first trooper to manage a successful career without working wrecks in the rain or wrestling drunks in a ditch on some godforsaken back road at two o'clock in the morning. Early in his career, Carter had managed to have himself placed in the Intelligence Division of the state police, where he

46

worked straight days collecting bits and pieces of information on gangsters in Baton Rouge. Since there were very few gangsters in Baton Rouge, his job was not complicated. In all of his years as an investigator, Carter had never arrested a single criminal, but he wrote excellent reports and understood the value of being a good writer, good listener and of keeping a low profile.

After leaving Simple Eddie's office, Mac took the elevator to the top floor of the headquarters building and Carter's office. He thought about the current governor of Louisiana. He was wealthy and elitist, having come from old money and prestige reminiscent of an effete southern aristocracy. Troopers assigned to his protective services detail said the move to the governor's mansion in Baton Rouge was a step down from his regular residence, which had been built by slave labor before the Civil War.

Mac entered the superintendent's office and approached his secretary. She looked to be about thirty-five years old with high cheek bones and a Doris Day haircut. Her dress revealed defined thighs and muscular calves. She looked fit and had the body of a younger woman. Mac thought she must work out often. Her dress was business, but also, tight and a little revealing, showing considerable cleavage when she sat down and reached for the phone to tell Carter that Mac was there. She was not wearing a ring and Mac briefly thought about asking her to lunch and was looking for the right approach when Carter walked into the room.

Carter was in his mid-fifties, slightly under six feet and a few pounds overweight, though not fat. Stocky would be a better description. His blue uniform was immaculate with perfect creases and freshly shined brass. His black shoes had a mirror finish; Mac noted that even the soles had been shined. His eyes were steady, but Mac judged that his thoughts were somewhere else.

"Good afternoon," said Carter, as he smiled and extended his hand to Mac. "Come into my office and have a seat."

The corner office was on the top floor and had almost floor-to-ceiling windows facing downtown Baton Rouge, the state capitol and governor's mansion. It was not as flashy and stylish as Kazan's office. Walls were not covered with expensive paintings but rather Army memorabilia. There was a dress sword on the wall above Carter's desk next to a picture of a young Army second lieutenant jumping out of the back of a C-130. A large Army knife was utilized as a paper weight on Carter's desk. Another wall had fifteen to twenty framed Army training certificates, promotions, and awards. Carter's Army medals were mounted against a black felt background. Mac would later say that, "Carter had more medals than a Mexican general." None of them indicated that he had ever seen combat. Carter was rear echelon all the way. The only picture that seemed to be out of place was one of John Wayne in a cowboy outfit.

"I understand that you were a Marine officer," said Carter, breaking the ice and establishing what he thought to be common ground. "I guess I will always be a soldier at heart."

"Yes sir," replied Mac, while taking a seat in front of Carter's desk. "But that was a long time ago. I did four years, and opted to get out. The Marine Corps is only fun if there is a war going on. When there is no war, regimental staff gets bored and holds inspections every other week. It's all spit and polish."

"What was your MOS (master occupational specialty)?" Carter inquired.

"Infantry when in Vietnam, but I transferred to Military Police when I returned stateside. I guess that's what got me interested in police work. Were you in Vietnam"? Mac asked, already knowing the answer.

Carter beamed, "I was stationed down in Saigon in 1966."

"You are the lucky one, Lieutenant. You are on the front line of the war against drugs. I would trade places with you if I could, but the governor wants me here, behind this desk."

"Why did you request to see me?" Mac wanted to get to the point.

"I know you came a long way today, so I'll get down to business. Colonel Kazan told me a little about the tug and barge you found in Vermilion Parish. Do you have any leads?"

"Not yet," Mac answered, "but the Region II team will find out who brought it in sooner or later. The marijuana has been distributed by now, so it's a historical investigation. We also have other investigations that are ongoing and have more of an adverse effect on the Lafayette area."

"Very good," said Carter. "I'm sure you can handle it. Life and business goes on, so to speak, and there are other matters I would like you to look into as well."

"Have you ever been to the governor's mansion and state capitol?" Carter asked.

Colonel Carter turned and walked toward the corner of his office and looked out of the massive window toward downtown Baton Rouge. "The governor's mansion, the nearby state capitol, and a few other historic buildings cover some twenty-seven acres of gardens and lakes along the Mississippi River," said Carter.

Mac wondered why he was getting a history lesson, but decided to let Carter continue uninterrupted.

"Come over to the window and take a look," said Carter. "The state capitol building in the distance was built by Governor Huey Long in 1932. It's the tallest state house in the United States. Long was assassinated in that building and is buried in its front lawn."

Mac looked out of the window as Carter continued his dialog. "Mac, are you acquainted with the Old Arsenal Powder Magazine and Museum near the mansion?"

"Not really, sir."

"It's the old red brick building on the grounds of the new state capitol. The history of the area goes back to 1720 when the French settled the area. Then England occupied the space until 1779 when Spain seized it. In 1810, a rag tag bunch of armed citizens took it by storm and declared it to be the Republic of West Florida. In 1836, it served as a military building housing guns and powder. In 1861, it belonged to the Confederacy, and after the war, it served as the campus for the Seminary of Learning, which would eventually become LSU. Legend has it that Ulysses S. Grant, George Armstrong Custer and Zachary Taylor served at the garrison. Now it's a museum."

Mac did not know where the conversation was going, but he knew it was more than a history lesson.

"The museum is in the middle of the park, and there are some walking paths under the oaks and magnolias that surround the building. It is a favorite place for the governor's wife to walk in the early evening," continued Carter.

"You know how the governor's wife is....old money, very aristocratic," continued Carter. "She says there are some undesirables hanging around the museum, and they make her nervous. She wants them removed. I instructed Colonel Kazan to

49

have them checked out, but he said our investigators in Baton Rouge are too busy right now, and he suggested you could handle this matter for us."

Mac thought to himself the reason the assignment is going to the Region II team is because it's a crappy assignment and Simple Eddie is covering for his Baton Rouge boys. Shit rolls downhill fast in LSP.

"Are the undesirables just run of the mill street bums and beggars, or is the park a meeting place for homosexuals?" Mac asked, as he considered similar issues that Lafayette had with city parks and I-10 rest areas.

"Colonel Kazan seems to think it may be a common location for homosexuals to meet. Anyway, the governor's wife has expressed that she doesn't have anything against gay people, she just wants them to conduct their business elsewhere."

Carter was walking toward the office door, indicating that it was time for Mac to leave. "Your assignment, Mac, is to do a little undercover work, and find a way to move the undesirables away from the park. Thanks for stopping by, and have a safe trip back to Lafayette."

The return trip across the Atchafalaya Basin toward Lafayette was due west and directly into a bright orange setting sun. Mac thought about the assignment. It was simple, any agent in Baton Rouge could handle it, so why was Simple Eddie assigning it to Region II? "Oh well," he said, aloud, "now this crazy job has got me talking to myself."

He thought about the right agent for the assignment. Hungry Harv wouldn't know a homosexual if one grabbed him by the dick. If a homo hit on Tatou Breaux he would whip his ass and drown him in the nearest lake. Hollywood would lose interest and just wander off to the nearest bar to chase women. Bubba Green can handle it, Mac thought. At least Bubba is educated enough to know the assignment is bullshit, he won't take it too seriously, and he has a morbid sense of humor. Perfect.

Darrell "Bubba" Green was one of the most educated investigators in the state police. He had a master's degree in history, and had been an instructor at a local college. He wrote the best reports in Region II. He was also almost always politically incorrect. He had a dry wit that most supervisors did not understand or relate to, and he had common sense. The tone and substance of Bubba's vocabulary had gotten him into trouble with the command staff on more than one occasion, and most of the time it was because they did not comprehend his intellect or humor.

The next morning Mac called in Bubba and explained the assignment.

Typical of Bubba, he accepted the job without a complaint and promised to do his best.

"This priority investigation needs a name," Bubba said, sarcastically. "How about Special Homosexual Investigative Team."

"Perfect," said Mac, thinking about the acronym. "The S.H.I.T. detail."

The next morning Bubba packed a change of clothes and drove his unit across the basin to Baton Rouge. Wasting no time, he parked his unit in the front capitol parking lot. At noon he decided to reconnoiter the grounds. He first walked past the statue and grave of former governor, Huey Long, after which he walked to the park area between the capitol and the governor's mansion.

Bubba was thinking about the history of Baton Rouge, which he had studied extensively. He knew he was walking the highest ground in the capitol city. It was close to the bluff, that according to legend, where a large cypress tree had been painted red to separate the hunting grounds of two area Indian tribes. The French had called the tree "Baton Rouge," meaning red stick, and the name stuck. The old state capitol, which Samuel Clemens had called the ugliest building he ever saw, was supposedly built where the original red tree had grown on a high bluff overlooking the Mississippi River.

As he continued his recon, Bubba thought about the Houma Indians who had occupied the area, followed by the French, then English, Spanish, and finally the United States, except from 1861 to 1865, at which time it was the capitol of Confederate Louisiana.

When he reached the Old Arsenal Building, situated between the capitol building and the governor's mansion, Bubba made a mental note that it was a short walking distance from the road that went from the mansion to the capitol, and there were several parking spaces under the trees that lined the road. The Old

Arsenal Building was surrounded by large oaks and magnolia trees. The terrain behind the arsenal sloped down to a lake. Bubba walked from the building toward the lake among the dogwood trees, hydrangeas and gardenias. The ground was littered with food wrappers, plastic water bottles, empty beer cans, and the occasional used condom.

Bubba walked back toward the capitol and stopped a hundred yards or so from the arsenal and sat at the foot of a large magnolia tree. He waited. At 6:30 p.m., when the sun was setting, he watched a late model Lincoln maneuver onto the narrow road between the mansion and the capitol and park under a live oak tree. A white male in a business suit exited the Lincoln and walked toward the arsenal. He was thin, had neatly trimmed grey hair, and appeared to be about fifty years old. He sat in a wood rocking chair on the porch of the arsenal. After twenty minutes or so he was approached by another middle-aged white male. They talked as if they knew each other. Bubba assumed the meeting had been prearranged. They went into the arsenal together. After another fifteen minutes or so, they emerged and walked their separate ways. Bubba wrote notes about times, appearances, and movements, but he was unable to copy the plate off the Lincoln.

The next morning Bubba met with two agents from the Baton Rouge narcotics field office. It was arranged that, in the afternoon, Bubba would wear a microphone and hang around the arsenal building. The Baton Rouge agents would monitor the listening device and tape the conversation.

"You hide in the bushes down by the lake," he instructed the Baton Rouge agents. "If I say something sexually related, come up the hill as quickly as you can and help me make the arrest."

"Got it," said both agents, who were clearly not interested in arresting homosexuals.

"Look," said Bubba, trying to get their attention, "monitor my conversation, and watch the corner of the building. If I get solicited for sex, you will hear in on the monitor, but in case the signal is bad, I will be standing next to the corner and will wave my right arm in large circles. When you see me waving my arm, come up the hill as quickly as possible."

"No problem," said one of the agents.

Bubba looked at the agents, and thought that, under the same circumstances, he wouldn't be enthusiastic either. Regardless, he did not have a good feeling about this operation.

That same afternoon, Bubba dropped the agents near the arsenal and showed them where they could hide behind some undergrowth close to the lake.

"Remember," said Bubba, "when I feel like I have enough conversation to make a soliciting case, I will say something sexual."

"Like what?" asked an agent.

"I don't know," replied Bubba. "Maybe I'll tell him he has a nice dick."

"Better you than me," said the agent.

"Har, Har," said Bubba. "This isn't my first choice in assignments either, but the governor wants something done about the homos and Simple Eddie assigned it to us."

The agents just looked at each other and said, "Right."

The two Baton Rouge agents checked their weapons and monitoring devices and walked slowly down the hill toward the lake. Bubba moved a wooden rocking chair next to the corner of the arsenal, sat down, and waited.

At six o'clock in the evening, Bubba sat quietly in the chair and watched the Lincoln drive under the live oak tree and stop. The same grey-haired gentleman exited the Lincoln and walked carefully up the hill toward the arsenal. Again, he was wearing a dark business suit. Bubba noted that this time the man was wearing glasses. When he saw Bubba in the chair, he stopped briefly, glanced over his shoulder, then continued the short distance to the building. He approached Bubba immediately upon reaching the arsenal.

"Hot today, isn't it, pal?"

"Hot every day this time of year," replied Bubba.

"What brings to the arsenal?" the man asked.

"Just resting in the shade," answered Bubba.

"Haven't seen you around here before. What is your name?"

"My name is Darrell, what's yours?"

"My name is Frank. Nice to meet you," he said while extending a hand to shake. "Tell me again, why you are at the park?"

"Well," said Bubba, "I was walking around the gardens, and I got a little tired, so I decided to rest. Why do you want to know?"

"I know what you came here for," Frank said, "and I am going to give it to you."

Frank looked around hastily to see if there were any other people in the area, then he stood directly in front of Bubba, unzipped his pants, and pulled out his penis.

Bubba, being caught off guard by the abruptness of the action, jumped up and said, "Hey, what the hell are you doing?"

Frank, who was now stroking his penis, said, "I'm getting my dick ready for you; let's go inside the building."

Bubba, who was regaining his composure, took a couple of steps toward the corner. He decided to get more conversation on tape.

"I'm new at this," Bubba said. "What is it exactly that you want to do?"

"I'm going to stick my dick in you ass, and talk dirty to you while I do it," said Frank. "That's why you are here, isn't it?"

"Up the hill, up the hill," Bubba was shouting.

"What are you talking about?" said Frank, who was puzzled.

The backup team heard the conversation, looked at each other, and decided that Bubba was not in immediate danger, so they lingered near the lake. They did not want to touch Frank, unless absolutely necessary.

Now Bubba was at the corner of the arsenal waving his right arm in large oval circles.

"Something wrong with your arm?" Frank asked.

"Uh, just a little bursitis," said Bubba, as he continued waving his arm.

Frank finally realized something was not right and proceeded to put his penis back into his pants. Bubba was aware that the backup team was not coming. He looked at Frank and said, "I'm agent Darrell Green with the Louisiana State Police, and you are under arrest."

Bubba made Frank lean against the brick wall and spread his legs while he searched him for weapons. He cuffed him and read him the standard Miranda rights.

The backup team, knowing that Bubba had secured Frank, had come up the hill to watch.

Frank, who had been scared, was regaining his self control and collecting his thoughts.

"Officers, I practice law in Baton Rouge. This is misdemeanor stuff, but I really don't need this kind of publicity, and neither does your supervisor," Frank said with an adamant voice.

"What are you implying?" asked Bubba.

"One of my best friends is Edward Kazan, whom I know to be in charge of all investigations within the state police."

"Just how friendly are you with Colonel Kazan?" asked Bubba, who immediately understood the innuendo.

"We run in some of the same circles and occasionally party together, and I know him well enough to tell you he would not approve of this type of attention any more than I would."

Bubba told the Baton Rouge agents he would handle the situation from here.

"Better you than us," they said, as they walked away. They gave Bubba the tape and said, "We didn't see or hear anything. That's our story and we are sticking with it."

Bubba left the cuffs on Frank, but placed him in the front seat of his unit where he would be more comfortable. He then drove to the nearest pay phone and called Mac.

"Lieutenant, we have trouble in paradise."

"What?" Mac asked.

"I arrested a middle-aged Baton Rouge lawyer for soliciting sex at the old arsenal. It appears he and Simple Eddie run in the same circles. He implied he will not go down alone. I'm not positive, but I have a strong feeling about this. It's a mine field."

Mac thought about the ramifications. The East Baton Rouge District Attorney would not have the time or inclination to pursue misdemeanor charges on an area attorney for soliciting sex. Allegations of misconduct against Simple Eddie would not cause him to lose rank or position in the department. He was too well-connected in the legislature, and Colonel Carter loved him.

"Bubba, if you arrest the homo, he will get off anyway, and the end result will be that Simple Eddie will accuse us of trying to hurt his reputation, and he will come down hard on us. It's a 'lose, lose' situation for us."

"What do you suggest, Mac?"

"In the interest of good judgment, my recommendation is to un-arrest the homo, tell him to go and sin no more, or at least don't do it around the park. Damn the governor's wife anyway."

"Roger that," said Bubba. "You advise to let the homo go with a warning."

"That's right. I know it's against procedure to release people after they've been arrested, but, if this thing got out of hand, no pun intended, our next assignment will be guarding the Henderson Swamp with a Daisy B B Gun."

Neither Frank nor Bubba spoke as Bubba drove back to the narrow road near the park, pulled up behind Frank's Lincoln, and parked.

Bubba walked around his unit, opened the passenger door, and helped Frank get out of the car, after which he removed the handcuffs.

Frank stood between his Lincoln and Bubba's unit, rubbing his wrists, and waited for instruction, or at least explanation.

Bubba, always the politically incorrect person, looked at Frank and said, "Carry your faggot ass away from here. If I see you near the arsenal building again, I'm going to cut your dick off and feed it to the fish."

Frank said nothing and started walking toward the driver's side of the Lincoln. Just before he got into his car he heard Bubba say, "Have a nice day, sir."

CHAPTER 6
Choir Practice

It had been five days since the discovery of the barge and tug at Fontenot's shipyard, and it was time to brief the Region II agents and catch up on administrative information coming out of headquarters in Baton Rouge. Mac arranged for "choir practice" at Doc Frederick's farm.

Dr. Sidney Frederick was a native of St. Martin Parish and one of Lafayette's first orthodontists. Mac met Dr. Frederick through his daughter, Dawn Frederick, when attending USL together. Dr. Frederick was an avid hunter and had purchased a hundred acre farm in rural St. Marin Parish, near the village of Arnaudville, where he maintained a rifle range, handgun range and small farm house. The farm was only twenty minutes from Region II Headquarters, and best of all, the farm was secured behind a heavy iron pipe gate, which he kept locked. There was a narrow gravel driveway leading to the farm house, which was shaded by a canopy of live oak trees. Doc had said the house was the oldest white frame structure in St. Martin Parish. Several years back Doc Frederick had given Mac a key to the farm so his team of narcs could shoot their guns without having to deal with the normal restrictions of a police firing range.

Mac had gotten into the habit of holding training sessions at the farm, where he, Hungry Harv and occasionally Doc Frederick, would purchase the ingredients for hotdogs and hamburgers, and have lunch on a large porch, typical of older Cajun structures. Beer was provided by the local Budweiser distributer, who had been Mac's college friend, and was a long-time supporter of law enforcement. Doc Frederick, who was a lifetime member of the NRA and huge fan of the second amendment, enjoyed listening to the enhanced police stories that always came with the beer.

Roy W. Frusha

It was at the Frederick farm that Mac would go over changes in policies and procedures and discuss any questions or concerns that the agents may have. The relaxed atmosphere of the farm was better suited than the office for making case assignments and obtaining verbal progress on existing investigations. The training session, which some of the agents called "choir practice," adopting the terminology from a Joseph Wambaugh novel, took place on the front steps of the old house.

After the training session was completed the agents practiced marksmanship with a beer in one hand and their service weapon in the other, a practice not generally allowed at the LSP range. They often switched hands quickly to demonstrate their dexterity and skill while shooting. Bubba considered it a sport worthy of a place in the Olympics, especially if you could do it without spilling any beer.

Hungry Harv, always trying to be practical said, "Actually, as much as the guys work undercover in barrooms, it's smart to practice shooting while drinking."

Mac thought about the men as they drank beer, laughed and shot their weapons.

The cousins, as they were called by the other agents, were born and raised in St. Martin Parish. Anthony "Hollywood" Bourdelle and Bennett "Tatou" Breaux had joined the state police one year apart. Their mothers were sisters and they had grown up together. Both were from wealthy families. Hollywood's father was a physician and Tatou's family owned one of the largest ship building companies in South Louisiana.

Hollywood was tall, well built and possessed the good looks of a movie star. He had dark thick hair, which he combed back, and had the brown skin of his Spanish ancestors. He regularly wore sunglasses, whether inside or out, and regardless of weather and lighting. His nickname came from the other narcs due to the sunglasses and extensive womanizing. Hollywood was married, but at any give time had at least two girlfriends. He was lucky that his mother was generous with his father's money. He had two former wives, or as he called them, "plaintiff number one, and plaintiff number two." Hollywood had a gift of gab, and it served him well as an undercover agent, and as a womanizer.

Hollywood once told Mac, "Lieutenant, hunting women ain't like hunting ducks. There's no limit on women."

58

Tatou, who was shorter, at five-foot-seven inches, had lighter skin, but the same dark, curly hair. He was heavyset, husky, high spirited and quick to lose his temper. When he was born he had short, fuzzy hair similar to that of a possum, thus his father had called him Tatou, which is French for possum. The name stuck. Tatou could have worked in the family business and been rich, but he preferred the risks, flexibility and adrenaline inherent to the job of a narc. Simply put, Tatou said, "I prefer fun over work."

As a road trooper Tatou subscribed to the theory that if a Hispanic male was driving through Louisiana in a vehicle with a Florida or Texas license plate there was the strong probability that he was carrying a load of marijuana, so he pulled them over and searched their vehicle. He did not always have probable cause, and rarely obtained a search warrant, and it was not always a legal search, but it was very, very effective.

On one occasion a Mexican male named Gonzales, had come to the Troop to file a formal complaint with Mac.

"What is your complaint, Mr. Gonzales?" Mac had asked him.

"Trooper Breaux stopped me and said that I was weaving in the roadway, so he was checking to see if I was drunk."

"Yes sir, and once Trooper Breaux realized that you were not drunk, what did he do next?"

"He asked me why I was in Louisiana, and I told him I was just passing through, on vacation to visit friends in Florida." Mr. Gonzales continued, "Then he asked me if I had some luggage in the trunk to prove I was on vacation. I opened my trunk and showed him my suitcases. He asked me if he could search the suitcases, and I said no to him. I had had enough and wanted to continue my trip."

Mac asked Mr. Gonzales what happened next, knowing it would not be good for tourism in Louisiana.

"He called me Poncho and told me to shut up or he would throw me in the swamp and feed me to the alligators. Then he searched one of my suitcases."

"Okay, Mr. Gonzales, these are serious charges. I need you to write a narrative of what you just told me on a formal complaint form. I'll forward it to Internal Affairs for further investigation, and see to it that Trooper Breaux is appropriately punished, maybe even terminated."

Mr. Gonzales seemed content, so he wrote his narrative, submitted it to Mac, and left the troop to continue his vacation.

Mac asked Trooper Breaux to come by his office when time permitted. Mac realized that the Fourth Amendment to the Constitution was not Trooper Breaux's strong suit. Many of his cases were thrown out of court for lack of probable cause, or even reasonable suspicion, or at least a general idea that a particular Mexican looked like a mule. However, Breaux led the state, if not the South, in marijuana and cocaine seizures, and that meant thousands of pounds of weed and coke would not hit the streets.

When they met Mac said, "Trooper Breaux, I appreciate all of your hard work, but bias based profiling is against the law. This fellow Gonzales has filed a formal complaint against you. Another supervisor may have followed up on it." Mac wadded the form and threw it into a trash basket. "If you are not more careful with this a news organization will pick up on it and set you up. It could be a big story. Try to mix it up out there; don't stop just minorities."

"Lieutenant, I haven't stopped a democrat in two weeks," Breaux said firmly. "I mostly look at the MAD people. You get better results with them."

Mac looked up from his desk, "Mad Mothers Against Drunk Driving?"

"No, Mexican Aliens with Dope."

Mac smiled and thought about a proper response. He remembered that Trooper Breaux had stopped the same Mexican mule, who was an illegal alien, three times in a six-month period on Interstate 10 in St. Martin Parish. The Mexican's name was Renaldo, and each time Trooper Breaux had seized a load of cocaine or marijuana headed to Florida. Each time Renaldo was turned over to immigration authorities, and each time he was temporarily sent back to Mexico.

The third time Trooper Breaux stopped Renaldo he did not have to turn on his emergency lights to pull him over. Renaldo recognized Breaux and knew that he would be stopped, so he simply pulled over voluntarily, got out of his car, and opened his trunk so Trooper Breaux could see the marijuana. Renaldo knew the routine.

Mac thought about the futility of stopping and arresting drug traffickers, knowing that neither the state government nor federal government would do anything useful to stop the flow of illegal drugs on the interstate system. The drug trade was bigger than U. S. Steel, and no one was going to stop it.

"You know what I mean, Tatou," said Mac. "Let's do us both a favor. Why don't you get off the road for a while and come to work in Region II Narcotics. You and your cousin Hollywood can have some fun."

Another agent who had been actively recruited by Mac was Grady "Rooster" Milam. Rooster had gotten his start with state police at Troop F in Shreveport. Mac liked Rooster because, like Mac, Rooster was somewhat of a North Louisiana redneck. Rooster had gotten the nickname at Troop F, because of a joke about a barnyard rooster who played dead so he could catch a circling buzzard and screw it. Rooster did not cull his women.

"If you cull your women," Rooster said, "you can't get into heaven."

Rooster had made a name for himself in police circles on two occasions. Rooster lived for a while in a rural parish north of Shreveport and hunted coons for sport. Rooster had two young children and his wife was continually nagging him about his coon dogs being overly aggressive toward the children. One day it happened. Rooster was coming home from a shift and his wife met him at the door, screaming and holding up a child to show Rooster the stitches the child had taken from one of his coon dogs. Rooster had had enough. He pulled his Smith and Wesson .357 caliber side arm and walked calmly over to his coon dogs and shot each of them in the head. Then he walked into his residence, picked up his wife's poodle by the scruff of his neck, walked out into the front yard, and shot the poodle out of his hand.

"We are out of the dog business," he informed his terrified and hysterical wife.

They were divorced shortly after the incident.

Rooster gave up coon hunting as a hobby and became an avid Civil War buff and re-enactor. He bought a grey horse and the uniform of a Confederate Colonel and attended re-enactments all over the South. Rooster was dressed in his confederate uniform when he was driving his marked unit to a re-enactment at Port

Hudson, south of St. Francisville.   Rooster was on Highway 61, headed south, when he clocked an on-coming car in excess of ninety miles per hour. It was too much for Rooster to take. He hit his brakes, fishtailed through the median and pulled the speeder over.   The speeder was in a late model Cadillac with Michigan plates. The driver was an African American lawyer, returning from a business trip to Baton Rouge.

Rooster approached the Cadillac and requested the driver to exit.

"Why are you wearing a sword, officer?" The man asked.

"None of your business. Sign the citation."

"I thought the Civil War was over."

"General Lee surrendered: I didn't," said Rooster.

The man took his speeding citation in good order from Rooster without further discussion, albeit he was a little pallid, or as Rooster would later say, almost white.

The letter the driver subsequently wrote to the governor's office and superintendent of the Louisiana State Police was a scathing denunciation of the unmitigated arrogance of a southern state that would dress its troopers in the uniform of the Confederacy. He demanded an explanation and an apology. He also sent a copy of the letter to NBC, CBS, ABC and various other news shows.

The governor and superintendent were initially in disbelief, but when they found out it was true they demanded Rooster give up his confederate uniform and be moved to another location in the state police, preferably one where he would not have daily contact with out-of-state civilians. Mac was glad to have Rooster on board with his Region II team. Rooster possessed courage and a good work ethic, although Mac might have to provide some Gee and Haw on occasion.

Hungry Harv sat on the front porch of the Frederick camp quietly sipping on a draft beer and watched the narcs shoot their pistols at the nearby range. Mac commented that agent Bertrand "Bert" DeBlanc was shooting a new gun.

"Bert is not like the rest of the agents," Hungry Harv said. "He is the only agent we have that is married to the same woman. He doesn't run the girls or the bars, but he likes new toys. He's the best tech man we've had. He keeps up with the latest in electronic gadgets. He has mettle, and enjoys participating on all the raids.

As for the new gun, he comes from money, and can have a new gun anytime he wants one. Like the rest of us; he is a police officer because he likes the chase and the action. He could be making a lot more money in his family business."

Bubba Green was intermittingly shooting right handed and then left handed from different positions, and never spilled his beer. Mac recalled when he recruited Bubba. Bubba was smart, educated and had served his country in the military. Not all of the agents had been in the military, but Mac preferred to recruit people with service records whenever possible. As a general rule they proved to be better disciplined and more dependable. They understood that LSP was a quasi military organization and it took less training to get them on step.

When Mac had interviewed Bubba he asked him if he had ever been in the military.

"Yes sir," said Bubba, "I was in the Air Force for four years."

"No, I meant military service," said Mac.

"Har har, Lieutenant. I heard you were in the Marines. I saw a lot of Marines where I was stationed, and I took a lot of ribbing about the Air Force not being a branch of the military."

"I was going to join the Marines, but they found out my parents were married."

Mac smiled, he liked his agents to have a sense of humor. "Where were you stationed?"

"I spent two years at Clark Air Force Base in the PI, Sir."

"The Philippines," said Mac. "Did you ever get over to Subic Bay and Cubi Point for a little recreation?"

Subic Bay was the home of the infamous Olongapo City, and Mac thought about the womanizing of some of the other agents and wanted to know if Bubba would fit in socially.

"Yes sir. Every airman in that part of the world knows about Olongapo. My first trip there I bar hopped around town some, then someone told me about the East End Club. That was a little too gross, even for me. I ended up hanging around a club called the U and I, just off Magsaysay Drive."

Mac remembered Magsaysay Drive being the main street in Olongapo. It crossed a deep drainage canal that separated the town from the Subic Bay military installation. The canal was called "shit river" by the military personnel who crossed it by the hundreds every day, walking into town for San Miguel beer and exotic entertainment. Young boys dove from the bridge into the canal for dimes that the sailors and Marines threw into the water.

"I remember the U and I Club," said Mac. It was almost totally a Marine hangout, though anyone with two pesos for a San Miguel, or five dollars for a girl, was welcome."

"The Marines didn't seem to mind a flyboy drinking with them, and I was having a good time listening to their stories about Vietnam, until someone played the Marine Corps Hymn on the jukebox."

Mac looked intently across the desk at Bubba. "Please tell me you stood up."

"Nope, wasn't my song, so I didn't stand."

"What did they do to you?"

"They beat me up pretty good, but actually that wasn't the worst part. They were trying to throw me through a window. I would have jumped through it, if I could have gotten loose. Anyway, they finally succeeded, and the glass cut me up some. The really bad part was the rehabilitation I had to go through after I got out of the hospital."

"Did you learn anything from the experience?" Mac asked.

"I stand up for the Marine Corps Hymn now."

Mac looked at Hungry Harv and returned his thoughts to the agents. "What are your thoughts on D K?" He asked Hungry Harv.

Patrick "D K" Celestine was the only African American agent in Region II Narcotics. D K had been a police officer in Patterson, Louisiana, near his home town of Morgan City, for four years, after which he ran for chief of police, and served in that capacity for another four years. Patterson was a small community and D K did not like the politics involved, nor did the job pay very well. He joined the state police, and had attended the academy with Mac. D K was tall, light skinned, good humored and smart. If he had any faults, it was his love for women, all of them. D K's first assignment was to Troop A, and the rural parishes north of Baton Rouge.

D K met his wife while working in the small town of Jackson, Louisiana, in agricultural East Feliciana Parish. She was a devout Southern Baptist. After their third child was born, she thought it was best for the family, and safer for D K, if he took a job with the state police that had regular hours. So D K volunteered for protective services and was assigned to Kathleen Babin, the lieutenant governor of Louisiana. His friends in the narcotics division began calling him "Driving Miss Kathy," and finally dropped it to D K, which stuck. He stayed with the lieutenant governor less than a year before becoming bored with the position. He volunteered for a narcotics slot.

His wife stayed at their country home just outside of Jackson, and D K rented a small apartment in Lafayette. He worked mostly cocaine cases in the north Lafayette area, but was often assigned under-cover cases in Houma, Lake Charles and other locations scattered throughout Southwestern Louisiana. He never complained and seldom failed to make a case. He worked closely with Duane "Dee" Pellerin.

Agent Pellerin had recently joined state police narcotics after a stint with the Lafayette Police Department.

"I don't know," said Hungry Harv, as he observed D K from the porch. "He seems to me to have something on his mind. I can't quite figure it out, but something is bothering him."

"Maybe we should send him home to Jackson for a few days of R and R," said Mac.

"He may be having family problems," said Hungry Harv, "but he knows he can go home anytime he wants. I think he has girlfriend problems. Some of the agents said he has fallen for a girl in his apartment complex."

"What about Buzzy," Mac asked Hungry Harv. "How is he doing since the divorce?"

Buzzy Bonin was the newest agent in the group. He had a degree in criminal justice, was articulate and wrote exceptionally good reports. He had worked as a road trooper only one year before being selected for undercover work. Buzzy had grown a long beard and had let his naturally curly hair reach his shoulders. He got tattoos and earrings and bought a motorcycle. It was a complete makeover for Buzzy. He ran lower-end bars and established contacts with strippers in five parishes. He developed snitches and bought drugs. He was good, but his devoutly Christian wife was not happy.

Justine Bonin had married a clean cut, well-mannered young man who took her to dinner on Saturday night and church on Sunday morning. She liked it when Buzzy was on shift because she knew exactly when he reported to work and when he was due home. She could schedule her life, and to some extent, his. Now she never knew where he was, and he looked like a tramp. He had become so ugly her children often cried when he came home late at night. The fear of losing Buzzy made Justine almost as crazy as her mother.

"Buzzy," Justine said, one evening after supper. "I've signed us up for dance lessons."

"Why would you do that?" asked Buzzy. "You know I hate to dance."

"My mother suggested it. She thinks it will be good for our relationship. We need to do more things together."

Justine and Buzzy had been taking dance lessons for several weeks before the tug and barge came up Vermilion Bayou. The dance instructor was a leggy brunette with store bought boobs. She was also about a foot taller than Justine. Three weeks into the lessons the instructor began giving special attention to Buzzy. Justine might have noticed, had she not been so happy Buzzy was dancing.

It was opportune that the life of a narc has to be flexible. Buzzy began taking late night lessons at the instructor's apartment, telling Justine he was on assignment.

Justine had suspicions, so she called Mac for an appointment.

"Lieutenant," she said, "my husband stays out late almost every night. Sometimes he doesn't come home until two o'clock in the morning. I think he might be having an affair with another woman."

"I'm not a marriage counselor, Mrs. Bonin," Mac stammered. "Maybe you should see a professional."

"I have, but Buzzy won't attend meetings with me. You, and my mother, are the only people I can discuss this with."

"Well," said Mac, "let's not jump to conclusions. All of the agents work nights. Night is when our clientele is active. Maybe Buzzy is doing some undercover work." Mac knew that Buzzy had not been assigned any recent undercover investigations, but he attempted to give Justine an out.

"A few weeks ago Buzzy and I started taking dancing lessons," Justine said abruptly. "I've driven by the instructor's apartment late at night and Buzzy's car is there."

Mac looked at her and said nothing.

"When his car is at her apartment all night, do you think it means Buzzy is sleeping with her?" Justine asked.

"I have to admit that it would look suspicious, but it's not necessarily proof," replied Mac, who thought to himself that if it were my car there all night I would be sleeping with her.

"Thank you for your time," Justine said, and began crying as she left the office.

Later that morning Mac called in Buzzy and explained what had happened. "Your affairs are none of my business, and the last thing I want to do is to get caught up in your marriage problems. Your wife came to me in tears and wanted advice. God knows I'm not qualified to give it. Hell, my ex-wife ran off with a dope-peddling, guitar-playing hippie. I was married for six years to a Crowley beauty queen when she walked in one day and said her new boyfriend showed her more love in one day than I did in a year. The son-of-a-bitch didn't even have a job. I thought she was doing Little Theater every night; it turned out she was doing her best man. Shit happens."

"Was your ex-wife happy?" asked Buzzy.

"She was for about twenty-one years," answered Mac, "but then she married me."

Buzzy did not laugh. "What did my wife say to you, Mac?"

"She said she followed you to your dance instructor's apartment on several occasions, and that you car was parked there all night. She asked me if that meant you were having sex with her."

Buzzy squirmed in his chair and looked at the floor, expecting bad news. "What did you tell her?"

"I said that she should realize that if you stayed with a woman, in her apartment, all night, that she should consider that is was possible you were having an affair, and that she should talk to you about it, not me."

Buzzy stood, paced the floor, and looked directly at Mac. "The truth is, Mac, I do have a girlfriend, and I've been seeing her at her residence, but we have not had sex."

It was hard for Mac to believe Buzzy was spending nights with a good-looking, hard-bodied home wrecker and not having sex. "Well, I guess you can move on to the next step and consummate the affair since I led your wife to believe you were doing it anyway. Sorry."

Buzzy got up to leave, and looked back when he reached the door. "Hey, Mac, don't help me anymore, okay."

The next morning Justine's mother, Mary Gautreaux, came to the office and requested to see Mac.

"Lieutenant, what are you going to do about Buzzy?" She demanded.

"Marriage counseling is not my area of expertise," said Mac, backing up, looking for an exit. "Buzzy asked me to stay out of his personal business, and I think that's what I will do."

"Did you know Buzzy's girlfriend was evil?"

Mac looked at the lady, briefly wondered what she meant, and moved a few steps closer to the door.

"The woman is a witch, and she cast a spell on Buzzy. We have to find a way to break the spell."

"Exactly what do you mean?" Mac said, with his mouth open, taking two more steps toward the door.

"I mean that Buzzy is the victim of a spell. It could be drugs, or witchcraft, but we have to break it."

Mac had meant to ask her to leave, but now he was curious. Voodoo and hoodoo had been practiced in Louisiana since the African slave trade, and was still active along the coast. He had heard several stories since moving to South Louisiana. One of the stories was about the famous blues singer, Robert Johnson, who supposedly sold his soul to the devil. He sang about it, saying "hot foot powder sprinkled all around my door." Tales of witchcraft around Acadiana had been rare until the recent charismatic movement.

"Are you Catholic Charismatic, Mrs. Gautreaux?" asked Mac politely. Mac knew the movement, which included speaking in tongues, possessing the gift of prophecy and supernatural healing, was currently popular in the Lafayette area. Mac's former wife had been involved in the movement for a short time, before she discovered unemployed dope-smoking guitar players.

"Yes," said Mrs. Gautreaux.

Mac stood up from his chair and started walking toward the door, indicating that it was time for Mrs. Gautreaux to leave.

"I'll talk to Buzzy some more, Mrs. Gautreaux, but he will have to work out his domestic problems on his own. Maybe you could suggest that he and your daughter talk to a professional."

One week later Justine and her mother followed Buzzy to his girlfriend's dance studio. They walked past the students and stood directly in front of Buzzy and the instructor. Mrs. Gautreaux spoke a few words that no one understood, and then hurled holy water on them. She caught them twice with the water as they attempted to run.

There was also Otis Ray Coody, who was as dark as D K with the same black curly hair. It was common knowledge that he was a "Red bone" from rural Beauregard Parish near the community of Merryville. Red bone was a derogatory term describing a group of people with a mixture of blood that includes Negro, Spanish, French, Indian and Caucasian. No one referred to the quiet, but quick tempered Coody as a Red bone. He was the only narc without a nickname. "You could not make up a better name than his given name," said Bubba. Coody's main goal in life was to improve the quality of his moonshine.

"Well, they are a good group. They work together well, and they are productive. They make a lot of arrests, and put a lot of dopers in jail, and that's what we are paid to do," Hungry Harv said.

"I don't like to get involved in their personal lives, unless they ask," Mac replied. "It's outside of my comfort zone."

"Mac, they remind me of the clay and Spanish moss mixture used to stabilize and insulate the walls of this old house. They trust and depend on each other, and together they make a strong team. They are our bousillage boys."

"Bousillage?"

"It's a building technique the Cajuns brought to Louisiana. The Cajuns would fix moss and clay dirt with water, and sometimes grass, and stuff it in the spaces between the wood posts used to frame a house. When it dried they could plaster and

69

paint it. It made for a strong wall and helped cool the house in summer and heat it in winter."

The agents holstered their weapons and gathered around in the shade of the porch.

Mac brought them up to date on the tug and barge saying, "Hungry Harv and I will concentrate on the 'Bulldog' investigation. Everyone else will continue with their on-going investigations, but keep an eye and ear open for any connections. My thoughts are that it is too big for any locals to handle, but locals had to be involved in order for it to be successful. As many as one hundred people may have been used, from off-loaders to drivers. Put some feelers out with your snitches, and offer some reward money for information. Let us know if you hear anything that may be related to the investigation."

Mac walked into the front yard, facing Hollywood and Tatou. "Hollywood, there's a report about two young black males dealing a new form of cocaine, 'crack' I think they are calling it, out of the Oak Trace Apartments on Pinhook Road, near the old Catholic Carmelite Monastery. You and your cousin see what you can find out about it."

"Also," Mac continued addressing the cousins, "Captain Landry, at Troop I, called to report that there have been several citizen reports of sexual harassment at the Interstate 10 rest stops just east of Lafayette. I argued that the Troop I shift lieutenants should handle it, but Landry said they were too busy. Anyway, at least check it out; who knows, they may be dealing drugs at the rest stops."

"Bubba handled the last shit detail, no pun intended," Mac said, as looked toward Bubba, and gave a synopsis of the Baton Rouge investigation. When Mac got to the part about the allegation that Simple Eddie may be a homo the cousins stuck their fingers in their ears and made incoherent noises. It was clearly information they didn't want to know about.

"Anyway," said Mac. "Remember, we work hard, and we play hard. Don't forget to have fun along the way." He was not through telling them to have fun, when Mac noticed that Hollywood sneaked away from the group. He filled an empty beer can with some gravel, and placed it under the driver's seat of Hungry Harv's unit.

Wrestling With Pigs

Hungry Harv was big enough to hunt bear with a stick, but his phobia regarding reptiles was legendary. When he applied the brakes as he was nearing the iron gates leading to Doc Frederick's farm the can rolled from beneath the seat making a sound similar to a rattle snake. The car had not stopped rolling when Hungry Harv jumped out of the door. Damage to the car was minor, but it was some time before the cousins would get within a few feet of Hungry Harv.

CHAPTER 7
Broussard Brothers

Three weeks had passed since the discovery of the tug and barge. It was the middle of July and the weather was tropical. Rain splashed on Mac's car in angry torrents from low, almost black clouds, obscuring the highway as he guided his unit south on Highway 167 toward Vermilion Parish. He drove slowly, knowing that the rain would pass in less than an hour. Hurricane season, when weather would become really dangerous, was months away. He turned on Highway 696. The rain had become a light drizzle and a thick fog enveloped the roadway. Visibility was less than one hundred feet, and speeds of more than thirty miles per hour were hazardous.

A local rancher's herd of cattle had broken through his fence and one had been hit by a pickup. Mac checked on the driver, who was not injured, and noted that the truck was totaled. He notified Troop I and called for the next 10-79 (wrecker). Troop I responded saying the lone trooper in Vermilion Parish was tied up with another accident near Pecan Island. Mac said he would begin the necessary paperwork to give him a head start. He was removing an accident report form from his trunk when he heard the cow's high pitched moan coming from the ditch where she landed.

The cow was attempting to stand on broken legs, and her piercing wails lamented her pitiful condition. Mac looked for a brand or some other identification so that he might contact the owner, but there was none. He thought about identifying the property owner by the hole in the fence, but previous experience told him that the owners would disclaim the animal to avoid any liability for the accident.

It was against state police policy and procedure, but Mac could not stand there and listen to the cow's suffering. He drew his Smith and Wesson .357 magnum and shot the cow between the eyes. Any time a shot is fired on duty the troop was to be notified and a shooting team would be dispatched to fully investigate the incident. Mac decided not to reveal the incident.

The driver just looked at Mac, as he holstered his weapon. "Standard procedure," Mac said.

The driver was nodding his approval when a late model BMW drove upon the scene and stopped. A middle-aged woman was driving and the female passenger appeared to be about fifteen, probably a daughter. Mac thought, "Rubber-neckers and do-gooders, they have a morbid sense of curiosity." Most cops try to avoid them.

"Is anyone injured," asked the lady, as she thrust her head through an open window of the beemer.

"No ma'am," said Mac. "Things are under control. No one is hurt. You can go now, and please be careful."

"Who was in the truck? Was it someone from here?"

"It's a police matter lady, please allow me to handle it. As I said before, be careful when you leave. It's pea soup out here. Visibility is next to nothing, and there are cows on the road." Mac turned his back on her, indicating that the conversation was over, and it was time for her to leave.

"The sheriff is my brother-in-law, and I want to know who was driving that truck." She was considerably louder.

Mac ignored her and proceeded with his paperwork.

The lady stomped her accelerator and the BMW peeled out, practically leaping down the narrow asphalt highway. She had not gone two hundred yards when Mac heard the screeching of brakes and the impact of the car with a cow. Mac threw down the accident report in disgust and drove to the second accident, which would mean a second accident report, another wrecker, possible injuries, and he would have to find transportation for the occupants.

The front end of the car was caved in and fluids were draining from the engine.

"Are either of you hurt?" Mac asked.

"No," said the lady. "My daughter and I are alright, but that poor cow is rolling around on the road, and blood is coming from her mouth. Oh, this is just awful."

Mac looked hard at the woman. "Are you sure you are not hurt?"

"We're fine officer, but look at that poor animal."

The woman was still talking as Mac walked to the cow and shot it twice in the head. The unexpected and explosive shots, combined with a two-foot flame coming out of the barrel, was sufficient to make the woman urinate on her plush leather seat.

"See what you made me do," Mac informed the woman. "Did I not tell you there were cows on the road, and that you should drive slowly and carefully?"

The woman did not say another word to Mac, but the next day she filed a written complaint against him, claiming he was rude and that he killed an innocent cow.

The rain had stopped by the time Mac arrived at Fontenot's shipyard. He parked his unit near the smaller of the two metal buildings and walked into the office. An overweight and bored secretary sat behind an antiquated metal desk smoking a cigarette. The tin walls of the office had been covered with cheap wood paneling that had become popular in the 1950s. The office was cooled with a noisy air conditioner that hung loosely out of a window. The off-white dropped ceiling was rust colored from years of neglect.

Mac introduced himself and asked for the yard foreman.

"That would be Clement Thibodeaux," she replied. "I'll get him for you."

Mac looked through the office window at the large shell yard, observing a dozen or so men moving about the yard. The tug and barge had not been moved since they had discovered the marijuana. One of the yard hands was using a boom lift, commonly called a cherry picker, to move supplies from a large storage building onto a docked supply boat. Mac noted that the cherry picker was mounted on a trailer so it could be easily moved around in the yard. Even with a cherry picker, or two or three cherry pickers, Mac thought it would take the better part of three days to off-load four hundred thousand pounds of marijuana.

"My name is Clement Thibodeaux," the man said as he entered the office, "and I am the foreman here." He spoke with a typical Cajun accent, not pronouncing the "th" or theta sound, saying "dis" for "this," or "dat" for the word "that." Thibodeaux appeared to lack formal education, but there was determination and authority in his voice. He was accustomed to telling other people what to do.

Thibodeaux was dressed in grease-stained denim coveralls and wore the white rubber boots preferred by the shrimpers in nearby Delcambre. Bubba called the white boots "Delcambre Reeboks." Thibodeaux was average height, stocky and had the rough, bull-like features you would expect of someone who spent his life working in the oil field. He had a large stomach from eating rice and gravy all of his life, but he was not fat, just big.

"Mr. Fontenot said you would be coming, Lieutenant. What can I do for you?"

"The tug and barge. Do you have any idea how they got here, or where they came from?"

"I don't have a clue, officer. We left work on a Friday afternoon and they were not here. We came back to work Monday morning and there they were." Thibodeaux fidgeted and looked away, momentarily lost in his thoughts. When he looked back at Mac, he blinked twice.

"How long have you worked for Lawless Fontenot?"

"Twenty-five years. It's a good job, and I don't want to lose it. I have a family to feed, Lieutenant." There was obvious concern, and maybe some resentment, in Thibodeaux's voice.

"In most places oil field work goes twenty-four hours per day, seven days a week. Is it normal procedure for all of your personnel to go home on week-ends? Aren't there crew boats and supply boats that operate on Saturdays and Sundays?"

"Sometimes we work weekends, sometimes we don't. It depends on the work load."

"What about security?" Mac turned and looked across the yard. "You've got cherry pickers, trailers, trucks, fork lifts, tools, a cash register, and a multitude of other equipment I haven't yet seen in this yard. Are you telling me that Lawless Fontenot does not have security personnel here on nights and weekends?"

"Like I said, sometimes we do, and sometimes we don't."

"Do the Fontenot boys, James and Jude, work here?"

Clement Thibodeaux looked thoughtfully out the window.

"They are good boys," said Thibodeaux. "They work here off and on. They've had other jobs too, and they went to that college up in Lafayette for a few months. I haven't seen them around the yard for a while. I'm not sure what they are doing now." Thibodeaux was evasive and uncomfortable.

Mac returned the conversation to the tug and barge. "Have you walked on the boat?"

"Yeah, I walked on the barge and tug. I know a little about boats, and that's not much of a tug. The tug is in my way, so I started the engine so I could move it, but I couldn't get it into gear. I think the clutch, or maybe transmission, is shot." Thibodeaux was glad the conversation had changed from the Fontenot boys and he spoke readily about the tug.

"Are you saying that this tug," Mac pointed toward the boat and barge, "did not come into this ship yard under its own power?"

"I'm saying that I needed to get it out of my way, so I tried to move it. The engine cranked okay, but the clutch is screwy."

"Then how did it get here?"

"Another tug could have pushed them into the yard and left them here." The tone of Thibodeaux's voice indicated that it seemed perfectly normal to him, but it had not occurred to Mac that another boat might be involved.

"If a tug broke down in the Gulf of Mexico, is there anyone around this area with the capacity to tow it through the locks and into the Vermilion Bayou?"

"Mais, yeah," said Thibodeaux. "Broussard Brothers has a field office between Banker and Abbeville. They could handle the job, no problem."

"I'll want to talk to you some more," Mac said as he turned and walked to his unit.

Mac looked at one of the many maps he kept in his trunk. Banker was an unincorporated area of Vermilion Parish, not ten miles distance from Fontenot's shipyard, except that there were no straight roads in that part of the parish. Elevation was often no more than two or three feet above sea level. It was just as well that he back track to Abbeville and choose another route. It was almost noon and he was hungry; Abbeville had restaurants.

The twenty mile stretch north to Abbeville was a mixture of farmland, salt marsh, saw grass and duckweed. Ditches were filled with water where dirt had been dug to elevate the road. Occasionally Mac passed an African American family fishing with cane poles. Depending on the time of year and the tides, the ditches in this area were home to choupique, garfish, chinquapin, channel cat, drum, and redfish, just to name a few. Mac mused that as long as there was a ditch with water in it the people native to Vermilion Parish would not go hungry.

Black's Oyster House in Abbeville had been a tourist spot for as long as Mac had been living in the Lafayette area. He ordered black coffee, knowing that it would be locally produced Community or Mellow Joy. There were no other choices in Acadiana. He decided on a shrimp po-boy with a side of homemade potato salad. As he was eating and watching the other customers he thought about the last time he was in Black's.

It had been six years, and the state police had assigned him to a security detail for the actor Walter Matthau, who was in Lafayette and Carencro to film a movie about a small-time Cajun horse trainer, who took a horse to the All American Futurity in New Mexico. It was coincidental that the movie, "Casey's Shadow," was based on a retired state trooper who trained racing quarter horses in nearby Erath.

Mac had stayed with Matthau sixteen hours a day for thirty days. He recalled Matthau being polite, organized, and a hard worker. He was far from the beer drinking slob he sometimes portrayed. Matthau had told Mac that his one true passion was gambling, and that he had lost over one million dollars to bookies during the past year.

The movie had been filmed in early winter, and the weather had been unusually sunny, cool and calm. Mac remembered the director's wife being astoundingly beautiful. She was tall, thin, about twenty-five, and had the legs of an athlete and the face of a goddess. But it was the boobs that people first noticed. Her dress code was consistent: she was always in cut off denims and a tee shirt. She never wore a bra, and the cool weather exhibited picture perfect nipples. Wherever she went on the set, her boobs got there a foot before the rest of her.

Mac's job was simply to stay near Matthau and keep tourists away when he was filming. The only time Matthau had an issue it involved the director's wife, who tore into Matthau when they were filming in front of Evangeline Downs in Carencro.

"I never said anything derogatory about you," stammered Matthau.

"My moral standards are as good as yours," she screamed.

"I never questioned your morals," Matthau shouted back.

"Just because I don't wear a bra, it does not mean I have loose morals." She was almost spitting on him.

Frustrated, Matthau got closer to the woman, bent over, and looked directly into her eyes. "I didn't say you had loose morals....I said you had loose tits."

Mac, unable to contain himself, had burst out laughing. The director's wife looked at him and said, "Where the fuck did you come from?" and promptly walked off.

After finishing off his po-boy and coffee Mac walked two blocks down Pere Megret Street in front of the ancient Catholic Church toward city center and the parish courthouse. At the courthouse he researched the little information that was available on the history of Abbeville, Henry and Banker, as well as doing a property search on Lawless Fontenot.

In 1760 Fusilier de la Clair had purchased land between Vermilion Bayou and the Teche Bayou from the Attakapas Indian chief, Kimino. In 1843 a Catholic priest named A. D. Megret paid less than a thousand dollars to Joseph LeBlanc for the land that would later become Abbeville. Henry was a small village south of Abbeville, and Banker was not much more than an intersection of two rural parish roads.

Like every community in South Louisiana Banker had a small Catholic Mission Church, a cemetery, and a small store that dealt in groceries and hunting supplies. If you were not a Veazey, Fontenot, Stelly, Guidry or Broussard, you were considered an outsider. If you were from somewhere north of Lafayette you were a damn Yankee, and not to be trusted. They still remembered Reconstruction and carpetbaggers in Vermilion Parish.

Mac drove south on State Street and then onto Highway 330 toward Banker, passing farms and cattle first, and then marsh. He drove slowly with his windows down. He could smell the stench of the saw grass and bulrush that floated on the murky water, never being dried by the sun and air above the water. Wherever the elevation reached two feet above sea level a few trees and bushes would sprout up, supporting the many types of wildlife indigenous to the area. The marshy environment was good for game, birds and fish, but it was tough on humans.

Highway 330 meandered south of Abbeville toward Banker, and Vermilion Bayou. From Banker the Vermilion curved and grew larger and deeper as it flowed on to Intracoastal City, some thirteen miles south.

There was a large community of workers in Intracoastal City, supporting offshore personnel, oil platforms, drilling rigs and shrimp boats. The Intracoastal Waterway ran through the village on its thousand-mile trip from Brownsville, Texas, to Carrabelle, Florida. The waterway had been designed and developed for barge transportation. Mac thought about the massive number of boats and barges using the waterway, and wondered how many of them carried drugs on a daily basis.

Mac pulled onto a long, narrow road made entirely of oyster shells, just wide enough for a large truck. Ancient live oak trees cast shadows across the lane as he drove onto the Broussard Brothers compound. It was similar to Fontenot's shipyard, in that it was made of tin buildings and had a dock alongside the Vermilion, but it was different in terms of the number of boats, cranes, equipment and personnel moving around the facility. It was busy. Mac indentified himself and asked to speak with a supervisor.

It wasn't five minutes before a middle-aged man in a white shirt and red tie arrived. His tan trousers were creased, his brown shoes recently shined. He walked with confidence and ease into the room and introduced himself. "I'm Felton Broussard, officer. My brother and I own this place. Please have a seat; I've been expecting you."

"Why would you be expecting me?" Mac asked, noting that Broussard was very relaxed.

"Every person in the parish knows about the barge load of marijuana. It was the lead off story on all the radio and television stations, and it was on the front page of the Daily Advertiser and Abbeville paper." Mac noted that Broussard was amiable and not the least bit intimidated or worried. His body language said he was comfortable with the conversation.

"Got any suspects?" Broussard continued.

"Not yet, but we will have. Do you mind if I ask you a few questions."

"Fire away, Lieutenant, no pun intended."

"What kind of company is Broussard Brothers, and what are some of the services you provide?"

"We are about as close as you can get to being a full-service oilfield company, and we've been in business since 1945. We rent heavy equipment, crew boats, dock space, cranes and marsh buggies. We build wood roads to platforms in the marsh. We construct levees and transport pipes and other tools to rigs in the shallow waters of the Gulf of Mexico. There are hundreds of oilfield service companies like us along the Louisiana coast, but we are larger than most. Our office in Banker is just a field office. Our main office is in Intracoastal City."

"How is business right now?" Mac asked.

"Business is a little slow. The oilfield is feast and famine. When oil and gas prices are high we have more business than we can handle. It's usually the opposite of the rest of the country. When everyone else is in a recession, we do very well."

"Are you acquainted with Mr. Lawless Fontenot, at Fontenot's shipyard?"

"I know him, but not well," answered Broussard. "He has a smaller operation, but I think he has done well over the years."

"Do you know his sons, James and Jude?"

"Not really," said Broussard. "There are a few stories about drugs and alcohol use, and some minor brushes with the law, but nothing serious that I am aware of."

"Does your company move oilfield rigs and platforms from one location to another along the coast?"

"Absolutely. We do it year round. It keeps the lights on," answered Broussard.

"If a barge or tug, or other boat that may have broken down in the Gulf, on the Intracoastal, or Vermilion Bayou, do you move them as well?"

"Sure, we get calls all the time to move barges down Vermilion Bayou to Intracoastal City and from beyond, from Texas to Florida. It's not as common to push around a tug and barge that has broken down on the river, but it happens occasionally."

"The foreman at Fontenot's ship yard seems to think the tug involved in the marijuana importation has clutch problems, and could not have pushed the barge into the yard under its own power. Is it possible that Broussard Brothers could have towed up to Vermilion to Fontenot's?"

"I'm not sure, Lieutenant. Let's check our records. What are the dates?"

"It would have been in the middle of June, on a weekend."

Felton Broussard and Mac sipped on coffee while his secretary went to Broussard's accounting office to pull receipts. She returned within twenty minutes with a handful of paper.

Broussard began going through them. "Here it is," he said, "on the eighteenth of June we got a call from Lafayette saying a tug and barge were broke down near the locks at Freshwater Bayou. We towed them to Fontenot's."

"How were you paid?"

"Cash," said Broussard.

"I'll need that receipt, Mr. Broussard. Would you like me to get a subpoena?"

"Not necessary, Lieutenant. It's yours," he said, as he handed the papers to Mac.

Mac took the receipt, thanked Felton Broussard, and began the slow drive toward Lafayette. He thought about the chain of events from the Freshwater Bayou Locks to Fontenot's shipyard. He did not believe Felton Broussard was involved. He was cooperative and happy to help. It did not seem likely that the dopers would have faked engine problems to give the appearance of business as usual. That would have created suspicion and increased the possibility of someone discovering the contents of the barge. Contacting Broussard Brothers also slowed the process, giving the dopers less time to unload the barge before workers began arriving on Monday morning. The tug developed clutch problems, yet the operation went off without a hitch. That meant that the dopers had contingency plans. They were smart and organized.

Mac looked at the receipt. Broussard Brothers had requested a "call back" number. It was a starting point.

CHAPTER 8
The Country Boy Grocery Store

The Region II Narcotics Field Office was not much more than one large room with twelve desks and the appropriate amount of chairs, filing cabinets and routine office equipment. The office was one of several housed within the Troop I building at the intersection of Interstate 49 and Pont des Mouton Road, which ironically, in French, meant "bridge of the sheep." The front door opened into the troop building, after which there was a reception area and three or four cubicles for secretaries. There was an adjoining room of the same size for detectives, and a smaller one for the LSP Intelligence Unit. The back door to the narcotics office, which was most used, opened onto a parking lot behind the troop. Agents parked in the back in order to keep, as much as possible, prying eyes from knowing their vehicles. Mac's small office was just past the secretaries' cubicle, and he also came through the back door on a routine basis.

It was just past nine o'clock on Monday morning when Mac came through the back door. A floor mat at the entrance had a peculiar fold to it and Mac reached down to straighten it out. As he lifted the mat a two foot snake came crawling out, causing Mac to jump backwards striking a nearby filing cabinet. He also said some nasty words.

Agents in the office turned back to their paperwork and tried not to laugh. The cousins left the room, thinking it was an opportune time to investigate the allegation about two young black males dealing crack cocaine near the Catholic Carmelite Monastery east of Lafayette.

"Well, I told y'all to have fun; I guess the joke was on me this time," Mac said to no one in particular.

"I think the snake was meant for someone else," said Bert.

In the front of the office Hungry Harv was sitting at his desk, large eyed, chewing tobacco, spitting in the trash can and watching closely to make sure Mac threw the snake out the back door. He made a mental note to leave the office through the front door.

"Bert, can you get a subpoena for a local phone number," Mac said.

"Ten-four, Mac. I'll have it for you by noon."

The cousins drove through the slum areas of Southeast Lafayette Parish and set up under a giant live oak tree at the monastery and watched the suspect apartments through binoculars.

"Not exactly how they do it on television," said Tatou.

"Not too glamorous," replied Hollywood. "Too bad we got Mac instead of Hungry Harv. That was a waste of a good snake; getting Hungry Harv would have been better."

The Oak Trace Apartment complex was government subsidized and located in a primarily African American part of town the locals called "Coontown." It bordered a rougher area the locals termed "Fightingville." Other areas were known as "New Jack City, Wine Alley and Death Row." Many of the residents in these areas made their living dealing coke, crack, preludin, marijuana, and pain pills.

By three o'clock in the afternoon the cousins had established one apartment that had had no less than twenty people go in, stay briefly, and exit. They made notes about how many of the people were white. On a few occasions the occupants of the apartment had gone to arriving vehicles and exchanged small packages for cash. The occupants appeared to be teenagers.

"I don't think they are more than seventeen or eighteen years old," said Hollywood.

"Old enough," said Tatou. "Seventeen and you are an adult. No requirement to call guardians. It makes everything a lot easier to deal with."

The cousins broke the surveillance at five o'clock to grab a beer and burger. They returned after dark and started the surveillance again. The steady flow of customers increased with the darkness. They took notes about times and movement, and wrote descriptions of people and vehicles. At ten p.m. Hollywood said, "Bro, we have enough information to establish probable cause for a search warrant. Let's take the rest of the night off for cocktails."

Roy W. Frusha

"I'm with you, cousin," replied Tatou. "Let's check out the watering hole on Bertrand Drive. They usually have some late night activity, and the bartenders are easy to look at."

The cousins slept late the next day, met for lunch, after which they drove to a district judge's office and obtained a signature on a search warrant. After the warrant was signed they returned to the bar on Bertrand and had a relaxing afternoon of drinking beer, eating burgers and shooting pool.

"Remind me to write some vouchers for this so we can get our money back out of the investigative expense fund," said Hollywood.

"Was there any question about it," replied Tatou, as he leaned over the pool table.

It was well after dark when the cousins returned to their surveillance location under the live oaks. Within an hour they observed several people enter and exit the apartment. It was enough. When they determined the apartment was empty of patrons Tatou said, "Let's hit the place before the fuckers run out of cocaine."

"Good by me," said Hollywood, and they drove the short distance to the apartment complex.

Hollywood knocked on the door. An unsuspecting young black male opened the door a couple of inches to look outside, but it was too late. The cousins, with a gun in one hand and a badge in the other, were on him and in the apartment, before he could react.

"Get down on the floor motherfuckers," screamed Hollywood. He was focused on the two black males and pointing his gun at them when he heard a shrill sound behind him. He turned quickly and saw a white, blond female, about forty years of age, standing in the corner of the living room naked except for her panties. She was in a total state of panic, screaming incoherently at the top of her lungs.

Tatou grabbed the two scared and panicky teenagers and threw them spread eagled on the floor. The almost naked woman continued to scream.

Hollywood placed his gun in his holster and approached the woman holding his badge out front to show her he was a police officer.

"I need to pithhhh," screamed the woman, as she covered her ears with her hands.

84

"It's okay," yelled Hollywood. "We're police officers."

Hollywood approached the woman as she braced to run. He dropped his wallet and badge and grabbed her from behind, pinning her arms to her side.

"I need to pithhhh," she continued.

"What?"

The woman could stand it no longer. She urinated as Hollywood held her, splashing his pants, and shoes, and making a direct hit on his wallet and badge, which was on the floor between her feet.

When the woman finally calmed down, she said, "I said I had to piss. I thought you were going to kill me."

"What are you doing here?" Hollywood asked, though he already knew the answer. She was a crack addict, and she was giving up sex to the teens in return for drugs. She ignored the question and began dressing.

While Tatou was searching and cuffing the teens, Hollywood searched the woman's purse, obtained her biographical information for future reference and then released her. "Go and sin no more, my child," he said.

Hollywood then went into the kitchen and returned with a large spoon to retrieve his wallet, which he placed in a trash bag. "The state is going to pay me for this."

The suspects were identified as Sha-rell "Sharkey" Senegal and Purvis "Tee-Boy" Batiste, high school dropouts who had moved out of their parents' homes to begin what was becoming a lucrative drug business. They had previous arrests for burglary and drug possession, but due to their age, and a lax Lafayette Parish judicial system, they had never spent a night in jail.

"You are a couple of scrawny little shits," said Tatou. They were dressed in jeans and white tee shirts covered in grease and dirt. "When was the last time you took a bath?"

"Look at this dump," said Hollywood. "It hasn't been cleaned in years." Clothes were on the floor, dishes with dried, moldy food were scattered on the floor. Half empty beer cans sat on a broken coffee table.

"Let's finish up and get out of here," said Hollywood. "I have to disinfect my wallet." Hollywood read them the Miranda warning and said, "Where are you brain surgeons getting the powder."

"I don't have to talk to you, Mr. Po-lice. I knows my rights. You can't talk to me unless my momma or auntie is here," said Tee-Boy.

"Dats right," quipped in Sharkey. "I wants to call my auntie."

Tatou said nothing, and showed no emotion, as he quickly and forcefully slapped each of them across the face with a cupped hand. It caused more noise than pain, but it got their attention.

Hollywood smiled at their shock, "In case you two entrepreneurs had a brain fart, and did not notice your last birthday, you are now seventeen. You are no longer subject to juvenile rights. You are adults, and you will be treated like adults."

"Let's put them in the cell with Brutus," said Tatou. "Brutus ain't had no pussy in a while. A couple of days with Brutus and these entrepreneurs will be glad to talk to us."

"Roger that," said Hollywood, as he stood and lifted Tee-Boy by the arm. "Let's book them at the jail, and go out for some cocktails. They will call us when they are ready to talk. We can check on them in a few days. I just hope Brutus don't fuck them up too much. These boys are young and pretty, but they will survive as long as they play the game."

"You know what they call them at the jail, don't you?" Tatou mused.

"What's that?"

"Gal-boys. It's standard issue at the jail to give an inmate a tooth brush, soap and Vaseline."

Tee-Boy Batiste had been watching the cousins closely. "Go fuck yourself, white men, you can't scare me."

As Tatou escorted the suspects to his unit Hollywood stayed behind and used the apartment telephone to call Region II. "Hungry Harv," Hollywood said. "I need a favor. Could you put on the orange jump suit we keep in the office, and cuff yourself to a chair in the squad room. We have a couple of teenage assholes who need to be brought up to speed on prison life."

Thirty minutes later the cousins arrived at Region II. Mac was waiting for them at the back door. The cousins pulled the cuffed suspects from the back seat of the unit and escorted them into the room. Hungry Harv, dressed in an orange jump suit borrowed from the Lafayette jail, was cuffed to a chair.

"They were just about to fuck a crack whore in exchange for a little dust when we arrested them," said Tatou. "They stink."

Hollywood grabbed suspects by the arm, removed the cuffs, and re-cuffed them to chairs about five feet from Hungry Harv.

"I want them boys," yelled Hungry Harv, as he pulled on his chair. "I want them for me, yeah."

"Who is that man?" said a very frightened Tee-Boy.

"That's Brutus," said Hollywood. "When we finish with the paperwork we will book all three of you at the same time. It will save a trip for us."

Hungry Harv was jerking his cuffed arm against the chair when Tatou said, "Hold on, Brutus. You can have them when we are through."

"Brutus is going to make your butt look like turtle sauce piquant," said Tatou, looking at Tee-Boy.

Tee-Boy Batiste had seen enough. "I'm ready to talk now," he said. He was close to tears. "I don't want to go to jail and I don't want to be in a room with that man. I want my mama."

"Ready to sing like the Four Tops," Hollywood said, as he grinned.

"Dat's right," said Sharkey Senegal, who caught the drift. "What you want, I got it."

The cousins separated the entrepreneurs and questioned them in detail about their sources and customers. Once they were satisfied they had the information they needed, they released them with instructions that they were on probation and could be re-arrested at any time. Further, they were made to understand that they would be called on later, in the status of a C I (confidential informant) to make "controlled purchases" of drugs from their supplier. The suspects understood that a controlled purchase meant they would be wired for sound and purchase the drugs under the supervision and protection of the cousins. The entrepreneurs were not educated, but they were street wise. They understood the concept of "trading up," and would have given up their mothers to avoid going to jail with Brutus.

"Okay," said Mac. "Take them into the interview room, and see what they can tell you."

One hour later Mac, Hungry Harv and Bert were talking casually about the Bulldog investigation when the cousins walked into the squad room with their case reports.

"Bring us up to date," said Hungry Harv, who was still in prison orange.

Hollywood began. "We busted Tee-Boy Batiste and Sharkey Senegal, two seventeen-year-old black kids dealing cocaine out of their apartment at Oak Trace, just off Pinhook Road. The horny little bastards were also trading crack for crack, so to speak. There was a forty-year-old white woman there trading sex for drugs. Real classy clientele."

"Did they give up their source for the coke?" Mac asked.

"Roger that. A guy named Alfred Patout, from Vermilion Parish. Anyone know him?" Tatou asked.

"I know of him," said Hungry Harv. "He lives off Highway 167, between Maurice and Abbeville. I heard he has a big swanky house and some acreage on the Vermilion River. There have been rumors about him smuggling for three or four years, but no one has gotten to him. Dopers in that area say he is a big user, and real paranoid. He stays holed up in his house, or at his duck camp. People in that area call him Freebase Freddy."

"Can your boys do a sting on him?" Mac inquired, looking at the cousins.

"The entrepreneurs will do anything to keep from getting butt fucked by Brutus here, but it might be tough. They said Patout will not talk to them on the phone. Standard procedure is for them to walk about two hundred yards down a dirt road leading to his house and leave an envelope with cash in it in a compartment in an old boat. The next day they go back and retrieve the drugs from the same compartment. They said he sometimes forgets."

"How does Patout know to check the boat?" Bert inquired.

"They call his residence, let the phone ring three times, and hang up," explained Hollywood.

"It's worth trying," said Mac. "Call your boys in tomorrow and shake some trees. Something may fall out."

88

Mac looked at Bert and changed the subject. "What did you find out about the call back number from Broussard Brothers?"

"The number is registered to the Country Boy Grocery store, southwest of Lafayette near the Judice community," said Bert.

A curtain of rain fell from a gloomy sky at mid-afternoon the next day when Mac and Hungry Harv drove down Highway 342 toward the Country Boy Grocery store. The temperature was in the mid-nineties with a hundred percent humidity. Mac wondered how the area was settled without benefit of air conditioning. Mac drove onto the gravel parking lot in front of the store, which was an old cypress building with a rusty tin roof. Two ancient ESSO gas pumps sat idle in front of the store. They appeared as if they had not been operational in thirty years. Two old Cajuns were sitting in home-made rocking chairs on the front porch eating boudin and drinking Dixie beer. An antiquated Hadacol sign was nailed to the front wall near the entrance.

Mac had not seen a Hadacol sign in years, but he recalled that the Hadacol founder was the former state senator, Dudley J. LeBlanc, from Vermilion Parish. LeBlanc had created the tonic he called medicine, though he was neither a doctor nor pharmacist. The tonic was twenty-four proof, and very popular all over the country. LeBlanc hobnobbed with famous people and movie stars, such as Mickey Rooney and Bob Hope. Once on national television, Groucho Marx asked LeBlanc what Hadacol was good for, and LeBlanc answered, "About five million last year."

The store was archaic and reminiscent of a time long departed from Lafayette Parish. During the time before the parish had improved roads and the residents had cars, the old store had served salt, sugar, flower, bread, milk and other basics to the citizens of the Judice community. Lafayette suburbs had grown steadily to toward the store, and area residents changed shopping habits. They now went to the local Winn Dixie. The old store managed to stay in business selling boudin, garfish balls, cracklings, pen-raised rabbits and cold beer.

Hungry Harv led the way into the store. The owner was a seventy-five year old Cajun who never got around to learning the English language; it just hadn't been necessary in rural Lafayette

Parish. Hungry Harv ordered two beers and some crackling in French. Mac listened to Hungry Harv and the old man talk.

"Bonjour, comment ca va après midi," said Hungry Harv.

"Cest pas trop mauvais," replied the old man. "C'est chaud." Mac had picked up a little French over the years, and understood that the old man had answered saying: "not too bad, and something about the weather being hot." Mac listened as they spoke for about fifteen minutes.

Hungry Harv turned and looked at Mac. "He said that for the last five or six weeks he has had several foreigners come in to buy beer, crackling and boudin, and to use the pay phone on the front porch."

"What does he mean by 'foreigners?'" asked Mac.

Hungry Harv spoke to the old man some more, then looked at Mac and said, "They were young white males, maybe twenty-five to thirty years old, and they were not from the area. He said all people who live outside the parish are foreigners. He said one of them was about six feet tall, had blond hair and a tan."

Mac and Hungry Harv drove toward the office to prepare a subpoena for the pay phone records covering the previous two months. When they arrived at Region II Hungry Harv sat down at his desk, opened a drawer and retrieved a can of Skoal chewing tobacco. He lifted the can toward his mouth and opened it to scoop out some tobacco. When he opened the can, a small, green grass snake came out. Hungry Harv screamed and fell backwards onto the wall.

"Fils de putain," he yelled, which everyone in the office knew to mean "son of a bitch." They all laughed, except the cousins, who were conspicuously absent.

CHAPTER 9
The Meeting

Leigh Ray Starwood had not wasted his time with the Army in Columbia. He had worked diligently in the Army's Counter Drug Section and had developed a reputation for being an intelligent, personable, Staff NCO with strong leadership and organizational capabilities. He had total access to the office's intelligence files, which detailed every major drug cartel in South America. Starwood wasted no time developing relationships in Barranquilla, Columbia, which in time, would get him introduced to Julio Nasser-David, known by the locals as "the old man." Nasser-David was intelligent and educated. He was an architect and land developer by trade. He was also one of the largest cocaine and marijuana smugglers in South America, if not the world.

Starwood began by working with the lower end elements of the Nasser-David organization, purchasing a thousand pounds of marijuana at a time, along with a few kilos of cocaine, sending the drugs to former pawn shop associates in Houston. The Nasser-David organization had all the contacts necessary to load the drugs into shipping containers and Starwood arranged for the drugs to be off-loaded at a Galveston shipyard where they would be picked up in trucks by Mexicans and driven to Houston for delivery. Starwood had been in Columbia less than a year, and he was clearing over two hundred thousand in cash. It was not enough. More importantly, he was developing contacts and relationships that would enable him to deal directly with Nasser-David. He could easily purchase and ship ten times the amounts he was currently handling, but he needed to organize a network of large-scale dealers in the states. He needed to bring his organization in the states to the next level in order to handle the massive amounts he was planning for the future.

The drugs Starwood was currently handling in Columbia allowed him a lavish lifestyle, but he was careful not to live better than his counterparts. He sent money to banks in Houston and in Grand Cayman. He was ready for a break, and ready to enjoy some of his earnings. He told his commanding officer he needed to visit his mother in Houston and asked for two weeks leave. It was granted, and he booked a flight to Key West, where he hoped he could have fun in a relaxed atmosphere where no one would know him.

Starwood stayed in a suite at the Casa Marina Resort in Key West and ate at the best restaurants the island had to offer. He toured the Hemmingway House, Harry Truman Little White House and the Mel Fisher Maritime Heritage Museum, taking in the island's scenery and history. On his fourth day he was drinking beer and listening to a local band at Sloppy Joe's on Duval Street when he spotted a tall, beautiful woman sitting alone on a stool at the bar. She had long, shapely legs and a short waist. Long, sand colored hair was neatly tied back in a pony tail. She wore cutoff denims and a white pull-over shirt. It was apparent she did not wear a bra. He walked over and sat on the stool next to her.

"May I join you for a glass of wine?" Starwood asked. "I'm Leigh Starwood, and I hope you don't mind if I offer you a glass of wine." Before she could reply, he called the bartender over and ordered a bottle of Chateaux Margaux and two glasses.

"I might have minded," she said, smiling, "but I know that wine, and I would love a glass."

She extended her hand, and said, "I'm Sherry Cox, it's nice to meet you."

They made small talk about the island, the people who lived there and the people who visited. Starwood learned Sherry was a pilot and had flown some customers to Key West from Jacksonville and would be in Key West for three more days. He was interested. The next bottle of wine Starwood ordered was Lafite-Rothshild, at just over a thousand dollars. Now she was interested.

That night he sent a limo for her and they dined at Louie's Backyard Restaurant. When he dropped her at her hotel she kissed him good night, but did not ask him to her room for a night cap. Starwood was patient, and thought it best not to push.

The next day Starwood met her at her hotel and asked her to walk around the island and take in the sights. It was a clear day with no clouds. It would have been hot, except for a strong breeze.

Wrestling With Pigs

They walked past white picket fences laced with firebush, orange geigers and marleberry bushes. The flowers on the island fairly exploded with color, and bouquets were present on every porch.

"I appreciate dinner and the wine, and I appreciate your company," Sherry said as they walked down a side street. I'm flying out tomorrow, and I'm not in the habit of jumping into bed with strangers." She stopped and looked at Starwood. "It's not going to happen."

Starwood saw a jewelry store just up the street, and walked toward it without speaking. He led her inside the store and casually looked at the bracelets, chains and rings under the glass. Eventually he asked a sales lady about a particular bracelet that held a single gold Spanish coin.

"Tell me about this bracelet," he said.

"That coin," she explained, "is from the Nuestra Senora de Atocha, a Spanish ship that sank in a hurricane just off the Florida straights in 1622. The ship, which was filled with gold, silver, emeralds and pearls, was just recently discovered."

The clerk handed the bracelet to Starwood who looked at the carving of the Spanish king on one side and lions and castles on the other. "How much?" he asked.

"Ten thousand dollars," the lady replied.

"Do you take cash," Starwood said, smiling.

Starwood handed the bracelet to Sherry as they walked out of the jewelry shop. "Something to remember me by," he said.

They drank wine and ate a sandwich at a French restaurant on Duval Street, after which they walked to Starwood's hotel. He removed a gram vile of cocaine from a drawer and drew out two lines of the powder on a hotel plate. He handed Sherry a straw. She snorted a line, and wiped her nose. As Starwood was snorting the second line, she said, "It's a trite question, but do you mind telling me a little more about yourself, like, where do you live, and what kind of job allows you to buy expensive wine and gold bracelets for women you barely know?"

"I live in Colombia, and I'm in the Army, but I will be getting my discharge in less than a year."

"Military men don't make the kind of money you are spending."

"I'm sort of an entrepreneur, an investor, you might say." Starwood smiled.

"Ahh, I think I understand," answered Sherry, as she removed the clip from her pony tail and let her hair fall over her shoulders. She unbuttoned her blouse and dropped it to the floor as she leaned forward to ingest another line of coke.

"You are salivating," she said as she stood and began removing her cutoff jeans.

The blood flowed from Starwood's big brain to his small brain as he sat and watched Sherry Cox pull down her panties. She moved next to him and he felt the tautness of her breasts and ran his hands down the narrow stomach, slightly full hips, long legs and tapered curves. She was in no hurry as she undressed him and took him in her hand. Thirty minutes later they sat cross legged and naked on the floor as Starwood drew out some more lines of cocaine.

"Just how lucrative is your business?" Sherry asked.

"About two hundred thousand right now, but there is potential for more, much, much more. The supply in Columbia is limitless. Demand in the United States is limitless. My problem is that I don't have the right connections to handle the supply."

Sherry did another line of coke, and wiped her nose casually. "Have you ever been to Michigan? I know someone there you might be interested in meeting."

"I have another week of vacation. When do we leave?"

"You can ride with me when I fly out tomorrow morning. I'll be dropping off my passengers in Jacksonville. From there we'll fly the King Air to Detroit. You can return commercial."

The next morning Starwood meet Sherry at the Key West International Airport. He was wearing a tailor made seersucker suit, starched white shirt with a blue tie. His black shoes had been recently shined and he carried one small, inconspicuous bag.

"You fly, you wear a tie," he said.

When Starwood left Key West it had been a blue bird day of ninety degrees, with a constant ocean breeze. It was raining and fifty-five degrees in Ann Arbor when Sherry Cox picked up Starwood from a local hotel and drove him to a restaurant she had chosen as a convenient meeting place. Vince Vargo had driven his new BMW. Sherry introduced them and then departed, saying, "I think you two may be able to conduct some business together, but it's best if I don't know any of the details. Call me when you are finished," she said, as she looked at Starwood, "and I will give you a lift back to your hotel."

Starwood was in a blue pin-stripe suit with a white shirt and dark blue tie. Vargo wore jeans, a cheap cotton pullover college sweatshirt. His brown loafers had never been shined. It was not a marriage made in heaven, but the relationship between Starwood and Vargo was a natural, in spite of conspicuous differences. Starwood was four years junior, smarter and better at organizing, but Vargo knew his job, and had a distribution network that was solid and productive. Vargo ordered beer and steak, and Starwood ordered red wine, sautéed mushrooms and smothered quail.

"Tell me about your organization," Vargo said.

"I work out of Columbia, but that will change in less than a year. When I come back to the states I'm thinking of establishing one residence in Florida and another one in Grand Cayman. There are several people and organizations I can go to for weed and coke, depending on the size of the load we want to put together, up to and including Julio Nasser-David, who runs one of the largest cartels in Columbia. So far my loads have been limited to a couple of thousand pounds. How much can you handle?"

"My distribution network has been extended from Ann Arbor to Detroit, Chicago, New York, New Jersey, Pennsylvania, and most recently, North Carolina," said Vargo. "Give me some details about what you can provide."

Starwood leaned back in his chair and sipped on a glass of Silver Oak cabernet before answering. "I'm very careful about what I do. Naturally, my organization includes Columbians, but I have been selective with them. I also have dock workers, electronics experts, former Army Rangers, former Navy SEALS, union officials, government workers, both Columbian and American, airplane pilots, seagoing boat captains, and a smattering of professional and experienced truck drivers. I have contacts in Texas, Florida and Louisiana."

Vargo exhaled slowly, and said, "Very impressive." Then he related the information about his higher level distributors and how Shine Armstrong routinely administered polygraphs to them.

"Good," said Starwood. "Between us, we have in the neighborhood of two hundred people. I have a forty-foot boat that is accessible to us now, and it can carry approximately forty thousand pounds, and we can throw in a thousand pounds of coke. We'll need some money to put down, but I can get most of the product fronted to us."

"No problem," answered Vargo, leaning across the table. "When and where do you think we should start?"

"You said you have sources in North Carolina; let's start there. I'll organize the first load and have my Florida contact, a man named Stephan Cahill, oversee the operation. You have trucks and drivers ready, and handle the distribution. We'll need to pay the Columbians in a timely manner."

"Consider it done," said a smiling Vargo, as he poured down his beer.

Two months later a forty-foot converted Coast Guard vessel chugged slowly up the Atlantic Intracoastal Waterway, six miles north of the Fort Macon Coast Guard base in North Carolina. Almost forty thousand pounds of marijuana and one thousand pounds of cocaine were loaded into waiting trucks at a rural landing. The next day the boat was gone, headed back south toward Florida with Cahill on board.

"It's been handled with no problems," was all Starwood said when he made the phone call to Vargo.

Starwood and Vargo were elated with their success, but neither was content to relax and enjoy the money they had made. Starwood told Cahill to find another boat for a second load to North Carolina. He quickly located an eighty-foot trawler for rent out of Houma, Louisiana. Cahill personally supervised the boat's movement to Columbia, where Starwood had another forty thousand pounds of marijuana and twenty-five hundred pounds of cocaine waiting at Barranquilla. Checkpoints were established on islands and boats all along the route using the latest in electronics, with escape routes and speed boats available. Like the first load, the second one also went down without a hitch. Precise planning was the key.

Vargo purchased a new porche, a fully restored antique corvette and a fashionable home in historic Barton Hills, within the Ann Arbor Township. There were only three hundred thirty-five residents in the gated community, and each house was built in the

1920s by a registered architect. The community, Vargo bragged to his friends, had the highest per capita income of any neighborhood in the state of Michigan, and he was the only resident without a job. His house backed up to Barton Pond, and was often visited by his friends and fraternity brothers from the university.

Starwood purchased a home on Grand Cayman Island for one point three million dollars. The house would later be visited by rock stars and famous actresses. For a backup banking account Starwood began depositing profits in a bank in Panama City, Panama. He was living the good life, and was three months from getting out of the Army with an honorable discharge as a staff sergeant. "Now I will have time to really raise the bar," he said to himself.

During the next several months Starwood and Vargo built a drug importation and distribution ring that would become responsible for over eighty percent of the marijuana and cocaine sold in the state of Michigan. Other outlets included Florida, North Carolina, Louisiana, Texas, New York and New Jersey. And they were just beginning. By 1980 they had smuggled over six hundred thousand pounds of marijuana and several thousand pounds of cocaine into the United States.

It was their fourth load of about forty thousand pounds of marijuana and three thousand pounds of cocaine that was scheduled to move from Columbia to the coastal water ways of North Carolina. Starwood had rented a shrimper called Lady Mouricette. It was complete with nets and riggings, and there was nothing to suggest that it was not a shrimp trawler. It was ten o'clock at night when the Lady Mouricette put in at a small landing not far from a coastal North Carolina fishing village. Vargo had stayed in Michigan. Starwood and Sherry Cox flew slow circles overhead. No one had thought about it not being professional shrimping season. One lone Customs official noticed the Mouricette, thought it suspicious, and called for backup to investigate. The smugglers escaped in speed boats, but the load was confiscated. They would not make that mistake again.

The next day Starwood called Vargo. "Let's change the format a bit."

"What do you have in mind?"

"Do you have people in place in Detroit?"

"Absolutely," said Vargo.

Over the next two months Starwood arranged for three flights of twelve thousand pounds each of cocaine and marijuana to be flown into Antrim County Airport in Detroit. The planes were off-loaded without a hitch. The dopers were on their way, or as they say in French at the beginning of a horse race, "Ils Sont Partis."

CHAPTER 10
Discovery and Progress

It was early and Mac couldn't sleep, so he drove to the office and unlocked the back door. It was late July, and he thought that the excessive temperature along the Cajun coast had to be experienced; it could not be sufficiently described. The density of the humidity, even in early morning, was thick like cane syrup. It was not like the heat on the Texas or Florida coast. Louisiana had no beaches with white sand and constant breezes. There was just marsh, heat, humidity and mosquitoes. He marveled at the strong Cajun people who settled the area without benefit of the conveniences taken for granted by the locals in this day and age. "I would move north, if it were not for air conditioning." Mac thought to himself.

The cousins had used a small nylon rope to tie a non-poisonous snake to the top of the door where the shades were fastened and then placed the snake on top of a nearby filing cabinet. When Mac walked into the room the rope pulled the snake from the filing cabinet onto his shoulder. Both knees bent a little, but Mac did not go down. "Motherfuckers," was all he could mumble. The agents, trying not to laugh, simply pointed at the cousins.

"Sorry," said Hollywood. "You're early. It was meant for Hungry Harv."

Mac took the rope off the snake and threw it out the back door. "You are going to give someone a heart attack one of these days. Either that, or Hungry Harv is going to kill one of you." Mac smiled, glad that the agents were having fun.

Mac looked at Bert and asked, "How is the subpoena for the Country Boy Grocery Store coming?"

"Got it all right here," Bert informed Mac. "Phone calls made during May and June 1983 went virtually all over the country. Most were to Michigan, but there were numerous calls to New York, California, Florida, North Carolina, Texas, New Jersey and some other states along the east coast."

"Okay, let's think out of the box," he addressed the agents in the room. "The pay phone is located at the Country Boy Grocery Store, which is a small, isolated store in the rural Judice area. The phone is located on the front porch of the store, and is likely only used by area Cajuns and a few blacks who cannot afford a house phone. This phone was used at least sixty or seventy times over in May and June for out of state calls. It's the same phone number used as a call back number when the dopers called Broussard Brothers for a tow to Fontenot's shipyard. What does this tell us?" He sat on the edge of an empty desk.

Bubba spoke first. "It tells me that a lot of dopers have been living in the area for several weeks, waiting for the boat to arrive so they could take possession of the drugs and move them to their final destination as quickly as possible."

"Good point," Mac replied. "Let's suppose the dopers were in Lafayette waiting for the tug and barge. Most likely it was not the hierarchy of the organization. It would have been muscle, people who could physically lift the bales of marijuana from the barge and place them onto large trucks, after which drivers would transport them God knows where. Would they have rented apartments or motel or hotel rooms?"

"Whoever masterminded the operation would have been in and out of Lafayette, but probably would not have stayed here. He would have too much to do," said Bubba. "I think some of the calls may have been related to the smuggling operation, but some would have been to family and friends back home."

"I'll call the Lafayette Utilities System and CLECO," said Bert, "and find out how many residences and apartments had electricity turned on during the last three months. Then I will prioritize the list according to those locations closest to the Country Boy Grocery."

"Excellent," answered Mac. "Also find out which residents in the area insisted on paying in cash."

Bubba spoke next. "I'll go to the airport, talk to people who work there about any suspicious activity they may have seen, check flight logs, and look for fuel receipts, flight plans, aircraft rentals, and whatever else is available there."

"Rooster and Dee will check Lafayette hotels and motels for any suspicious behavior, such as patrons who lack proper identification, or those who demanded they be allowed to pay in cash," said Mac.

"The cousins will work on some area dealers, try to trade up and shake some trees in Vermilion Parish," said Mac. "Speaking of Vermilion Parish, that is home turf for Hungry Harv. He can check the records at Freshwater Bayou Locks. The tug and barge had to go through there and there may be some documentation."

"As much as I hate to do it, I think the next step is to get the feds involved. I'll call the FBI and give them the list of phone numbers. If we can get them interested they can trace the numbers and come up with names and locations."

The next morning, as Mac was on the phone with the SAC (Special Agent in Charge) of the Lafayette FBI office Buzzy returned from the Lafayette Utilities System and SLEMCO.

"LUS said they have no new customers on the south side, especially near the Country Boy Grocery Store. However, SLEMCO, which provides electricity for the Judice area had better results. They verified that they had a new customer just off Ridge Road, near the old Ferdinand Stutes bar. It's half a mile from the Country Boy Grocery and they've been connected for two months."

Buzzy looked at his notes. "I located the owner of the residence and learned that utilities and rent payments were in cash and in advance. The property was rented to a man calling himself David Williams. The property owner described him as about twenty-eight to thirty years old, blondish hair, blue eyes, clean cut, tanned skin, about six feet tall and about one hundred seventy pounds."

"That's pretty close to the same description we got from the old man at the store," said Hungry Harv.

"Did the property owner obtain any identification from the renter?"

"No, only a phone number, which is the same one as the Country Boy Grocery pay phone," replied Buzzy.

"Bingo," said Mac. "Good work. You and Bert write up a search warrant for the residence. Let's hit it this afternoon."

At two o'clock that same day the agents arrived at the residence. It was a ranch style three-bedroom, two-bath, brick house with a double carport. It was typical 1950s style, located on the fringe of an old neighborhood, just outside the Lafayette city limits. The house was surrounded by wax leaf ligustrum bushes and chicken trees, providing a relative amount of privacy. The grass had not been cut in three or four weeks. There were several cheap lawn chairs near the carport, scattered around a large barbeque pit on wheels. Weight lifting equipment and workout benches were scatter under the carport.

Doors to the residence were locked. Mac made the decision not to contact the owner for a key, as owners typically do not want their residences searched, and they always want to be involved, usually getting in the way.

Hungry Harv was broad shouldered, with short muscular legs and a size fourteen shoe. The first kick caused a crack around the door frame, but the dead bolt held. The second kick caused the frame to separate from the wall. Mac, Hungry Harv, Buzzy and Bert walked into the residence. Mac and Hungry Harv methodically searched each room while Buzzy made a written list of the evidence taken.

"Looks like my kids live here," said Hungry Harv, referring to the mess. It was as if a small tornado had entered the house and dispersed household items in all directions. Cheap furniture was scattered throughout, and did not appear to have been functionally organized. Partially eaten food was left on dinner plates on a table that looked to be made of cardboard. Half empty bottles of beer sat on tables and window sills in all of the rooms. No less than ten empty pizza boxes were dispersed on the floor. Mac opened the refrigerator; it contained frozen food, leftovers in paper containers, soft drinks and beer. The dishwasher was open and full of dirty dishes. Each bedroom contained three sets of bunk beds. All of them had sheets and blankets, and all of them appeared to have been used. Not one bed was made. Dirty clothes were scattered on bed-room and closet floors. The two bathrooms contained toothpaste, soap, shampoo, washcloths and bath towels. Several towels were on the floor.

"Looks like a scene from Animal House," said Buzzy, "or worse, the Twilight Zone."

"I lived in a frat house for two years," replied Mac. "It was bad, but not this bad. This place smells like an armpit."

"Looks like they left in a hurry," said Hungry Harv, as he pulled damp clothes from the washer.

"They have no intention of returning," said Mac. "Apparently we've found a safe house where some fifteen or twenty men lived while waiting for the tug and barge to arrive. When they got the call they bolted out of here, drove to Banker, off-loaded the boat, and departed for areas unknown."

"Dust some beer bottles for fingerprints, and look for anything, such as a receipt or note, that may give us an identity," said Mac.

"They have good taste," said Bert, picking up an empty Rolex box. "They don't sell Rolex watches just anywhere; I'll follow up on this."

Mac picked up a yellow legal pad from a chair and looked through it for some writing. "At least some of them wrote notes, but these pages are empty."

"Let me see it," said Hungry Harv. He held it in the light near a window. He showed Mac the front page. A note had been written by a strong hand, after which the page had been torn from the pad. Indentions had been left on the second page. Hungry Harv went to his unit, obtained a number two pencil, and slowly worked the lead over the indentations, as a grade school kid may have done. Almost magically a letter formed. It described the pending importation, and named a few individuals.

"It's addressed to someone called Shine Armstrong," said Hungry Harv.

Bubba found a torn piece of paper on the floor. "It's a note addressed to J.D., Don and George," he said. "There's also a signature and phone number. It's signed by Fred Patout. His penmanship is different in that it is partially written and partially printed."

On the kitchen table was a New York Times Atlas of the World. Bert thumbed through the pages finding a rough drawing of a map indicating a route from Barranquilla, Colombia, to the Louisiana coast. It was marked with dates, times and probable locations of the tug and barge. "They had an estimated time and date of arrival," said Bert. "They were just waiting for the call."

That evening Mac contacted the owner of the residence, and informed him that the state police would pay for his door. Mac learned that the house had been rented for cash to a man who looked like a "Florida boy" who called himself David Williams. No identification had been obtained, but he said he could pick him out of a photo lineup. The landlord didn't care as long as he got cash. The renter had purchased all of the furniture, including refrigerator, washer and dryer, chairs, couches, beds and tables. The landlord asked Mac if he could keep the furniture that had been left behind.

The following night the cousins returned to the apartment rented by Tee-Boy Bastiste and Sharkey Senegal. They picked up the entrepreneurs and transported them to Maurice, just south of Lafayette. They instructed the young dopers to write a letter to Free Base Freddy asking him to sell them some cocaine. They placed ten crisp one hundred dollar bills inside the envelope and instructed the boys to place the envelope in the compartment of the old boat. They called Patout, let the phone ring three times, and hung up. They returned the entrepreneurs to their apartment. It was against procedure to front cash, but it was worth a try.

Twenty-four hours later, under a rising moon, Tetou and Hollywood sneaked down the narrow road leading to Patout's residence and retrieved the envelope from the boat. It contained the thousand dollars with a note that said there would be no more cocaine for the entrepreneurs, and for them to never come on his property again. They returned the money to the investigative expense fund, and gave the handwritten note to Mac. It was partially print and partial script. The handwriting matched the note bubba found in the house, and it would prove to be valuable later in the investigation.

CHAPTER 11
The Interstate 10 Rest Areas

It was Tuesday morning and had been almost a week since they had found the safe house on Ridge Road. The feds were working on the phone numbers and Region II was continuing with routine area narcotics investigations. The region secretary leaned into Mac's door, and said, "There's a phone call for you on line one. It's Colonel Kazan."

"How is the smuggling investigation going, Lieutenant?" Simple Eddie inquired.

Mac explained about the search and phone numbers, but knew that Simple Eddie did not give a shit about an investigation that was not centered in Baton Rouge, unless it affected a politician.

"I have a couple of assignments for you," said Simple Eddie. "First, there have been reports of violence at the Interstate 10 rest stops near Lafayette. I want you to send some of your boys out there, find out what is going on, and fix it."

"What kind of problems can they have at a rest stop?"

"I don't have details, but reports are that travelers are being harassed, or maybe robbed."

"What about Troop I personnel?"

"I spoke with the Troop I commander; they are too busy," said Simple Eddie.

"Right," said Mac, "we wouldn't want an investigation to interfere with their latte breaks at the Pitt Grill. They might have to get out of the air conditioning. Do you have any written complaints, and would it be too much to ask to send me a written request to perform this investigation."

"I'm giving you verbal instructions, Lieutenant. Handle it, it's just that simple."

"Roger that, consider it done." Actually, Mac had been hearing rumors about the rest stops. They were known for homosexual activity. He made a mental note that this was the second time Simple Eddie had assigned an investigation to Region II that centered on homo activity.

"What is the second assignment?" Mac inquired.

"I don't know. Colonel Carter said he wants to see you. He said to make an appointment with his secretary this week."

"Okay boss," said Mac, hanging up and thinking that encounters with state police superintendents were rarely productive.

The next day Mac called in the cousins and asked them to check on suspicious activity at the rest stops.

"Have there been any reports of fights or any types of violence called in to Troop I?" Hollywood asked.

"None, I checked with the troop dispatchers." Mac answered. "Just do some late-night surveillance and write a report. Maybe that will make Simple Eddie happy."

It was almost midnight when the cousins drove east on Interstate 10 toward the rest stops. The almost daily rain had let up, but the temperature was over ninety with a corresponding humidity. The cousins were not pleased with the temperature or the assignment. Only the mosquitoes were happy. Traffic was average for the season, which meant it was heavy.

They pulled into the westbound rest stop first, and noted six vehicles parked in front of the building containing restroom facilities. A single white male, about forty years old and weighing maybe one hundred and eighty pounds, sat quietly on concrete steps smoking a cigarette. He wore faded jeans and a white tee shirt. The cousins approached him.

"How are things going tonight buddy?" Hollywood asked, as the cousins stood directly in front of the sitting man.

"Things are okay, I guess," said the man, without much conviction. He didn't look up. "I'm just passing through. I took a piss break and grabbed a smoke. I don't do cigarettes in the car."

Hollywood thought the man's story sounded good, but decided to cut to the chase. "Are you looking for some male company, or maybe a little drug action?"

The man stood up, closed his fist and braced himself. "Hell no, I ain't looking for male company. Do I look like a damn queer to you?"

"No offense, buddy," said Tatou, trying to avoid a fist fight with the man. "That's just my cousin's sense of humor. His daddy dropped him on his head when he was young."

The cousins bid farewell to the irate man, returned to their unit, and drove west toward Lafayette. They had gone a mile down interstate, when Hollywood cut through the median and headed for the eastbound rest stop. Hollywood parked near a pay phone and watched the man in the tee shirt with a pair of binoculars. The man was still sitting on the concrete steps of the rest stop smoking cigarettes.

"What do you think he is up to?" asked Tatou.

Hollywood thought about it before answering. "He is obviously not a homo. He's not into drugs, unless it's a little personal use marijuana. My guess is that he is just a transient who is claiming squatter's rights to the rest stop. I think he is living in the bathroom, and is one of the beggars who have been fleecing drivers at the main intersections into Lafayette, 'will work for food,' that type of thing."

Hollywood and Tatou sat quietly in their unit at the eastbound rest stop watching the man on the steps through binoculars. They were startled when the pay phone near their unit rang. Tatou looked at his cousin and said, "Who would call a pay phone at midnight at a rest stop?"

"It's probably Farrah Fawcett," answered Hollywood. "I heard she was looking for me."

Hollywood exited the car and answered the phone.

"Hello," he said. "Uh, my name is Bill, what's yours." Hollywood listened, and replied as he looked at Tatou. "Yes, I might be interested in meeting you in a few minutes. How old are you, and what do you look like?" He paused. "Of course I'm interested; otherwise, why would I be answering the pay phone at a rest stop in the middle of the night. If you can be here in ten minutes I'll show you the time of your life," Hollywood said, with a slight lisp.

Hollywood listened to the man for another few seconds and said, "I'll be waiting for you on the steps of the westbound rest stop, near the entrance to the bathroom. I'm wearing faded jeans and a white tee shirt. See you in a few minutes, sweetie."

Tatou looked at his cousin. "Bro, you have always been a shit stirrer."

"Mac told us to have a good time," answered Hollywood, with a grin.

The cousins sat quietly and watched the westbound rest area. It was not long before a white Ford pickup raced into the rest area and parked near the bathroom facilities. The driver, a fiftyish white male dressed in a blue suit, exited the truck and walked directly toward the man in the white tee shirt. A few words were spoken, after which the man in the tee shirt stood quickly and lunged at the suited man, catching him with a solid right cross that sent him to the concrete. The tee-shirted man continued kicking the suited man as he attempted to crawl under his truck.

Hollywood used the pay phone to make an anonymous report to Troop I about a severe beating taking place at the rest stop. A few minutes later two unhappy uniformed troopers arrested the two men and cleared the rest area.

The cousins considered it a successful operation and drove into Lafayette to see if any ladies were still hanging around Legend's bar. The next day they submitted a report to Mac relating how the Interstate 10 rest areas were once again safe for travelers.

It had been two days since the agents had searched the residence on Ridge Road. Mac, Hungry Harv, Buzzy and Bert returned to the residence in a truck and searched it again. Once they were satisfied that they had not missed any evidence, they loaded up couches, chairs, weight-lifting equipment, washer and dryer and miscellaneous other furniture and hauled it to Troop I. They would do the appropriate paperwork to have the items forfeited to the state police, where it would be used for the next several years in various offices at the Troop I complex.

Mac placed one of the smaller sofas in his office and sat on it. He looked at Buzzy and Hungry Harv and asked, "How many people do you think stayed at the Ridge Road house while they waited for the barge to dock?"

"Fifteen to twenty," answered Buzzy.

"That's not enough people for the work they had to do. The information leading to the discovery came from SLEMCO, but you said LUS did not have any new accounts."

"That's correct," replied Buzzy.

Early that afternoon Mac drove to the main office of the Lafayette Utilities System. It was a busy place, and many of the civil service employees who worked there were overloaded and had to deal constantly with rude, uncooperative people. Mac showed his credentials to a receptionist and asked to speak with a clerk.

"Miss," he said, "could you check your files for the previous three months to see if you have any new accounts under the name David Williams. It sounds like a common name, but it's really not that common to this area."

The clerk rolled her eyes. "I would have to search it by hand, and I really don't have the time."

"It could help solve a murder," Mac lied in a tone just short of begging.

"Well, if it can help you with a murder investigation, I guess I can look at some records. Wait here."

The clerk returned in thirty minutes. "There was a David Williams who paid for an electrical hookup three months ago. He paid in cash, three months in advance. There is still a surplus, though he will be billed again at the end of July."

Mac returned to the office with the new address and picked up Hungry Harv.

"We have another hit on David Williams," Mac said. "I believe it will be a similar place, one that was used for living accommodations for several men."

They drove south on the Evangeline Thruway, then turned east toward Moss Street. The address turned out to be a mobile home in a secluded trailer park on the opposite side of Lafayette from the Ridge Road address.

"It was smart of them to have two off-load crews. I doubt that one crew knew about the existence of the other crew," said Hungry Harv. "The link between the two residences is David Williams. It was well organized."

They pulled into the concrete driveway and the single car garage attached to the mobile home. It was cluttered with beer cans, ice chests, and weight-lifting equipment.

"When this is all over, we'll have enough exercise equipment to start our own gym," said Hungry Harv.

"Whoever was in charge wanted his people to be in shape," answered Mac.

They entered the trailer through an unlocked back door. Like the Ridge Road residence, it was filled with cheap furniture. "It has more bunk beds than a Nazi prisoner of war camp," said Hungry Harv.

Beer, bread, and rotting frozen dinners were left on the kitchen counters. An oversized television sat behind a worn-out pool table.

"Whoever rented this place did not want his hands going in and out of Lafayette for entertainment or supplies," said Hungry Harv. "They ate, drank, watched television, worked out and partied here."

"That was smart," replied Mac. "It they had been allowed to go out on the town they might have gotten into trouble in a local bar and left evidence of their stay in Lafayette. If no one sees them, no one can identify them."

Hungry Harv picked up a piece of paper from the floor. It was a handwritten note describing how the tug and barge had entered into Vermilion Bay. It was notification that the marijuana had arrived, and it was time to immediately depart for Banker. The note was not addressed to anyone in particular, and it was not signed. Mac noted that the note was partially printed and partially in script, an exact match to the note found in the Ridge Road address. He placed it into an evidence bag. They continued searching the trailer and picked up a few small items to submit for prints. When they were satisfied that there was no more evidence, they returned to the office.

Mac let himself into the evidence vault and retrieved the note that the cousins had obtained from Freebase Freddy Patout. It was printed in the same fashion as the note Hungry Harv had found in the trailer. A professional analysis would establish that they were written by the same person.

"Freebase Freddy is our link to the smugglers," Mac said to Hungry Harv. "Assign a couple of agents to steal his garbage for a week or so and look for writing specimens. Follow up with a search warrant for his residence for additional writing samples. Then have Bert obtain a subpoena compelling him to give us a handwriting sample. Once we have all the samples we can contact the FBI for a forensic graphology expert to do the comparisons.

The result will be sufficient for us to squeeze his nuts for information."

Mac thought about the situation for a few moments, looked at Hungry Harv, and continued. "Also get the guys to put some pressure on our snitches for information on Patout. Let's go after him from every possible angle."

"Will do," said Hungry Harv. "Where are you going?"

"Simple Eddie said the colonel wants to see me."

"I heard the colonel's secretary is a looker," said Hollywood, who was listening to the conversation. "Have you seen her, Mac?"

"Yes, I've seen her. She's a little on the butch side for me, but very well put together." Mac looked at Hungry Harv and said, "As they say in Kaplan, she could make a weak dog break his chain."

Mac thought it prudent to do a little fact finding, and called Bugger Red before going to Baton Rouge.

"Pilot's section, can I help you?" said Bugger Red.

"Bugger, this is Mac. How are thing at the puzzle palace," he said, referring to LSP headquarters. Mac knew that Bugger Red's job description was to fly police-related missions, and Bugger Red dearly loved to clock speeders, participate in rolling surveillances, and find marijuana fields, but he also knew that eighty-five percent of what Bugger Red did was fly the colonel, or one of his cronies, around the state on an LSP helicopter.

"Just living the dream," said Bugger Red. "What's up?"

"Buck Carter wants to see me. Do you have any idea why?"

"I heard him talking about creating some new positions, but I don't have any details, and I don't know how that may concern Region II Narcotics. Maybe he just wants to be briefed on the smuggling investigation. He knows Simple Eddie is not up to it."

"What is the deal with his looker secretary?" Mac changed the subject. "I hate to waste a trip to Baton Rouge. Is she available?"

"Better let that one alone," said Bugger Red. "She is the colonel's steady squeeze. You know how I am, and about some of

111

the adventures I've had in the copter, but Carter's got me beat. He and his secretary have worn the leather off the back seat of my bird."

"You are shitting me," said Mac. "Carter is married and has some kids. Are you sure?"

"I watched them in my rear view mirror," said Bugger Red. "She could suck a golf ball through a garden hose."

"Roger that," said Mac. I'll keep the information to myself."

"Keep your head down and your powder dry," said Bugger Red. "Say, when are you coming to the puzzle palace?"

"I'd rather go to the zoo and sandpaper a lion's dick," answered Mac, taking a line from Bill Spencer, "but I'll probably be there tomorrow or the next day."

CHAPTER 12
A Lesson in Politics

Mac chose the following Wednesday to make the trip across the Atchafalaya Basin to the hallowed halls of the LSP headquarters building in Baton Rouge. When he had made the call to Carter's secretary he thought he heard a little extra sweetness in her voice. No big deal, but different anyway. He had just driven upon the Interstate 10 expanse bridge across the basin and was looking south past Lake Henderson and Lake Bigeux and was almost to the Pelba swamp area when he came upon a minivan overturned in the outside lane of the bridge. He pulled up to the van and stopped.

A middle-aged, heavy-set woman ran toward Mac's unit, screaming. She was crying hysterically, flailing her arms erratically and muttering something about her child. Mac thought he heard her say, "My baby is in the water, my baby is in the water." He made a quick observation of the scene, noting that there were skid marks indicating the location where the van had spun out of control striking the heavy concrete railing of the bridge. Broken glass was scattered around the area and the back window of the mini van was busted out. He looked at the woman again, who was now out of breath, but was still flailing her arms about and pointing to the railing.

Realization struck Mac like he had been hit in the face with a rolled up newspaper. He ran the few steps to the railing and looked over the side. A small girl was about twenty feet down and over twenty feet out, struggling to stay afloat in the water, her head bouncing up and down in the water lilies. It was clear now what had happened. When the van had spun out of control the rear of the van impacted the concrete railing. The girl had been lying in the back seat and was thrown through the large glass window, over the railing and into the basin water below. She was lucky to land in the water, Mac thought. Alligators and poisonous snakes are

113

plentiful, but the cottonmouths are the worst. Where most snakes will avoid human contact, cottonmouths are curious and vicious, seeking contact. But landing on the ground, or worse, a stump, would have killed her.

"She can't swim," screamed the mother, reminding Mac he did not have time to fully analyze the situation.

Mac had to react quickly. He ran to his unit, called Troop I on the radio. "NI-3, Troop I, this is a signal thirty-seven emergency. There is a signal twenty (vehicle accident) at mile post one twenty-three, eastbound, on the basin bridge. A little girl was thrown over the railing into the water. Send help immediately. I'm going over the side. Out."

The area was mostly shallow water, mud, scrub trees and rotting cypress stumps, but the lucky kid had landed in deep water. Mac could not see the bottom; he took a deep breath, and crossed his legs as he jumped, hoping he would not land on a cypress stump, or worse, an alligator. "Jesus, I hate snakes," he said, as he jumped. It was deep where he landed, and when he came to the surface he began swimming toward the girl, watching for snakes and gators in all directions. He thought to himself, "I don't even have a plan."

Mac reached the little girl, told her to relax and kick her legs to stay afloat. "We have people coming to help us," he said. "They will be here in just a few minutes." Mac was not a particularly good swimmer. He had been placed in a remedial swim class when he was on active duty with the Marines while training in Pensacola. He had been required to swim a mile in a flight suit and tennis shoes, and finished last in his class by over thirty minutes.

"Why me?"

"What?" replied the little girl.

"Never mind. Are you hurt, are you bleeding anywhere, and do you think you have any broken bones?" Mac visually checked as much of her as he could observe.

"I'm not hurting," said the little girl, "I'm just scared. I was sleeping and when I woke up I was flying through the air."

Mac looked at the girl's arms, face and neck. There were scratches and bruises, but amazingly, no lacerations that would require stitches. He began collecting nearby water lilies and placed them under her arms. They supported her weight.

114

"I'm not sure what we are going to do next, but we are getting out of here soon," Mac said, as he tried to smile at the little girl. Mac was still treading water when his leg struck the little girl's leg. His eyes got big, thinking maybe it was an alligator.

"That was my leg you hit," said the little girl, sensing Mac's fear. She smiled at him.

Troop I personnel arrived within ten minutes. One of the troopers had the common sense to stop a fisherman and take two life vests from his boat. Mac left the little girl, who was amazingly calm, supported by the lilies. He swam to the bridge, obtained the vests and swam back to the girl, and placed both vests around her waist, tying them together. She would need the extra thickness to prevent rope burns. Mac pulled the girl back to the bridge. A trooper had seized a thin nylon anchor rope and lowered it to Mac, who tied it to the little girl. Ten seconds later she was standing on the bridge with her mother.

Another twenty minutes and Acadian Ambulance arrived and was examining the girl. They announced to the mother that it had to be a miracle she did not have any serious injuries, and was lucky to be alive. Reporters had arrived from two television stations and were interviewing the little girl.

"When I woke up from my nap," she told the reporters, "I was flying through the air and two angels flew by my side and lowered me gently into the water. Then when that man (she pointed to Mac) was in the water with me he kicked my leg and thought it was a snake. He was scared." The little girl laughed. The next day, a small independent newspaper would carry the story under the headline, "And You Think You Have Problems." Mac was not amused.

It was late afternoon when Mac finally called Colonel Carter's secretary and informed her he would need to set a new appointment.

"Colonel Carter does not like to be stood up," she said, with some ice on her words.

"Can't be helped," Mac said, too exhausted to explain.

"What should I tell Colonel Carter?" she said.

"Tell him I'm going to get drunk, and that I'll be there early tomorrow," Mac said, and hung up. He fully intended to have a late night celebrating not being alligator bait.

That night the rescue of the little girl was the lead story on every major television station from Lafayette to Baton Rouge. For the past several years he had been the primary spokesman for major drug arrests and seizures in the Lafayette area, and was accustomed to dealing with the media. Mac routinely used media contacts to help create new cases or enhance ongoing cases. On several occasions Mac had used the media as leverage by ensuring a suspect that a lack of cooperation would guarantee his picture would be on the front page of the local paper. He trusted the media and considered them to be a huge asset. But now he paid little attention to the newscast, and concentrated on downing some beer.

An hour or so into his boozing Mac felt like some company. He used the house phone at Legend's Bar to call Marcelle, hoping that she would not be on duty at Lafayette General.

"Well, long time no hear from, Tarzan. I saw you on the six o'clock news. Nice work."

"That's nothing," replied Mac. "Did you know that they have a statue of me in Washington D. C.?"

"Really?" Marcelle asked, doubtfully.

"That's right. I was one of the flag raisers at Iwo Jima."

"Wasn't that in World War II?" History was not Marcelle's area of expertise.

"I also won the Edgar Award for literature."

"The what?" Literature wasn't at the top of the list either, Mac thought to himself.

"Never mind," said Mac. "Why don't you drive over to Legend's and meet me for cocktails."

"No can do, Tarzan. I haven't heard from you in six weeks. I'm dating someone."

"Who is the lucky doctor?" Mac was guessing.

"In fact," Marcelle said. "It is a doctor. I'm dating Bobby Feldon."

Mac knew about Feldon; he was a Lafayette gynecologist, and a known womanizer. A couple of years back Mac had dated a nurse, whose roommate was also a nurse, and was seeing Feldon on the side.

"Feldon has a wife and three kids," Mac informed her.

"He said he was going to leave his wife and marry me."

"Feldon has had more love affairs than anyone in Lafayette. He majored in it. It was a class requirement in order to become a gynecologist," Mac continued.

"I'll hook you up with my new roommate. She's not dating anyone at the present."

"Who is your roommate?" asked Mac, somewhat interested, and hoping the night wouldn't be a complete loss.

"Diane McDaniels. Do you know her?"

"I know of her," replied Mac. "She's seen more dicks than a urologist." Mac was about to say something else when he realized Marcelle had hung up on him.

Jared Doise, proprietor of the bar, walked over to Mac and said, "Lieutenant, I saw you on the six o'clock news. Good work. Let me buy you a cold drink."

"A double margarita would probably be some good medicine right now," replied Mac.

"A double it is. Why the dejected look?"

"Rejected look is a better fit. My girlfriend just dumped me for a married guy." Mac said as he looked around at Jared's bartenders and waitresses. "Legend's has the most beautiful bartenders in Lafayette, and seemingly smart as well."

"All of my girls have a college degree, or they are working on one. It's one of my rules." Jared pointed to a beautiful blonde behind the bar. "That's Crystal, one more year and she will be a registered nurse. The taller blonde at the end of the bar is Kelly. She has a degree in General Studies. Stacy, in the back office, is my manager. Lisa is in school, and Ami, the tall brunette, is a graduate student. All of my girls are beautiful and sharp; that's why we have customers like you, Lieutenant," Jared said, with a smile.

"Don't ever move the beer box," said Mac, as he watched Ami bend over the box to serve a drive-thru customer.

Jared grinned and handed Mac another double margarita.

Early the next morning Mac took two aspirin and washed them down with black coffee. At eight o'clock he began another trip east toward Baton Rouge. He intentionally joined the morning commuter traffic in order to avoid another swim in the snake-infested waters of the Atchafalaya Basin. As he drove past mile marker one twenty-three he slowed to look at the place where the little girl had been thrown into the basin water below. The path Mac had made swimming through the water hyacinths was still visible, like a well used deer trail through the woods. There was a small circle of open water in the lilies, where the girl had landed, pushing the green plants outward. A large alligator floated, stationary in the hole, as if claiming squatter's rights, or maybe hoping for another passenger to be dropped into the basin. Mac shivered slightly and turned his attention back to the road. The little girl and her mother would never realize how close she had come to being gator bait. Mac thought it was just as well that they remained naïve.

LSP Headquarters Building contained a small cafeteria where troopers and administrative staff met regularly for breakfast and lunch. It was a good place to pick up on the latest rumors. Mac had long believed that police officers were worse than the Junior League for gossiping and rumor mongering, and troopers were worse than most law enforcement agencies. The secretaries at Headquarters regularly knew more about the inner workings of LSP than the troopers. They always seemed to have advance knowledge of who was being punished, transferred or promoted.

Mac sat alone in the cafeteria, downing an additional two cups of coffee, after which he walked down the long hall leading to the superintendent's office. Buck Carter's long-legged secretary was wearing a dress that said "I'm a bad, bad girl; don't mess with me." She led him into the inner sanctum of the LSP puzzle palace.

"Welcome back to Baton Rouge," said Carter. "I read the article in the Morning Advocate about your heroic rescue of the accident victim on Interstate 10. Good work, Mac. Excellent representation of the state police."

"She was a very lucky kid," said Mac. "I don't think she will ever realize how fortunate she is to be alive. She and her mother were taking a first ever vacation to New Orleans, when her mother saw a shadow in the road and slammed on her breaks, losing control of her van, and t-boning the railing. Her mother said they were returning to Missouri, and never coming back to Louisiana. It's just as well."

Buck Carter rose from his desk and walked toward the massive office window. "How many narcotics agents are there in the state police?" He asked.

Mac hesitated, inherently knowing that it was a rhetorical question. "The last time I checked it was around fifty-five, or so." Mac thought it was a good time to make a point and continued, "There are only twelve in my region. The other two regions have about twenty-two each." Mac was aware that Region III, the north district, was Carter's home district. Region I was the south district, headquartered in Baton Rouge, and had long been a favorite of the state's politicians. It was an aggravation to Mac that his district had less than half the agents of the other districts, but was just as productive, if not more so, in terms of arrests and seizures.

"Do you think there is justification for adding forty more drug agents to LSP Narcotics?" Carter was looking directly at Mac.

"Absolutely," answered Mac, somewhat taken back, and wondering where the conversation was headed.

"How is the smuggling investigation going?" Carter asked.

"We are making progress," said Mac. "We've identified some of the players. As soon as one person gives it up, others will get in line. It's first come, first serve. When you start showing them the inside of Angola, they trade up fast."

"Good," said Carter, returning to his desk. He sat down and picked up a folder. "I've looked over the arrest and seizure statistics in the state as a whole, and your area has been very productive during the past two years. A lot of major seizures came from the Criminal Patrol Unit, and your team developed some excellent follow-up investigations. The statistics speak for themselves. You can't pick up a newspaper without reading about drugs. It affects everybody, no matter what your level of society. The legislature is in session, and I think now is a good time to push for a hundred person narcotics team for the state."

Carter looked over his desk at Mac, and said, "What could you accomplish if you doubled, or maybe tripled, the number of narcotics agents you have?"

Mac took the bait, excited at the prospect of increasing the number of agents in the Region II office.

"I could turn Acadiana upside down," he replied. "We could branch out, become more accessible to the area's smaller departments, and become more involved with the feds, working in a task force concept. I could create a field office in Morgan City,

119

where we know there is smuggling activity involving some Cubans. Customs has been after us to work more closely with them; we could establish a water patrol unit and in conjunction with Customs we could intercept suspicious boats on the bayous and in the coastal areas. There's no limit to the positive impact we could have on the drug war if we doubled or tripled our personnel."

"I've looked at your file, Mac. You have degrees in Speech and English, and you've established good contacts with the media. Can you make a case for us in front of the budget committee at the state legislature?"

"I think so, Colonel. When and where?"

"Next week. I'll set it up for you."

The next day Mac and Hungry Harv began pulling a year's worth of files from a secondhand metal filing cabinet in the secretary's cubical. They agreed that a year of stats pertaining to arrests and seizures should be sufficient to establish the severity of the drug problem in South Louisiana, and justify the hiring of forty more agents for the state.

The sun was rising over the basin as Mac and Hungry Harv drove east toward Baton Rouge and the state capital. Mac squinted into the bright light as he passed the commuters who lived in Lafayette but worked in Baton Rouge. They exited on College Drive and stopped for coffee at the Morning Call, which was a spin off of the famous Cafe' du Monde in New Orleans. They sat quietly as Hungry Harv ate two orders of sugar coated beignets. Mac silently went over a mental list of items to discuss before the budget committee.

As they walked up the steps to the historic state capitol Mac thought about former Governor Huey Long, who built the capitol, was later assassinated in it, and was buried on its front lawn. They walked past the many politicians and lobbyists in the halls and stopped briefly to look at the location of Long's assassination. Small indentations in the walls were still visible where state trooper's bullets had ricocheted off imported marble. Dr. Carl Austin Weiss had walked up to Long, according to the most reliable reports, and shot him twice with a thirty-eight caliber revolver. One bullet struck Long, after which he ran down the hall screaming. The trooper bodyguards unloaded on Weiss with automatic weapons. One account said Weiss was hit thirty-two times; another said as many as sixty times. There is still controversy as to whether Weiss's bullet killed Long or that of a trooper.

After visiting the location of Long's assassination they took the elevator some four hundred feet above Baton Rouge, and looked down upon the city and the grave of Governor Long.

Hungry Harv turned to Mac, and said, "I can't put my finger on it, but I don't have a good feeling about this assignment."

The budget committee was in session and Mac was called to speak just prior to the noon break.

"Colonel Carter has requested consideration for forty new positions within state police in order to almost double the size of the narcotics division," said the committee chairman. "Lieutenant, do you agree with this assessment?"

"Unequivocally."

"Tell us about your organization, Lieutenant, and the type of work you do."

"Well," Mac began, "The Louisiana State Police Bureau of Investigation Narcotics Section is divided into three regions. I supervise Region II, which comprises seventeen parishes, and is headquartered in Lafayette. There are currently ten full time agents in my region. The other two regions have over twice that number." Mac glanced toward Colonel Carter, who sat in the rear of the room. Carter rolled his eyes, knowing that Mac had used the opportunity to point out his lack of equal personnel and resources.

"What kind of illicit drugs are prevalent in Louisiana?" The chairman continued his questioning.

"Marijuana, cocaine and a newcomer called crack are the current heavyweights," explained Mac. "Ecstasy is becoming very popular with the young crowd, and LSD is making somewhat of a comeback. Methamphetamine is the drug of choice with bikers and dancers at the topless bars. And, of course, there are the usual prescription pills that sell for ten to twenty-five dollars a pop on the street."

"What kind of successes are you having in the Lafayette area," asked a committee member.

Mac held up a recent copy of the Baton Rouge Morning Advocate. A front page article stated, "Drug Dealers are Winning the War in Lafayette." "We've arrested a lot of people and seized record numbers of drugs in Acadiana, but it's not enough. There are too many drugs and dealers; we need more agents and assets."

"Just how many cases have you made in the past twelve months," asked a committee member.

"First, I would like to explain that we do not make cases on users. We could arrest users by the hundreds, but that would not solve the problem, and the stats would be inflated. There is not enough time to mess with users. We concentrate on large-scale dealers, smugglers, and distribution networks. We go after organizations. In that respect we have arrested three hundred forty-seven people during the past twelve months."

"Give us some specifics regarding the drugs you are seizing," said the chairman.

Mac looked at his notes. "We seized forty-three hundred dosage units of hallucinogens such as PCP and LSD. We seized in excess of forty pounds of cocaine and three thousand pounds of marijuana, not counting twelve tons or so that was left on a barge south of Lafayette a few weeks back. We seized close to a million dollars in cash and over fifty thousand prescription pills such as stimulants, depressants and pain killers. These seizures are in addition to those made by our Criminal Patrol Unit, which is also seizing drugs in record amounts."

"Tell us what happens when the Criminal Patrol Unit makes a seizure."

"They bring the drugs and suspects to Region II, and we pick up the case from that point, releasing CPU to return to the highway and look for other suspects."

"How do you handle the CPU cases?"

"We call DEA and Customs because the drugs routinely come from Texas headed east."

"What is the response from the federal authorities?" the chairman asked.

"Thus far, they have never picked up a case," Mac said, as he looked at Colonel Carter, who was squirming in his seat.

"What is their response to you?"

"They say they are too busy, or don't have enough advance notice. At that point we routinely contact a federal or state agency where the drugs are headed. We belong to an organization called SDEA. That stands for the National Alliance of State Drug Enforcement Agencies. SDEA meets twice a year to provide classes on the latest drug trends, major smuggling organizations, and other issues relevant to illicit drugs in the United States. More importantly, the organization provides us with a network of names and contact numbers across the nation."

"Be more specific as to how this affects your unit in Lafayette."

"We deliver the suspects and drugs to that agency for what is commonly called 'a controlled delivery.' For example, the Criminal Patrol Unit seizes a hundred pounds of marijuana. We interview the mules, (the person transporting the drugs) and learn that the load was going to Atlanta. We call DEA and they are busy. We then call SDEA members in Atlanta and learn they are part of a local task force. We make arrangements to deliver the suspect and marijuana to them. We take no enforcement action, as it is out of our jurisdiction, but the case leads to some major arrests in Atlanta. It is a national problem, so we work with the other states to make a difference. It's very time consuming, and we could accomplish a lot more if we had more agents, and better cooperation from the feds."

"What was the total value of the seized drugs you seized in Lafayette last year?" asked a committee member.

Mac looked at his notes. "Five million."

It was getting close to lunchtime and the committee chairman wanted to move on. "Do you have anything else to add?"

"Drugs and drug abuse are in our schools," Mac continued, "the work place, and our social units. I doubt there is a person in this room who does not know someone who has addiction problems. It affects every aspect of society in Louisiana. Eighty-five percent of the people incarcerated in this state are locked up because of drugs. And, by the way, Louisiana leads the nation in incarceration rates."

"In your opinion, how do we solve the problem?" asked a committee member.

"Some people believe we should legalize and tax drugs," Mac continued. "I'm not in favor of that approach. Another approach is demand reduction, but more education and treatment programs will be needed. A third approach is supply reduction. That's my area. We seize drugs, arrest dealers and bust up distribution networks. The largest load of marijuana, and possible cocaine, in the history of the United States recently came through the locks in Vermilion Bay. The smugglers got away with as much as four hundred thousand pounds. It was a well organized and financially successful venture, and it happened right under our noses. We have some leads, but have had very little time to fully investigate them."

"What could you accomplish if you had twice the number of narcotics agents in the state police?" said the chairman.

"I believe we could make a huge difference in the illicit drug business in Louisiana. The growth rate of our arrests and seizures would increase exponentially. It would enable us to increase our efforts with local and federal task forces. Louisiana would no longer be a safe haven for dopers."

The chairman looked at Colonel Carter, and said, "Has Lieutenant McCullough asked you for additional personnel, Colonel?"

"Damn near been a pest about it," said a smiling Carter, ever the congenial politician, knowing the legislature would fund the extra slots.

The chairman thanked Mac for his service and for his testimony before the committee and adjourned for lunch.

Mac and Hungry Harv were walking out of the committee room when they were approached by Simple Eddie. "I heard what you said about DEA and Customs, and I didn't like it. From now on, I am ordering you not to participate with NEDA or SNEA or whatever the hell that organization is you talked about in front of the committee. You, and none of your people are to leave the state for any reason, it's just that simple."

Mac chose not to respond, and he and Hungry Harv walked down the steps of the capitol to begin the boring drive back to Lafayette.

"What is Simple Eddie's problem?" Hungry Harv asked.

"I don't really understand the psychological complexities of psychopaths. But, I know this much, Simple Eddie is a self-interested, self-serving, Perrier-drinking bureaucrat . He is a power hungry politician who lives to control other people. He's never had an original thought, and he is jealous of other people's success. He is also a cunning little prick who is happiest when he is stirring shit. He lives for the smell of it."

"Mais, I think he has visions of having your head on his trophy shelf," Hungry Harv said. "And if you lose your job you're screwed."

"Maybe I could sell cars or insurance for a living," Mac said, beginning to smile.

"You couldn't sell a prostitute on a troop train," said Hungry Harv. "I guess it's like 'catch twenty-two' for you Mac."

"Do you even know what catch twenty-two is?" Without waiting for an answer, Mac said: "A character named Yossarian was a pilot in World War II. He didn't want to fly missions over Germany. If he flew them he was crazy and didn't have to, but if he refused to fly, then he was sane and had to."

"Like I said," Hungry Harv repeated himself, "it's 'catch twenty-two.'"

"By the way," Hungry Harv continued, "my barber knows more about state police politics than you do."

At four o'clock that afternoon Mac received a call from Colonel Carter's secretary saying the measure had passed and Colonel Carter said thanks.

The following Monday Mac received a call from Bugger Red. "I just want to give you a heads up on the new slots," he said. "The word around headquarters is that none of them are going to narcotics. Buck Carter used five to promote his closest friends to lieutenant colonel, five were used to promote various people to major, and ten were used for captain's promotions. He used one position to hire a secretary for his secretary. He's keeping the other positions in reserve for future use."

Mac was in shock as he hung up the phone.

"You look you saw a ghost," Hungry Harv said.

"I should have seen it coming," said Mac, dejectedly. "None of the new positions funded by the legislature are going to narcotics personnel. Buck Carter used them to promote friends, and create new power bases around the state enhancing his position as superintendent. He pissed down my leg and told me it was raining."

"Same old state police. Don't take it personal, Mac," said Hungry Harv. "That's the way it has always been in Baton Rouge. It's like Captain Spencer said, you wrestle with pigs you get dirty, and the pigs like it."

"They have no notion of what this job takes, and no notion of what it takes out of you. Not one of them gives a shit about the public we serve. The only thing I have going for me right now is my willingness to humiliate myself in front of the legislature."

"I'm just the colonel's whore," Mac continued, looking dejectedly out of the driver's window.

CHAPTER 13
Guilty as Sin

Maurice, Louisiana is a small community just inside Vermilion Parish, located on Highway 167, about ten miles south of Lafayette. The town has one traffic light and one police officer, who refers to himself in the third person as "the chief," and whose sole job is to write speeding tickets, which pays his salary and the mayor's. Maurice has a combined service station and convenience store that is a known late-night hangout for dope peddlers and dope users. The cousins were sitting in the store parking lot drinking beer hoping for some leads into the smuggling case when they heard Maurice's only cop call for assistance on the sheriff's office frequency.

A young black male known to the locals as Ty-rone was tripping on LSD and had climbed a tall magnolia tree in a subdivision on the edge of town. He was yelling at the residents, threatening to jump out of the tree and kill himself.

"I hate myself," Ty-rone screamed to the gathering crowd. "I hate the world, and I'm going to jump out of this tree and kill myself."

The cousins arrived on the scene at one o'clock in the morning. "What is that snow bird doing up a tree at this time of the morning; does he think he is a monkey?" Tatou asked the chief.

"Far as I know a damned coon dog may have treed him," said the politically incorrect chief. "He sure is messing up my night. All I'm trained for is to write tickets, and I'm thinking about giving him one for disturbing my sleep. Do you think I should call the volunteer fire department?" The chief was walking back and forth, running his hand through his grey hair.

"Calm down and keep talking to him," said Hollywood, "I'll call the Lafayette Parish Sheriff's Office. They have a SWAT

Team and a Hostage Negotiation Team. They'll know how to handle it for you."

Someone called the local television stations, and the situation quickly became a media event. The Lafayette Sheriff's Office arrived and set up a perimeter, making the area around the magnolia tree as sterile as possible. A public information officer set up a briefing area, and the SWAT Team wrote an operations order. It was a detailed plan, and the cousins thought it was a lot of work for just one democrat up a tree, but they were content to watch.

"One monkey don't make a circus," said Tatou.

"It's a Chinese fire drill," retorted Hollywood. "It's Friday the thirteenth, and a full moon. Every derelict and fruitcake in the parish comes out of the closet when it's a full moon."

"I'll go back to the store for some popcorn and beer," said Tatou.

It was now two o'clock in the morning and the democrat was still screaming about his shitty life when the negotiators from LPSO arrived on the scene. Ms. Billie Jean Wilson, and her SIT members (Suicide Intervention Team) were there to save the day.

The cousins had heard about Billie Jean after she had joined the Lafayette Sheriff's Office, transferring from a correctional facility in Boulder, Colorado. The Lafayette sheriff was a democratic liberal who had made a priority of rehabilitating convicts, believing that they were the same as law-abiding citizens, just not as educated, or maybe the product of a broken home. Inmates in the politically correct Lafayette facility were called clients. Billie Jean had a PhD in Clinical Psychology from the University of Colorado. Her job with the sheriff's office was essentially that of a mental health worker. She evaluated and educated prisoners and arranged for an early release for those convicts who were not considered an immediate threat to the general public.

When the Lafayette sheriff had interviewed Billie Jean he said, "Why would you want to leave such a beautiful place as Colorado to work in Louisiana?"

"Well," said Billie Jean, "it's just so confusing up there, what with the women trying to be men, and the men trying to be women."

Wrestling With Pigs

The cousins had heard about Billie Jean from Tee Joe Thibodeaux, whom they had incarcerated for crack distribution. Tee Joe was a deckhand in the oilfield around Vermilion Parish, when he was not high on crack. He had been incarcerated for crack possession, distribution and remaining on premises after forbidden. His offenses were not considered violent or excessive, so he was an excellent client for Billie Jean's feel good class. All he had to do was attend the class, behave, and he would be back on the street before Billie Jean could get off work.

Billie Jean began her classes with twelve students sitting on the jailhouse floor cross-legged in a large circle. She explained her instructions slowly and carefully.

"I want everyone to hold you head back, place your index finger to your thumbs, and close your eyes," she instructed the students. "I am going to teach you the spiritual practice for cultivating a steady mind."

Billie Jean was on a roll. She was positive she could help the inmates by enhancing their inherent understanding of themselves.

"Now concentrate on feeling good," she said, with a smile. "Think about something you enjoy. This will give you insight into the behavior that caused your inappropriate actions. This will happen through motivation."

A coworker tapped Billie Jean on the shoulder. "Miss Billie," she said, "you might want to check on Tee Joe."

Billie Jean opened her eyes and looked at Tee Joe, who was sitting directly across from her masturbating feverishly while staring at her.

Billie Jean screamed once, then composed herself and yelled at Tee Joe. "I said meditate, not masturbate, you moron."

As Tee Joe was being forcibly removed from the room, the inmate sitting next to him asked what had happened.

"Tee Joe was jerking off," said another student.

"I can't believe he disrespected me like that," he said. "I would have beat the shit out of him if I had known he was doing that next to me."

Another one of the students took that comment as a challenge, stood up, unzipped his pants, and began masturbating in front of Billie Jean and the rest of the students. Pandemonium broke out, and Billie Jean ran for the door, slamming it behind her. SWAT had to be called in to quell the mini riot.

Thereafter, Billie Jean had a sign on her office door that said, "Meditation, not Masturbation."

Ty-rone was still in the tree threatening to jump out. He looked down at Billie Jean and said, "You better get out of the way, lady; I'm going to jump."

"Why don't we climb up there and throw him down?" asked Tatou, who was becoming bored.

"Very funny," said Billie Jean. "Can't you see that this young man is crying out for help? He is probably bipolar. If I can just establish a meaningful information exchange with him, I'm sure I can talk him down."

"Whatever," said Hollywood, who knew that Ty-rone was just tripping on LSD. "We would all be better off if the turd just fell out of the tree."

Billie Jean took almost forty-five minutes to talk Ty-rone down from the Magnolia tree, after which he was taken to the mental health ward of the University Medical Center in Lafayette, where he was fed, clothed, and given counseling and medication. He rested at the medical center for three days, after which a judge released him based on Billie Jean's recommendation.

Two days after Ty-rone's release from the hospital, he climbed the Magnolia tree and began screaming that he was going to jump.

The cousins were just south of Maurice retrieving trash from the driveway leading to the Alfred Patout residence when they heard the chief call for help.

They arrived at the Magnolia tree in two minutes. "We will help you," said Hollywood, "if you let us handle it without calling for any outside assistance."

The chief was happy for anyone to take over and relieve him of the responsibility.

Tatou opened the trunk of his unit and removed a rifle and six canisters of CS gas, which is the preferred gas for riot control situations.

The cousins walked calmly to the Magnolia tree.

"Where is the woman?" Tee Joe yelled to the cousins.

"She is not coming," said Tatou. "You have about one minute to get your doper ass down from that tree, before I light you up with this 'act right' gas."

"You ain't got the guts to shoot me, motherfucker," said Ty-rone, who knew his rights, but did not know Tatou.

The first shot narrowly missed Ty-rone, striking a nearby limb.

"Hey, motherfucker. You almost hit me," cried Ty-rone, whose eyes were starting to burn from the gas.

"Stand by, asshole," said Tatou as he fired the second round.

Ty-rone took three direct hits out of the six canisters that Tatou shot at him. Hollywood later reported that snot flowed twenty feet down the tree as Ty-rone tried desperately to dodge the canisters.

"He looks like Curious George," shouted Hollywood, as he watched Ty-rone come down the tree.

The cousins took Ty-rone to the Maurice car wash and sprayed him with a high pressure hose until most of the gas and stench was removed.

"Ty-rone, you can go to jail, this time in Vermilion Parish, where they won't treat you as well as Lafayette, or you can talk to us," said Hollywood.

Ty-rone, whose eyes and nose were still running, just wanted to go home. "Don't want to go back to jail," he said, without expression.

"Good," said Tatou. "Tell us what you know about Freebase Freddy."

"I used to run some stuff for him, and I helped him off load some bales from crew boats, but I quit because he don't pay. He always manages to forget about paying you, ask anybody in Maurice."

"Who does Freebase Freddy hang around with?" Hollywood asked.

"Freddy be married to one of them Rochon women from Abbeville, the ones who owns the boat place," said Ty-rone. "He hangs around with his brother-in-law."

131

"All right," said Hollywood. "We may want a written statement from you later, but for right now, go home, and don't climb any more Magnolia trees."

The next day the cousins briefed Mac and Hungry Harv on the information received from Ty-rone.

"Isn't that interesting that smugglers are using the Vermilion Bayou, that the Rochons have crime connections, and own a boat dealership on the Vermilion River?" asked Mac.

"I don't believe in coincidences," said Hungry Harv. "What do you know of the Rochon family?"

Mac had heard of the Rochon family. They had been established in Abbeville for several generations. Their ancestry was mixed with Cajun, but they were originally Italian. The Rochon family became famous in federal police circles during the 1960s due to its connection with New Orleans crime boss, Carlos Marcello.

When Huey Long was governor of Louisiana, he met with New York mobsters Dandy Phil Kastel and Frank Costello to introduce illegal gambling into the state for a piece of the pie. At the time, Silver Dollar "Sam" Carolla was the New Orleans crime boss. A young Carlos Marcello worked for Carolla, managing his gambling interests. In 1947, Carolla was deported by federal authorities, and Carlos Marcello took over the crime syndicate in the city.

Later, when Bobby Kennedy became Attorney General of the United States, he held congressional hearings in which Carlos Marcello repeatedly had to take the fifth amendment. Afterwards, Marcello said to a federal informant, "If you cut off a dog's tail, he can still bite you, but if you cut off his head, it will no longer be a problem." The statement was interpreted as a threat to kill President John Kennedy. The rumor was furthered when Carlos Marcello met with Jack Ruby and Santos Trafficante just before President Kennedy was assassinated.

Bobby Kennedy could not convict Marcello of a crime, so he used his position as Attorney General to have Marcello deported to Guatemala in 1961. Carlos Marcello secretly returned to the United States via Vermilion Bayou. It was well known that the Rochon family in Abbeville brought him back into the States. They even named one of their sons "Carlos" after Marcello. After reentering the States, Marcello quietly returned to his Metairie mansion and continued to run the New Orleans syndicate. Proof of his connection with the New York crime bosses came in 1966 when he was arrested after attending a Mafia Crime Commission meeting.

It was early October and the heat and humidity of the Louisiana summer was subsiding when Mac drove to the Lafayette Correctional Center and knocked on Billie Jean Wilson's office door. She was between sessions with her inmates.

"I need your help with an interview," Mac said. "I'm going to Abbeville to interview a member of the Rochon family. I think he is involved in a multi-million dollar smuggling operation, and I would like your insight into his reactions."

"Why not?" replied Billie Jean. "Sounds like more fun than watching inmates masturbate."

As Mac drove south toward Abbeville, he described the Vermilion Parish smuggling operation to Billie Jean. "I have no direct or indirect evidence linking Peter Rochon to the operation, but we know that he hangs with his brother-in-law, Alfred Patout, and we currently have enough information to establish that Patout is a user, dealer, and smuggler."

"What do you hope to accomplish today?" she asked.

"Rochon will not give us any information, but I want him to feel that we are close to solving the investigation. I want him to sweat. If we push, he will call other people who are involved and people will scramble. Somebody will make a mistake. The first dopers to fold will get the best deals, and they know it. I want Peter Rochon to feel like he has an opportunity to be the first to work with us."

"All right," said Billie Jean. "Try to establish some rapport with Rochon. Questions are tools. Try to avoid words like confession, doper, and smuggler. Use terminology that is user friendly. Don't antagonize or bully him. Look for signs of weakness."

"Give me some examples," said Mac.

"If he becomes nervous, he will sweat, his mouth may become dry, and his facial complexion will change. If he becomes tense and restless, he will avoid direct answers. He will be deceptive," she replied.

It was early afternoon when they arrived in Abbeville. Mac drove across the Vermilion River and pulled into the gravel yard of the Rochon boat dealership. There were a few bass boats scattered across the front parking lot and a couple on the showroom floor. Four or five larger off-shore fishing boats lined the back parking lot. Mac thought the dealership had a run-down appearance, like they were not that interested in selling and repairing boats. He looked around and did not see a service department. The roof was rusty, corrugated tin, and tiles were missing from the floor. The walls were constructed of rough, unpainted cypress. Mac led the way inside and asked the lone employee, a receptionist, for Peter Rochon.

Peter came out of his office and introduced himself. Mac estimated that he was slightly less than six feet tall, appeared to be in his early thirties, and weighed about one hundred eighty pounds. He had dark, receding hair and brown eyes that showed no emotion. Mac identified himself and Billie Jean as law enforcement officers and handed Rochon his credentials. Rochon squinted when looking at the identification card, then looked up at Mac and Billie Jean quizzically.

"Please come into my office and have a seat. Would you like some coffee or perhaps a soda water?" Rochon said, as he sat behind a cheap imitation oak desk.

Mac ignored the offer and sat down in front of the desk, pulling his chair close.

"We are investigating a smuggling operation that recently occurred in Vermilion Parish." Mac was direct. "We've located two houses in Lafayette that some of the players lived in while they waited for the barge load of marijuana to arrive at Fontenot's shipyard. Evidence has been gathered, and some of the suspects have been interviewed." Mac lied about the suspects, but thought it might give Rochon something to think about.

"There is evidence that your brother-in-law, Alfred Patout, is involved."

Rochon did not change facial expression, so Mac continued, "Can you tell us where you were on Friday, June eighteenth?" Billie Jean looked at Mac, who immediately realized that was a trite question, but it was a starting point.

"I don't recall that far back, but I was likely here at the boatyard," Rochon responded.

"Can you verify that you were here? Are there witnesses, maybe a receptionist, or some customers? Do you have any documentation, such as sales receipts, with your signature? Perhaps you paid some bills that day and wrote some checks."

Rochon was silent.

Mac continued, "Would you mind if we got with your secretary and looked through your sales receipts for the month of June?"

Rochon sat upright in his chair, regaining his composure, but avoided direct eye contact. "I prefer you didn't look at my books," he said.

"Never mind, then. I'll get a warrant for them, but you might not like my demeanor when I return."

Rochon sat motionless.

"Is it possible that you and Alfred Patout were together that weekend?"

"Freddy is married to my sister; we socialize often, but I don't know if we were together that particular weekend."

"Your brother-in-law is known in certain circles as 'Freebase Freddy,'" said Mac. "Do you have any idea why people would call him that?"

Rochon ignored the question. His eyes clouded momentarily, and he looked out of his office window, as if embarrassed of himself.

"You were born and raised in Vermilion Parish," Mac continued. "Do you think it is strange that a shipyard could close down for three days, allow a tugboat and ocean-going barge to dock and off-load a few hundred thousand pounds of marijuana and cocaine, and no one in the area have any knowledge of it?"

"I agree that is unusual, but it doesn't have anything to do with me."

"Do you know the Fontenot brothers?" Mac asked.

"I know them, but not well. We don't socialize."

"When was the last time you saw them?" Mac was pushing.

"I don't remember."

"You don't remember much," said Mac, as he leaned forward in his chair, staring directly at Rochon. "But remember this. It took over fifty men to manage the movement of that much

135

dope from a barge onto trucks. There had to be vehicles watching the roads and boats on the water for surveillance. It's also likely that there was air surveillance. In all, there were at least sixty or seventy people involved, if not a hundred. The Fontenot family is involved and your brother-in-law is involved. The first people to give it up and write a statement will get the best deals." Mac stood up to make a point. "Ask yourself if you will be the first one to go to jail when others get suspended sentences."

Billie Jean stood up, and she and Mac began walking out of the room. Mac looked over his shoulder at Rochon, smiled, and said, "I'll be back."

Once they were in Mac's unit and headed north toward Lafayette, he looked at Billie Jean and said, "What do you think?"

"Guilty as sin," she replied. "He is not only guilty of involvement, he feels guilt and shame. He is not an inherently bad person. He got caught up in something he regrets, and I think he will come around at some point."

CHAPTER 14
James Fontenot

It was a given that Peter Rochon would call Freebase Freddy, probably before Mac and Billie Jean had gotten out of the Abbeville city limits. "I probably have enough evidence to obtain a wire tap," Mac said to Billie Jean. "But wire taps are time intensive and would necessitate federal involvement, and I hate for the investigation to get screwed up before we get started good. I'll call the feds at some point, but not yet."

"What's the next step?" Billie Jean inquired.

"As I said, Rochon will contact Freebase Freddy to discuss options. They will come to the conclusion that we don't have enough evidence yet, because we haven't arrested them. They probably made enough money to run, but they won't. Cajuns seldom run; it would be out of character. They are uncomfortable anywhere except South Louisiana. They would rather go to jail than leave home. My guess is that they will notify other players that we are on to something. Rumors will start; people will talk, and sooner or later, one of them will make a deal. Anyway, it's time to push the investigation to the next level."

Mac dropped Billie Jean at the Lafayette Parish jail, thanked her for her assistance, and returned to the Region II office. He called the Vermilion Parish sheriff and asked for an address on Lawless Fontenot.

He learned that Lawless Fontenot lived a few miles south of Abbeville in an antebellum home on Vermilion Bayou. It was early evening when Mac made the journey down the small, bumpy parish road leading to his residence. Mac drove under a sign held in place by hand-carved cypress posts that said "Vieux Chenes," meaning old oaks. Wisteria vines with its purple flowers covered red brick fireplaces on each end of the two-story Cajun style house. There was a gap where the bricks were beginning to separate from

137

unpainted cypress wood. The tin roof was covered in leaves from nearby water oaks, and the lawn had not been mowed. The old mansion, like its owner, thought Mac, had long been devoid of any pride or dignity.

A black housekeeper answered the door. She wore a flowered dress, reminiscent of the days when women made dresses from flour sacks. She was light-skinned, with graying hair and round cheeks, and dark brown sad eyes.

"May I help you, sir?"

Mac handed her his credentials and asked to see Lawless Fontenot.

"I'm afraid Mr. Fontenot is not home, sir. He is up in Alexandria, attending a big meeting for the Masons, and Mrs. Fontenot is at her women's league meeting in Kaplan."

"How about Mr. Fontenot's children: James and Jude. Are they home?"

"No sir, they don't stay here anymore."

"Do you know where I can find them?" Mac asked.

"I think Mr. Jude stays up in Lafayette, but I don't know where. Mr. James has a house over in Indian Bayou."

"Could you write down his address and phone number for me?"

"Yes sir," replied the housekeeper, "but only if you promise not to tell him where you got it. Mr. James can be real mean sometimes. Mr. Fontenot is polite enough, and his boys are from the right side of the tracks, but they act like they are from the wrong side, if you know what I mean."

She wrote down the information and Mac promised not to reveal where he got it.

Mac left the Fontenot house, drove to Abbeville, and used a pay phone to call James Fontenot and verify that he would be home. Fontenot answered the phone, and started the conversation by saying, "This is a private number. Where did you get it?"

"I got it from someone at the shipyard," Mac lied. "I would like to talk to you in person, if you have a few minutes." James Fontenot reluctantly agreed, and Mac left Abbeville for Indian Bayou.

Indian Bayou was not far from Abbeville, but the roads were in disrepair. Mostly rice fields and crawfish farms bordered the narrow, potholed blacktop highway. Indian Bayou was a small community consisting of a few farms, a general store, and a Catholic Church. It was evening and swarthy clouds foreboded a gathering storm. Small drops of rain began bouncing off Mac's hood and roof. It was well after dark when he located Fontenot's ramshackle house. The old wood residence had a rusty tin roof and wood walls that had not seen paint in thirty years. There was a front gate, but large sections of the fence were missing. A pit bull was chained to a post near the front door. Pools of water stood where the dog had dug holes in the yard.

Mac's gut feeling was not good. He wished he had brought Hungry Harv with him. As a caution, he used the unit radio to call Troop I. They would have at least one uniformed trooper in the parish. He gave his location to the desk sergeant and asked that the trooper be in the general area, if possible.

The pit bull barked and strained against his chain as Mac knocked on the front door of the Fontenot residence. A woman, about thirty years old, answered the door and invited Mac inside. She had large eyes, thin lips, and long stringy brown hair. She was tense and uncomfortable but tried to be social. She smiled slightly as she smoothed her dress to cover her knees.

"We were just having a beer," she said. "Can I get one for you?"

Mac thought about the beer. It was late and he was thirsty. He also thought the gesture might put the Fontenots at ease. He took the beer and sat on a torn, dirty sofa. The small living room had no less than four Lazy Boy recliners facing an overly large television which sat on a cheap coffee table. The room had the appearance of a movie theater, and was as dirty as an oil rig.

He smelled Fontenot before he saw him. "I'm Lieutenant McCullough with the state police," Mac began speaking to the woman as James Fontenot walked into the room holding a Dixie beer. He was at least six feet tall, and weighed a little less than two hundred pounds. He was built like a fighter, with broad shoulders, short stocky legs, and arms that seemed too short for his body. He had long, curly, scraggly hair soiled with grease. He wore leather work boots, torn jeans, and a stained tee shirt. Under heavy black eyebrows, his eyes were glassy and wild, and had a crazed look about them.

139

"Why are you here?" Fontenot was belligerent and pointing a dirty finger at Mac's face.

Mac set his beer on a coffee table and stood up, facing Fontenot. "There is no need to be rude, Mr. Fontenot. I think you know why I'm here. A barge-load of marijuana and cocaine was docked in the Fontenot shipyard, and I would like to ask you a few simple questions about it."

"Where did you get my phone number and address?" he continued.

"It's not important where I got the number. I could subpoena you to Lafayette and question you, but I thought this would be easier for everyone."

"My phone number is unlisted, and you are going to tell me who gave it to you, or I'm going to whip your ass," Fontenot was yelling, as he placed his beer on a table and clinched his fist toward Mac.

The woman was backing up toward a door leading out of the living room. She was clearly scared as she looked at Mac and then toward her common-law husband. She wanted to say something but was too terrified.

It had been a mistake to come to the house alone. Fontenot's eyes were bulging and his face was beet red from alcohol and drugs. He was looking for a fight. Mac started for the door when Fontenot put his hand on Mac's shoulder and jerked him around. Fontenot smelled of beer, sweat, and cheap deodorant. He was anxious and hyper, and Mac assumed he was on methamphetamine or a similar drug.

"Touch me again, and I'll put your ass in jail," Mac said, knowing it was a foolish statement because Fontenot had worked himself up for a fight before Mac arrived at the house.

Mac was in the front door when Fontenot came at him with the determination of a wrestler, intent on taking him to the ground. They went through the door, turning and twisting, and hit the ground together. Mac rolled away, stood, and when Fontenot came at him, he swung a hard right, striking Fontenot a glancing blow below the left eye. Fontenot backed up a step, put his head down, and lunged forward from the balls of his feet, catching Mac with a left to the temple, almost knocking him down. Mac responded with another right, this time striking Fontenot a solid blow to the forehead.

Fontenot was briefly stunned, but backed up and said, "Bubba, if that's all you got, I'm going to trash your ass." He was not a boxer, but a street fighter who always charged like a bull, attacking, wild-eyed, and with the viciousness of a trapped animal. He was on Mac before he could maneuver out of the way. They went to the ground a second time. They were temporarily locked together. Fontenot was in good physical condition, and he fought like a demented animal. He was clawing and scratching and trying to bite Mac's ear. Mac's chest was burning for lack of oxygen. He rolled like a gator, unable to release himself from Fontenot, then he remembered in-service training and managed to get a solid knee into the common peronal nerve of Fontenot's left leg. Fontenot was stunned, wondering why a blow to his leg would make him go limp, but it allowed Mac time to get away. He sprinted the short distance to his unit, opened the door, grabbed his microphone and called Troop I screaming for a backup.

Mac thought he heard Troop I dispatch Trooper Ray Mata as he turned to face Fontenot, who had regained his balance and was lowering his head for another charge. Mac was getting really pissed at the absurdity of the situation. Someone was trying to beat him to death because he wanted to ask him a few questions. He stooped low and came from the legs, catching Fontenot with a right upper cut, followed by a kick to the groin. Fontenot was momentarily stunned and was regrouping when Mac grabbed a five cell metal Maglite flashlight from his car seat. Mac swung the light with his right hand and caught Fontenot on the cheek. It only served to make Fontenot more furious. He lowered his head again and ran toward Mac, swinging wildly with both fists. Mac assumed a forty-five degree stance, holding the flashlight with both hands. He swung it like a baseball bat with all the force he could muster. Fontenot tried to duck, but it was too late. Mac caught him in the top of his scalp. Fontenot screamed as his feet left the ground, and he literally flew backwards landing in the mud.

Mac now had tunnel vision and had lost all sense of reason. He was dirty and sweating, and his chest was burning from lack of oxygen. He pulled his magnum revolver and was on Fontenot's chest, striking him in the face with the gun. He cocked the hammer, placed his finger on the trigger, and said, "You are a dead fuck." Mac knew he could kill Fontenot and get away with it, and reasoned that it would be a service to society. He had killed people before and not lost a night's sleep over it. The circle of light which he had focused on his adversary was dissipating and finally broke when he heard a woman screaming behind him. "Please don't kill him; please don't kill him," the hysterical voice said.

He had forgotten about the woman. She was holding her hands over her face, sobbing. Mac stood up, lowered the hammer on the revolver, and placed it inside his belt. He walked calmly to his unit, took out a pair of cuffs, and walked back to the still unconscious Fontenot, rolled him over, and cuffed his hands behind his back. He dragged Fontenot roughly to his car, opened the back door, and crawled in, pulling Fontenot in behind him. He stared at the pitiful woman but said nothing as he brushed himself off and got into his unit. The Vermilion Parish jail would not accept Fontenot with injuries. He would have to transport him to the Abbeville hospital before he could be incarcerated.

Normal procedure would have been for Mac to call Troop I and announce that he was code four (okay), after which he would say he was ten-fifteen (had a prisoner), and en route to the hospital. But he was covered with blood, sweat, and mud, and was so exhausted and stressed, he forgot to call in. The adrenaline rush had depleted him.

Mac started his car and drove away from the bewildered woman still standing in her front yard. He was less than a mile from Fontenot's residence when he spotted a state police unit, with lights off, parked under some trees in a farmer's driveway. It was Mac's bad luck that the Troop had sent Trooper Ray Mata, the Cuban Cajun, as his backup. Trooper Mata's mother was pure Cajun and his father was a Cuban immigrant. He was known in Troop I circles as a blow hard who constantly bragged about things he never did. The coward had hidden in some bushes and was monitoring the situation by radio. So much for brotherhood, thought Mac. He would deal with Mata later, but right now he was content with calling Troop I.

"I'm code four," Mac said. "You can tell Trooper Mata he can come out of the bushes now." Mata mumbled something on the radio about not being able to find the house. Mac ignored him.

"Lieutenant McCullough, are you saying that Trooper Mata never arrived to back you up?" The desk sergeant asked.

"That's exactly what I'm saying," replied Mac. "He is a cowardly piece of shit."

"Don't use that kind of terminology on the radio. If you want to file a complaint, come to the troop and handle it through procedures," ordered the desk sergeant.

Mac was en route to the Abbeville General Hospital when James Fontenot came to his senses and sat up in the backseat. The head wound had stopped bleeding, but Fontenot's long, greasy hair was caked in blood and dirt.

"You look like a character from Dawn of the Dead," said Mac with a smile.

"Go fuck yourself."

"Mr. Fontenot, before I take you to the hospital, I want you to understand that you have the right to remain silent, and that anything you say can and will be used against you in court. You also have the right to an attorney," Mac was giving him the short version, knowing that Fontenot would not cooperate.

"Before I take you to the hospital," Mac continued, "and then to jail, I want to give you an opportunity to answer a few questions about the load of marijuana that was docked at your family's shipyard."

"Go fuck yourself," he repeated.

"You sure have an extensive vocabulary," said Mac, who was exhausted and losing patience. "Be careful you don't fall down on your way to the hospital. By the way, if you bond out of jail tomorrow, be sure to check the Lafayette newspaper. I intend to give your family business a little free advertising."

"You leave my family out of this, or I will beat the shit out of you," Fontenot said.

"Yeah, well, I hope you do better than you did tonight," Mac said, as he pulled into the Abbeville General Hospital emergency room parking lot. The hospital was small by most standards, having about sixty beds. However, due to the propensity of drunk drivers and all-night bars in Abbeville, the hospital maintained a fully staffed twenty-four hour emergency room.

It was after midnight when Mac escorted Fontenot into the Abbeville hospital. The bright lights amplified the blood covering Fontenot's face and shirt. Mac showed a waiting nurse his credentials and explained that Fontenot was a prisoner. She sat Fontenot on a bed covered with white paper, looked contemptuously at Mac, and called for the doctor.

Fontenot was sitting quietly when the on-call doctor arrived ten minutes later. The doctor looked at Fontenot's scalp, where Mac's flashlight had left a deep two-inch laceration. "Do you know who this is?" the doctor asked, looking in Mac's direction.

Mac ignored the question.

"He hit me with a bat after he put the cuffs on me," Fontenot said to the doctor.

"Do you like beating up people?" said the doctor. It was a statement, not a question. "Brutality is against the law, and this kid is from one of the most influential families in the area. I have enough shit to do around here without taking care of crap like this. Take the cuffs off this man so he can lie on his back while I sew him up."

"I will cuff his hands to the front, if that will help, but I will not take them off of him," Mac replied.

"Do as I say!" the doctor yelled at Mac, "or I will not attend to this man."

"I don't think it is a good idea," Mac replied, knowing Fontenot's aptitude for violence, "but it's your call, and if he goes ape shit, it's your responsibility." Mac removed the cuffs, and the nurse helped Fontenot to lie on his back. He was complacent and cooperative as the nurse washed his face, hair and wound. She looked again at Mac with a frown on her face, as if she were saying, "I told you so."

Fontenot was meek as a lamb, even dozing off, until the doctor began shaving the scalp around the wound, at which point Fontenot sprang from the table like a rabid dog. He grabbed the doctor by the throat and threw him backwards on the floor. He then overturned the bed and threw a chair at the doctor. The nurse screamed at Mac to do something.

"Stop him," she screamed at Mac, "he's wrecking the emergency room."

"You wanted the cuffs off him; you stop him," said Mac calmly.

Fontenot looked at Mac, sizing him up for another round, but Mac was in no mood to fight again. He pulled his revolver and advanced toward Fontenot. Fontenot sensed that he had pushed his luck far enough for one night and took a prone position on the floor, allowing Mac to once again cuff him. The doctor shaved the hair around the wound and placed fifteen stitches in his scalp without benefit of an anesthetic. Fontenot screamed and cussed the doctor like a dog. The doctor never said another word to Mac. When he was through, he just walked out of the room.

Mac looked at the nurse, who was very attractive, and said, "Would you like to go to dinner this weekend?"

She walked out of the room without further conversation, and Mac escorted Fontenot back to his unit, and drove him to the Vermilion Parish Correctional Facility, where he booked him for battery on a police officer and resisting arrest violently. As the steel gate closed on Fontenot, he shouted at Mac one last time, "I'll kill you, motherfucker."

It was almost two o'clock in the morning when Mac arrived at Legend's. He needed a drink to unwind and think about the day's events. Stacy gave him the usual margarita without asking, and said, "Hello, Mac." She looked at her watch and said, "You're late," before scurrying off to another customer.

Mac drank the margarita and thought about the lack of response from Trooper Mata, and the desk sergeant being complacent about the matter. "One parish, one trooper," Captain Spencer used to say. Mac would have to deal with it. He should have had a better plan, and he should have brought another agent with him. The only witness to the fight was Fontenot's common-law wife, so he was sure there would be a civil suit filed against him. All in all, it had not been a good day, but some value could come of it, if he played it right.

He ordered another margarita and thought about the fight. Physical aggression was not uncommon for troopers. Lafayette was the hub of oil field country. Hands working on rigs for weeks at a time came to town like sailors and Marines after being at sea. They were full of piss and vinegar, and if they couldn't find female action, they fought. Barroom fights, domestic beatings, getting drunk, and wrecking jacked-up four-wheel drive trucks were regular stuff.

Mac sat quietly and thought about his days in the Marine Corps. On his way to Vietnam, he had gone through staging at

Okinawa. While he was there, he visited the Marine Officer's Club at Fetuma air base. It was a Friday afternoon, and the old tin building was crowded with young men in fatigues. He ran into Lieutenant Marty Olson, a young helicopter pilot that he had known at The Basic School in Quantico, Virginia. They were drinking and laughing at the bar when a Navy commander, considerably higher ranking than Mac or Olson, said something about them being too loud. Normal procedure would have been for them to move on, but Olson would have none of it. "Go away before I whip your ass," he said to the commander.

The Navy commander had never been addressed in such a fashion and was not quite sure how to handle the situation. He gave it some thought, then walked over to a table of senior Marine officers and asked if one of them was the commanding officer of Lieutenant Olson.

"I'm Colonel Conroy," the senior man said, "and I'm the commanding officer of MAG (Marine Air Group) Thirty-Six. The young lieutenant is a pilot in HMM-164. How can I help you?"

"Colonel, Lieutenant Olson is drunk, loud, and obnoxious. I ordered him to leave the officer's club, and he threatened to beat the shit out of me."

"Commander," said Colonel Conroy. "Are there any women at the bar?"

"No sir," replied the commander, somewhat puzzled by the question.

"Good, then," said the colonel, firmly, putting his beer down on the table. "If Lieutenant Olson can't be fucking, he should be fighting. He's a Marine."

Mac smiled as he recalled the events. The colonel at the bar had been Colonel Donald Conroy, later to become famous as the Great Santini, the subject of novelist Pat Conroy's first book. "Too bad the state police doesn't have supervisors like Conroy," thought Mac.

At midmorning the next day, Mac called Bill Decker at the Daily Advertiser.

"What's shaking, Mac?" Bill inquired.

"My knees feel like I've been in a knife fight with a midget, but otherwise, I'm well. Sorry to bother you, but I may have a story for you and also a favor to ask."

"I'm in the business of writing stories," Bill answered. "What have you got for me?"

Mac told Bill all he knew about the bulldog investigation, including evidence seized and the recent altercation with James Fontenot. He made it clear that he wanted as much press on the subject as possible, hoping that the attention would bring some pressure on the local players.

The following morning there was a picture of James Fontenot, detailing his arrest in Vermilion Parish, on the front page of The Advertiser.

CHAPTER 15
Boats against the Current

Two days after the Advertiser ran the picture and story about James Fontenot, Mac got a call from Simple Eddie. As expected, he was livid. "You stupid son-of-a-bitch. Do you know who you arrested?"

"I arrested James Fontenot, who is a punk, a doper, a smuggler, petty thief, bully, and would-be gangster, except that he is not smart enough. Never mind that he tried to kill me," Mac responded.

"Fontenot's father is the number one Freemason in Louisiana. Do you know what that means? He is connected with unions and the legislature, not to mention the governor's office. He could use his contacts to influence the budget committee," said Simple Eddie.

Mac had minored in history and had read articles about Freemasonry. He had never joined but knew the organization had been in Louisiana since before the American Revolution. Freemasonry had roots in Ireland, Scotland, England, and France. Even George Washington had been a Mason. It was only natural that the secret society would be entrenched in Louisiana. He also remembered his rookie year when an old state police captain had told him that most of the senior supervisors in the state police were masons, and that if he wanted to be promoted he should find a sponsor and join. However, before today, Mac had not understood the depth of the influence that Masonry had over local and state politics.

"Are you listening to me?" Simple Eddie continued. "Half the legislature is calling me asking that the charges be dropped on James Fontenot. A couple of them hinted that Fontenot's arrest could affect our budget. I'm asking you to consider the importance of this situation."

Mac did not reply.

"Another thing, Lieutenant, I got a call from Fontenot's lawyer. He is going to sue the department and you specifically, for police brutality. Did you use an unauthorized weapon to strike Fontenot on the top of his head?"

"James Fontenot attacked me and I defended myself with my flashlight. The reason I hit him on the top of his head is because he ducked. I was trying to hit him between the eyes. I guess you could call it a clear case of brutality by Everready," responded Mac, sarcastically. "I can send you a copy of the report if you like. Fontenot has knowledge, and probably participation, in the smuggling operation. If he wants to work something out, all he has to do is contact us."

Simple Eddie was quiet.

"Is there anything else you wanted, Colonel?"

"Yes. As a matter of fact, there are three more things I want to discuss with you. First, a doctor at Abbeville General Hospital has filed a complaint on you for allowing Fontenot to rough him up. I'm turning it over to Internal Affairs. They will be checking on that as well as the brutality issue."

"Internal Affairs can kiss my ass," said Mac, growing tired of the conversation.

"Second," said Simple Eddie. "Your name has been in the news too much. I'll be sending you a written directive ordering you to stop giving news releases. I'll have someone from Baton Rouge handle all future releases from your area." Mac could tell from the inflection in his voice that Simple Eddie was enjoying himself.

"Headquarters cannot effectively handle news releases in Lafayette," Mac said flatly, knowing that effectiveness did not matter to Simple Eddie. "A Public Information Officer in Baton Rouge giving releases concerning Lafayette is stupid. He will not know shit from Shinola, and the media in Lafayette will not be interested unless they can do live sound bites. The bottom line is that the public will not learn about the good things that LSP is doing for them, but that doesn't matter to you, does it?"

Mac was losing his temper, which is exactly what Simple Eddie wanted. He needed to shut it down. "What is the third thing you wanted, Colonel?"

"We have information that the CEO of Charity Hospital in Houma, a guy named Simon, is abusing his authority. Some of the accusations have to do with drugs. I'm assigning you to go to Houma, get a motel room, and stay there until the investigation is completed."

"Roger that, sir," Mac said, trying to sound cheerful. He did not want to give Simple Eddie the satisfaction of knowing he hated Houma. He decided to get the last word in.

"By the way, Colonel, can I ask you a question? Are you a Mason?"

Simple Eddie hung up.

Mac was in no hurry to go to Houma, and had slept little during the three days that had passed since his conversation with Simple Eddie. He laid awake at night thinking about ways to kill the simple son-of-a-bitch, and may have given it some serious thought, except that Simple Eddie was not worth going to prison. It was noon on Friday when the cousins came in with a Mexican courier they had caught transporting seventy-five thousand dosage units of valium on its way to Memphis.

Hollywood had been driving to work on Interstate 10 when he saw a Hispanic male walking beside the roadway with a gas can. He picked up the Mexican and drove him to the nearest gas station. He was waiting for the Mexican to fill up the gas can and was going to return him to his vehicle, when he noticed that the Mexican only put two gallons of gas in a five gallon can.

"Just to be on the safe side," said Hollywood. "Why don't you fill up the can?"

"No, two gallons will do," said the Mexican. "My gas tank only holds two gallons at a time. I have to stop often, but this time I ran out of gas."

"Does your gas tank have a hole in it?"

"No, it's just small," said the Mexican, who was fidgeting and avoiding eye contact.

"Right," said Hollywood, who excused himself and called Troop I for a drug dog.

A trooper and drug dog met Hollywood at the Mexican's car. The dog began scratching around the gas tank. The Mexican and his car were taken to the Troop I garage, where the tank was dropped. It had been modified, and the valium was neatly wrapped in the tank.

Hollywood incarcerated the Mexican, and Mac called the newspaper, against the orders of Simple Eddie. The next day the Advertiser ran the story, along with a picture of Mac holding a trash bag full of valiums, on the front page. The headline stated, "They Will Be Singing the Blues in Memphis." Mac knew the release would send Simple Eddie to the moon. He felt better now, and called for a verbal "after action report" to be held at Legend's at five o'clock.

As the agents were drinking beer and staring at USL co-eds in their tank tops, Bert asked, "What's next with the Bulldog? We have enough information for the feds to get some conspiracy warrants."

"Probably," responded Mac. "But I'm not quite ready to bring them on board. Think about the manpower it took to put this thing together. We know they rented at least two places to house twenty to forty people, but twice that number may have been involved. We know that the Fontenot brothers, along with Peter Rochon and Alfred Patout, were involved, but we need some more evidence."

"I know Vermilion Parish," said Hungry Harv. "Those are my people, and I understand them. If they made some money, they are going to spend it, and soon."

"Exactly," said Mac, thinking about what Hungry Harv meant. "I have a little investigation to check on down in Houma. While I'm gone, you, Hollywood, Buzzy, and Bert beat the bushes around Vermilion Parish. Go to the courthouse; find out if anybody recently purchased some property or a new house with a cash down payment. Check the Abbeville airport for any extravagant rental flights. There are a lot of cattlemen in the parish, check the receipts at the auction barn. Shake some trees, something will fall out."

It was late Monday morning when Mac packed a suitcase, called Troop I, and logged himself ten-eight (in service) en route to Houma. It was normally a two-hour trip, but he was not in a hurry and decided to take the back way, along Highway 182, also known as the Old Spanish Trail. The scenery might help get his mind straight for the assignment.

As he turned from US-90 to LA-182 Mac looked out at the multitude of metal oilfield buildings that had sprung up like mushrooms out of cow manure after a rain. They littered both sides of the highway. It had been only a few years back that bean fields, oak trees and the occasional farmhouse were visible in the area. There had been a giant live oak where Mac had parked his unit in the shade and clocked speeders. It had been replaced by a Pizza Village. The road had become so thick with drunks traveling from Morgan City to Lafayette that it was now called "blood alley" by area troopers.

The cool morning was giving way to the sultry heat common to the area as Mac entered downtown New Iberia. He drove to Clementine's restaurant on Bayou Teche and stopped for coffee. He looked down the street and saw men dressed in the uniforms of union and confederate soldiers. They were marching toward the Weeks Mansion, known to everyone in the area as Shadows-on-the-Teche. Mac finished his coffee and walked the short distance to the mansion. Civil War enthusiasts were setting up tents on the lawn, and a few old cannon were guarding the front gate. The tents were exact in design and measurement. Some were napping in the tents. People were taller now, and their bare feet stuck out in the sun. Authenticity was a priority with the re-enactors. Mac suspected that none of them had been in the military, much less in an actual gun fight.

Mac thought about the Civil War as he walked under the ancient oaks and looked at the old house with its eight gigantic columns. The Weeks family had owned sugar cane plantations and had built the house with the sweat of slave labor. The shaded yard extended to Bayou Teche and was covered with camellias, azaleas and aspidistra. It all seemed romantic and beautiful, but prior to the War Between the States, a small minority of people owned almost all of the land. The wealth to poverty ratio in the Old South was not pretty. There was very little middle class, and most people in rural Louisiana were dirt poor.

The pretentious and well-bred southern aristocracy, with its rank and privileges, had brought ruin on everyone. Ninety-five percent of confederate soldiers had never owned a slave, but they fought and died by the hundreds of thousands for a system that served only the wealthiest of people. Mac thought it similar to Vietnam, where politicians ran the war but kept their families far removed from it. It took the South over one hundred years to revive from the war and following period of reconstruction. He appreciated the beauty of the buildings and surrounding grounds, but he was not a fan of the Weeks family, nor did he truly understand why so many men fought for a feudal system that served a privileged few. Young men from the south fought a power with a hundred times the men and resources. Did they believe they could win against such overwhelming odds? Or maybe, like William Faulkner implied in his books about the antebellum south, it simply had to do with the intangibles of pride, duty, and honor.

He walked up East Main Street, which was part of the Old Spanish Trail, and tried to envision what it may have looked like during the war years. In 1864, Union General Nathanial Banks and his army of thirty-five thousand men had marched from New Orleans to Morgan City, and then along this very road through New Iberia and on to Lafayette. Banks had been intent on a final destination of Shreveport, where he hoped to destroy the confederate army led by General Richard Taylor, the son of President Zachary Taylor, who was a Louisiana native.

Banks had caught General Taylor at Mansfield, just south of Shreveport, when Taylor turned to fight. Although Taylor had only eighty-five hundred men, he gave Banks a resounding defeat. Brigadier General Alfred Mouton, of Lafayette, was killed in the battle. As Banks retreated through the towns of Alexandria, Lafayette, New Iberia, and Morgan City, the bitter and demoralized Union Army burned every house and barn in its path and killed every farm animal and chicken within ten miles of Highway 182. Women and children would freeze and starve that year, but somehow the Banks family had managed to salvage the mansion and continue living there. Mac considered that somehow things may not have changed so much after all.

The rest of the drive to Houma was slow, tiresome, and banal. Traffic was heavy, and there was little to look at except oilfield facilities and run-down bars scattered along the route. Houma, named for the Houmas Indians, was a small city of about twenty-five thousand, built on the bayou. It was only about ten feet above sea level, and large canals crisscrossed the town. Locals were oilfield hands, shrimpers and crabbers, and a few fishermen. Run-down Cajun and blues dance halls seemed to be on every block. It was early afternoon when Mac arrived and checked into the local Holiday Inn. He had made the decision not

Roy W. Frusha

to make it an undercover investigation. Rather, he would approach it in a historical fashion, questioning various hospital employees, gathering information, and then submitting a report to the local district attorney for any potential charges and follow-up prosecution.

At eight o'clock the next morning, Mac rose and dressed in a tan suit, which was the only suit he owned. He drank coffee in the hotel lobby, and drove the short distance down Industrial Drive to Leonard Chabert Medical Center. It was a new building and named for a local politician, and was one of several large state-run charity hospitals. Mac parked his unit and walked the grounds. It seemed to Mac that everything in Louisiana was somehow tied to politics. It was becoming redundant.

He entered through the front door and began a slow walk through the corridors. The hospital looked and smelled clean. Workers were friendly, and he observed that most of the rooms were filled with patients. Mac checked in at the front desk, identified himself, and asked for the pharmacy supervisor.

Jessica Cormier looked to be about thirty years old. She had an oval face with larger than normal, dark brown eyes. The only makeup she wore was bright red lipstick on full lips. Long black hair flowed comfortably over her shoulders. Singularly, her facial qualities would not have seemed attractive, but together they created a distinctly beautiful young woman. Her degree from Northeastern College in Monroe hung on the wall behind her desk. Mac sat in front of the desk as she advised him of her duties and explained about the hospital pharmacy providing medications for the hospital patients.

"How many beds are there in the hospital and how many outpatients do you serve?" Mac asked.

"We have about one hundred fifty beds, and we serve over one hundred thousand outpatients each year."

"Do you have any idea how big the hospital budget is?" Mac continued.

"The hospital has a budget of several million and employs about eight hundred people," she answered. "We also recently created an Internal Medicine Residency Training Program."

"Do hospital employees have access to controlled drugs in the pharmacy?"

"Yes," Jessica answered, "as long as they have a valid prescription. In fact, anyone can purchase their drugs here. But, as you can see, we are located on the third floor of the hospital, which makes it somewhat inconvenient for those patrons who do not have a reason to be here."

"Who is the hospital CEO?" Mac asked.

Jessica had been friendly and cooperative until now. She sat upright in her chair and stiffened. "The CEO of the hospital is Victor Simon," she said flatly.

"Do you know any details regarding his education and past record of employment?"

Jessica leaned forward and looked directly into Mac's eyes. "Is this on the record or off the record?"

"Any way you want it," he responded, as he placed his notebook on her desk and returned his pen to his shirt pocket.

"I want it off the record," she said, and proceeded to tell Mac that Victor Simon is a certified public accountant and self-proclaimed workaholic. He had graduated from the University of Southwestern Louisiana in Lafayette. It was rumored that he was the chief financial officer of a large hospital in Lafayette but had been terminated for unknown reasons. Simon had been at Chaubert Medical for three years. "Furthermore," she said, "he is conceited, domineering, and rude. He is not well liked by the staff, but he does not care because he is politically connected."

"Does he obtain prescription drugs from your pharmacy?"

"He does," she responded plainly, without breaking eye contact.

"Does he have valid prescriptions?"

"Not always. He is so arrogant he simply comes into the pharmacy, walks onto the drug aisles, and takes what he wants."

"What types of drugs does he take from your stock?"

"Mostly narcotics, such as codeine and hydrocodone, but he will also take amphetamines, such as Dexedrine."

Mac smiled, "If he is taking all that, it may explain his rotten attitude." He thought for a moment and continued, "If I could get the Diversion Unit of DEA to audit your records, would it show that certain drugs are missing from your inventory?"

"I keep immaculate records," she said, smiling back, "and I am not going to jail for anyone."

"Thank you for your time, Miss Cormier. Let's keep our conversation private for now. I'll be in touch," Mac stood to leave.

"Au revoir," she said, speaking French, which was common in Houma.

"Parlez-vous francais?" Mac responded, turning to face Jessica and hoping he could mix a little pleasure with business.

"Oui," she said. "Et vous?"

"Un peu," Mac replied, though he knew only bits and pieces he sometimes used to get a date. "Voulez-vous diner?"

"No," she smiled, "mais merci pour demander."

"Oh well, another time it is," Mac said, and walked out of Jessica Cormier's pharmacy.

The next stop was the hospital security office. The security staff had the appearance of retired police officers. They were a reasonably fit group of older men who wore starched khaki uniforms with black belts and shined black boots. They wore badges and carried hand-held radios, but had no weapons. Mac asked to see the security supervisor.

Mac was introduced to Captain Tony Auzenne. He had broad shoulders and large arms and sported a graying thick mustache which was well trimmed. "You look like POST certified law enforcement," Mac said to him.

"Retired chief deputy from the Terrebonne Parish Sheriff's Office," Auzenne said. "Would you like some coffee?" Captain Auzenne did not wait for an answer, but rather poured Mac a cup and did not offer cream or sugar.

Mac had known many men like Auzenne. Auzenne stood erect, removed his cap, or "cover" as they called it in the Corps, immediately upon entering his office. He spoke in terse sentences with a deeper than normal voice. Men like Auzenne would have considered it effeminate to use cream and sugar in their coffee. He was a proud man who would not compromise his character or integrity.

"How long were you in the Corps?" Mac asked.

"I guess it still shows, huh? Some things you can't get rid of. I was active for four and in the reserves for another sixteen. I mustered out as a First Sergeant."

"And the Terrbonne Sheriff's Office?"

"Thirty years," answered Auzenne. "Started in the jail, then worked my way up through patrol, detectives, and finally to chief deputy. I would have stayed longer, but I maxed out my salary and would have been working for nothing. I've been with the hospital about a year now. It's not hard work, and I have a good staff that includes a secretary and twelve former cops."

"What are some of the duties of your men?"

"They walk the parking lot to prevent thieves from breaking into vehicles. They tour the hospital floors with the nurses to make sure things are safe and orderly. Occasionally, a drunk will try to sneak some alcohol or drugs to a patient, and we respond, but unless they become violent, we just escort them off the grounds. We also help the nurses subdue mental patients, but that's pretty rare."

"Who is your boss?" Mac asked. He got the same physical response as he did from Jessica Cormier. Auzenne stiffened ever so slightly.

"I work directly for the CEO, Victor Simon."

"How is he to work for?"

"I've had better. Let's cut to the chase, Lieutenant. What do you want?"

Mac spoke frankly, one police officer to another. "There are allegations of malfeasance and criminal activity by the CEO. I've been assigned to investigate those allegations. I've come to see you to determine if any of the allegations involve your department."

"There are some things Simon does that I don't agree with, but I don't know if they are illegal," Auzenne responded.

"Give me an example."

"The security department has a budget which covers salaries, insurance, uniforms, vehicles and office supplies. Simon lets me make the decisions on how the monies are spent, and I sign off on the budget at the end of the year. I handled the budget for the Terrebonne Sheriff, and I know what I am doing. Here's the thing, the numbers don't match. Mr. Simon says we spend about a hundred thousand more than we actually spend. I keep good records, Lieutenant, and I'm not going to jail for anybody."

"Sounds familiar," replied Mac.

"What?"

"Never mind," said Mac. "I can probably get some state police auditors to go though his records and crunch some numbers. Do you have any specifics I can use?"

"Probably." Auzenne stated. "Simon purchases a new Cadillac every year with funds clearly marked for the security department." Mac thought about this and knew inherently that the allegation wouldn't hold water. It was the same situation at USL in Lafayette where high ranking university officials were known to drive vehicles paid for from the budget of the university police department. It was just business as usual in Louisiana.

"Roger that," said Mac, who was taking notes. "When I was walking the grounds earlier today, I saw some parish inmates on the property. What are their duties here?"

"I'm glad you asked, Lieutenant. The security staff is supposed to supervise the inmate work crews with garbage details, dumping trash, mowing the grass, cleaning floors, painting the building, routine stuff like that. But half the time they are at Simon's house or camp."

Mac looked up. "Are you saying Simon uses parish inmate labor at his personal residence and camp?"

"That's about the size of it, Lieutenant."

"I'll get some auditors to look over Simon's records, and I'll contact the sheriff for permission to interview the inmates. There are some other allegations I'm also investigating. I'll be in touch." Mac stood to leave, shook hands with Auzenne and said, "Thanks, and Semper Fi."

"One more thing, Lieutenant. Simon is hooked up politically. Be careful."

It was time to confront Simon and inform him that the investigation was in progress. Mac took the elevator to the top floor of the building, identified himself to Simon's secretary, and requested an audience with him. The secretary escorted him into Simon's office, which was a large room, taking up most of a corner of the building. Floor to ceiling custom windows offered a nice view of downtown Houma on one side of the office and the Intracoastal Waterway on the other, with its constant flow of tugs, barges, and fishing boats. A crystal chandelier hung over a hand-carved mahogany desk. They seemed out of place in a non-profit charity hospital. The floor was long leaf pine, or heart pine, as it was known locally. It was not indigenous to South Louisiana, and it was very, very expensive.

There was a large oil painting of State Senator Richard Chaubert hanging behind Simon's desk. There was another portrait on the far wall of Francis Bonaventure. Mac recognized him immediately. Bonaventure was a short, bald, fat man who made millions in the shipbuilding business in Houma, Thibodeaux, and New Orleans. He had financed the current governor's campaign, and typical of Louisiana politics, the governor rewarded him by making him the Director of the Department of Public Safety. Bonaventure was over the state police, and, in reality, Mac's boss. He had seen him around the headquarters building, dressed like a clown, wearing a jump suit and rubber boots. Bonaventure often bragged about all his pretty secretaries and personal fleet of helicopters, all paid for by taxpayers. He was a joke, but it was no joking matter. Mac did not feel good about the picture of Bonaventure.

Victor Simon was six feet tall and weighed no more than one hundred fifty pounds. His head was shaved, and his nails were polished. He wore a gray suit that matched his eyes. He had an elitist appearance, though Mac supposed he had never accomplished anything other than obtaining CPA certification and kissing ass. He suspected Simon was the type of person who considered it cool and fashionable to always send something back when eating out at a restaurant.

Simon was standing, looking out a window toward the river. He did not sit, nor did he invite Mac to sit. "What can I do for you, Mr. McCullough?"

"It's Lieutenant McCullough, Mr. Simon," Mac said, hoping Simon would catch the implied sarcasm. "I've been sent here to conduct an investigation. I've come to your office to notify you in person and request your assistance."

Simon turned from the window and looked directly at Mac. "What type of investigation?"

"There have been anonymous allegations of misconduct regarding the hospital pharmacy, hospital security equipment, and budget matters. Other issues may be forthcoming."

"And who might be the target of these allegations, Lieutenant?" He pronounced "lieutenant" like some grumpy old

159

master sergeant who had no respect for brown bar second lieutenants. Mac thought his tone of voice was that of a patronizingly superior manner, and it was pissing him off.

"Quite frankly, Mr. Simon, you are the primary target, though others may surface. I would like your cooperation, but either way, I'm here to conduct the investigation."

Simon smiled, and said, with some authority in his voice, "There will be no investigation at my hospital, by state police or any other organization."

Mac started to reply, but Simon held up a hand, walked to his desk, and dialed a number. He turned on the speaker phone. It rang twice then a gravelly voice said "Hello."

"Francis, this is Vic. I have you on the speaker phone; I hope you don't mind." Mac recognized the voice of Francis Bonaventure.

"What can I do for you, Vic?" Bonaventure inquired.

"Francis, there is a state trooper in my office, and he says that he is investigating allegations of misconduct in the hospital. In particular, he is focusing his investigation on me. I run a tight ship here at Richard Chaubert Hospital, and there is no criminal activity here. Can you talk to the trooper for me?"

"Absolutely," said Bonaventure. "Trooper, can you hear me?"

"I'm not a trooper, Mr. Bonaventure," Mac said, knowing his shit was going downhill fast. "I'm Lieutenant McCullough, and I was sent here by Lieutenant Colonel Edward Kazan to conduct an investigation."

"What kind of investigation?" Bonaventure quizzed.

"There are allegations of hospital monies being misused, if not outright stolen. Controlled drugs are missing from the hospital pharmacy, and hospital equipment and personnel are being utilized for personal gain," Mac said flatly.

"Francis," Simon interrupted. "None of these accusations are true, it's just the result of some unhappy employee who wrote an anonymous letter to the state police. However, if it will make you happy, I will conduct an in-house investigation, and send you the final report."

Mac was incredulous. He took a step toward Simon. "Are you saying you will investigate yourself?"

Bonaventure heard the mockery in Mac's voice and interrupted. "Trooper, are you staying in Houma?" he said, ignoring Mac's rank, or possibly not knowing the difference.

All Mac could think to say was, "Yes, I have a room at the Holiday Inn."

"Good," said Bonaventure. "I want you to return to your room. Someone will be in contact at the motel and give you your orders."

Mac approached the phone, "Mr. Bonaventure, am I understanding you correctly that as the Director of Public Safety in Louisiana, you want me to drop this investigation regardless of any proof and or witnesses I may have corroborating allegations of theft, drug abuse, misuse of convict labor and hospital equipment? If we drop this investigation, do you also think that the media might consider it to be corruption?"

Bonaventure would not be coerced. In a booming voice, he said, "Don't threaten me Trooper, or your ass will be working the night shift in one of my shipyards. Now do as I instructed you. Go back to your room. This conversation is over."

"Fuck you, fuck Simon, and fuck this corrupt state," Mac was screaming, but Bonaventure had hung up.

"Have a nice day, Trooper," said Simon, who was smiling.

Rather than walk to the door, Mac walked to the painting of Bonaventure, pulled it from the wall, and threw it at Simon, who scrambled behind his desk and ducked. The frame broke as the picture bounced off the wall behind Simon and landed on the floor. Shattered glass was hurled across the room, some of it landing on Simon.

Mac drove back to the motel, packed his clothes, and went to the motel bar. He knew that Simple Eddie had set him up. He was not a rocket scientist, but Simple Eddie understood Louisiana's corrupt political system, and he knew about Simon's relationship with Bonaventure. There would be no investigation regardless of witnesses or tangible evidence. He was on his third beer when the call came from Simple Eddie.

"You knew the investigation was doomed, didn't you?" Mac said.

"Of course," Simple Eddie responded. "You think you are such a hot shit, I just wanted to teach you a little lesson about Louisiana politics."

"I'm going to write a detailed report about the investigation and the conversation I had with Bonaventure. What are you going to do with it?"

"Throw it away," answered Simple Eddie. "Let me explain something to you about Louisiana politics. Simon will investigate himself, find that he is doing a great job, and write a report to cover his ass and Bonaventure's. Nothing will change. Your problem is that you think you can make a difference. This is Louisiana; nobody makes a difference. Your problem, Lieutenant, is that you don't know how to play the game."

"What about the people who gave me information about Simon?" Mac inquired.

"They will probably be terminated. Fuck them, they should have been more loyal," Simple Eddie said, then hung up.

Mac ordered another beer. He was still at the bar an hour later when the second phone call came.

"Mac," said Hungry Harv, whose voice hinted uncertainty or unwillingness to get to the point. "How is the investigation going?" he stammered, inarticulately.

"It's just boats against the current," answered Mac.

"What?" answered Hungry Harv.

"Nothing, it's just a line from a book I read a long time ago. The investigation in Houma is not going anywhere. C'est fini. What is going on in Lafayette?"

"Bad news," said Hungry Harv. "Hollywood's wife kicked him out of the house."

"No problem there, he can move in with me until he finds a place to live. What else is happening?" asked Mac, who realized he had interrupted Hungry Harv's train of thought.

"D K is dead."

Mac paused and caught his breath. "What the hell happened to D K?"

"No one is sure yet, but it looks like suicide. It may have been an accident, but all indications are that it was self-inflicted. There may have been a woman involved, possibly a female snitch that he fell for. He didn't leave a note, so no one really knows what happened."

"Okay," said Mac, who really did not have the words. "I'm ten-eight en route to Lafayette."

Roy W. Frusha

CHAPTER 16
Patrick "D K" Celestine

On the day of the funeral, lightning illuminated fast-moving pearl blue clouds in the distance.   The temperature was in the mid-thirties, and the sky rumbled as fat drops of rain danced noisily off the tin roof of the small whitewashed Baptist church in rural Tangipahoa Parish, some forty miles northeast of Baton Rouge. Agent Celestine's wife had been born and raised in the area. This was her church and her people. It was standing room only inside the church, and there were a hundred or so people waiting outside with black umbrellas and raincoats, looking through antique stained glass windows. Mac watched agent Celestine's family, including a wife and three young children, sitting quiescently, heads down, in the first pew. They seemed more in shock than mourning. They were suffering unremitting, inconsolable grief. Mac had supposed there would be more outward expression.

"Everyone suffers differently," Hungry Harv said.

Most southern Baptist preachers will not miss an opportunity to preach the saving grace of Jesus Christ, and this preacher was no different. He knew there were disbelievers in the crowd, and understood that this was his chance to preach the gospel. His message was for them more so than the Celestine family. He was saying, "Sorrow is better than laughter: for by the sadness of the countenance, the heart is made better. The heart of the wise is in the house of the mourning: but the heart of fools is in the house of mirth." Mac was not sure of the intended meaning, but thought that it came from the Book of Ecclesiastes. "Fear God and keep His commandants," the preacher said. "There is a time to mourn, and a time to dance; a time to weep and a time to laugh; a time to be silent and a time to speak; a time for war and a time for peace."

"It was a good sermon for the occasion," Mac said, as the preacher completed his service.

The narcotics agents walked quietly from the church to the nearby graveyard wearing raincoats, but without umbrellas.

164

The cemetery was on top of a small hill under the limbs of water oaks and giant cedar trees. There were no more than a hundred tombstones, some dating back to World War I. The choir sang "How Firm a Foundation." Someone in the distance played Amazing Grace on the bagpipes as they lowered the casket into the grave. It was a fitting and emotional service for a fallen warrior.

"Colonel Carter and Simple Eddie did not attend the service," said Hungry Harv.

"Neither one of those assholes gives a shit about the people who work for them," replied Mac, as they walked slowly toward their units.

The following day, the agents sat around the squad room and told cheerful stories about Agent Celestine.

"I went through the academy with Celestine," Mac interjected. "He was a good trooper and narcotics agent. He should have been promoted years ago. Maybe he was just in the wrong place at the wrong time, or maybe it was because he was black. In case you haven't noticed, Simple Eddie surrounds himself with white people."

"Will the state police take care of his family?" Bert asked.

"Probably not," said Hungry Harv. "It's rotten, but that is the way it is if you don't have enough years to retire."

"I want to write an article about D K for the newspaper," Mac said, staring into space and thinking of a plan. "Simple Eddie has been playing a game of 'catch me, fuck me' for about a year now. Maybe I can arrange a little payback."

"What do you have in mind?" Hungry Harv asked.

"Simple Eddie has ordered me to stay away from the media. I'm going to write an article praising D K and his work. Hopefully, it will be of some comfort to the Celestine family, but I guarantee you it will send Simple Eddie into a rage. It may also cause him to make a mistake."

That night, the Region II agents gathered at Legend's to reminisce about D K and get commode-hugging drunk. Handling grief can be individual or group. With the agents, it was group psychotherapy at happy hour. There were no words or ceremonies to help them comprehend what went wrong with D K. Every decision made as a narcotics agent, whether personal or

165

professional, leads to unforeseen consequences. It's a vicious game that they play each and every day of their lives. Dealing with the death of a brother in arms cannot be forced. Grief is not a weakness, and they did not want to appear uncaring, but expressions of logic, or even a little common sense, were lost on them that day.

"The best way to take the attention off our grief," Mac said, "is to drown it. Have fun, replenish your belief in yourself. Tomorrow is another day, and then it is back to the grindstone."

"If you have the same number of holes in you at the end of the day that you had at the beginning, you had a good day," Hungry Harv said. "D K had a bad day. Make sure it doesn't happen to the rest of you. Look out for each other. Say something if you see strange behavior in your partner."

"Tatou always acts strange," said Hollywood, nodding in the direction of his cousin.

"Why wasn't Simple Eddie at the funeral?" Bert asked.

"He hates narcs, unless they are federal," answered Mac. "Hatred is malignant with some people. We investigate and arrest dopers every day, but I don't hate them. In fact, they are a lot easier to understand and deal with than politicians and high level state police supervisors. The crazy son-of-a-bitch thinks I'm crazy, which is a good indication that I'm sane. Anyway, I'll deal with him tomorrow."

At one o'clock in the morning, Rooster passed out while sitting on the can at Legend's. Bubba, who was only slightly more sober than Rooster, picked him up and drove slowly and carefully toward his residence on the south side of Lafayette. Bubba was half a block past his house when he realized he had missed his driveway. Rather than stop the car with the brake, he instinctively threw the car into reverse. Unknown to Bubba, his door was not closed and the sudden change in direction threw him out of the car, which summarily ran over his foot. Rooster, who had been sleeping, suddenly woke up to the realization that the car was in reverse, and looked up to see Bubba chasing it. He wasn't sure what to do, so he bailed out of the car, rolling onto the asphalt road. The car struck the culvert of Bubba's driveway, coming to a dead stop.

"Nice landing," said Rooster.

"Help me into the house," answered Bubba, who was now limping. Bubba's future ex-wife met them at the door. She pointed at Rooster and said, "After tonight, you are no longer welcome at this house." Then she looked at Bubba, who was puking on a nearby water oak, and said, "I want a divorce."

"Don't pay any attention to her," Bubba said, as he wiped his mouth on his shirt sleeve. "She gets a little edgy sometimes, but she'll get over it."

"It's not easy living with you assholes," she screamed. "You are all a bunch of alcoholics. Next time I'll marry an axe murderer, before I marry another narc."

Hollywood, who had that afternoon moved a few clothes into Mac's residence, was in a dark corner of the bar feeding martinis to a black-haired beauty queen that could have won a Gina Lollobrigida look-alike contest. She had pearl white skin, red lips, and a matching red mini skirt. It was lust at first sight. If Hollywood was grieving over his recent separation, this was guaranteed to get him past it.

"Tatou, order me another drink while I ask Susie Home Wrecker what kind of car she wants," he said to his cousin.

At midnight, Mac excused himself and drove the short distance to his house and went to bed. At two o'clock in the morning, Hollywood arrived with the Italian beauty, who, like Hollywood, was drunker than ten Indians. Mac's house was no more than one thousand square feet, with two bedrooms and one bath. It was not exactly a house where a person could get lost. Hollywood managed to get his date's clothes off just prior to passing out. Gina Lollobrigida needed to go to the bathroom but opened Mac's door by mistake and turned on the light.

"Shhh!" she said, in a little girl voice, as she brought her index finger to her lips motioning for Mac to be quiet. She wore black lace panties, and nothing else. "I am totally drunk, and I can't find the bathroom." She giggled.

"I am totally mystified," Mac answered back, as he sat up in bed. "But the bathroom is the next door."

She turned off the light and closed Mac's door. Five minutes later, she re-entered Mac's room and flipped the light on again. This time she walked to edge of Mac's bed. She had a few freckles near the top of her breasts, and there was just a hint of perfume.

"Do you like my breasts? They are not as big as some, but they are firm, don't you think?" She was holding her breasts in her hands, caressing them carefully. She took one of Mac's hands and held it to a breast. "Do they feel firm to you?"

Mac, who hadn't been laid in six months, stammered. "Well, I'm no gynecologist, but they look pretty good to me. Uh, I don't even know your name, and you've had too much to drink. I assume Hollywood is sleeping, and I'm not real comfortable with this situation. Maybe you should reconsider this. You can sleep on the couch."

"You look like a deer in a headlight," she said, as she removed her panties and climbed on top of Mac. "I'm going to regret this," Mac said, "but not tonight."

For the next twenty minutes, they made love with such passionate intensity that it bordered on violence. They had not even taken the time to exchange names.

At five o'clock in the morning, Gina Lollobrigida woke. "Where am I, and who the fuck are you?" It was not a good way to start the day.

"It's a long story, but the short version is that my name is Miles McCullough, and you are in my home."

"When did you take me here?"

"Well, actually, I didn't. Hollywood did. He's in the next room."

"You are a perverted piece of shit, and I should call the police," she screamed as she jumped from the bed and began looking for her clothes.

"I'm a state trooper, so technically, I guess I am the police," Mac responded, meekly. He desperately wanted to calm her down and find out her name. He also realized that his ambitions of having a legitimate date with her were dwindling fast.

After she was dressed, she returned to Mac's room. "Get out of bed, asshole, and take me home."

She stormed through the living room and flung open the door to the carport only to find that her car was in the driveway. She had followed Hollywood to Mac's house. She strutted into Mac's bedroom like a banny rooster one last time and shot him the finger.

"Wait, I think we should talk about this," Mac said, as he followed her to her car.

"Fuck you," she said, and sped down the street giving him the finger for the second time.

"Love is twenty minutes of bliss and two hours in the heavyweight division," Hollywood said, from somewhere in the house.

"Love hurts," Mac responded, and walked dejectedly back into his small house.

Later that same morning, Mac went to the office, took a handful of aspirin, washed them down with black coffee and sat down at his desk to write a column for Trooper Patrick Celestine. The next day it, would be underscored by different captions, and carried by the Lafayette Daily Advertiser, Baton Rouge Morning Advocate, and the New Orleans Times Picayune.

In bold letters, the Daily Advertiser caption said: PATRICK CELESTINE PERSONIFIED DUTY, HONOR, COURAGE, PRIDE. The column read as follows: "Narcotics agent Patrick Celestine, Louisiana State Police, shot himself Thursday, October 23, 1983. He left a wife, three young sons, family, and fifty-four narcotics agents wondering how and why. We think it was an accident, but even so, it's difficult to understand. How could a professional law officer make such a lethal error in judgment?

"Celestine had been in narcotics enforcement for six years, and he was one of the best. He was brave, loyal and intelligent. He worked many successful operations, most of which were in an undercover capacity. He wrote excellent reports and was organized and articulate when interrogating suspects and testifying in court. He had a competitive score on his promotional examination and should have been promoted numerous times, but for whatever reason had been passed over.

"Celestine appeared to be happy with his work, but working as a narcotics agent is scary business and outward signs are not always accurate indicators of inner stress. Drug abuse and related crime are adversely affecting virtually every aspect of our society. We are involved in a war, and Patrick Celestine was in the trenches, at the front, trying to make a meaningful difference. He worked often as an undercover agent, assuming various identities,

169

Roy W. Frusha

living and socializing with scum, placing his life in danger every day, attempting to make cases on drug dealers.

"He recently rescued another agent who was in a ditch fighting for his life with a dealer. It was dark, radios were not working, and the pre-set meeting took place at the wrong location. The drug deal had gone bad, and guns had been pulled. Patrick did not hesitate; he followed the sound of the fight to the agent's location and threw himself onto the violator. It was all in a day's work for Patrick. He was that kind of cop, but six years of this type of work can do its damage.

"Narcotics enforcement is different from any other type of law enforcement. Cops like Patrick Celestine assume many roles, working insane hours, and regularly place themselves in precarious and perilous situations.

"The role playing becomes so serious that transition back into the norm is often difficult. It's tough on family life. Most narcotics agents have been married at least twice, they avoid normal social situations, and they are never very far from a gun. They deal with an uncaring public and an ineffective judicial system.

"Yet people like Patrick Celestine continue to step into the gap and take a stand. It is difficult to understand why they continue to fight with such dedication when many believe the war is already lost. Maybe the answer cannot be explained but implied in terms of feelings about people and life situations. William Faulkner touched on it in a short story called 'The Bear.' Faulkner spoke of his grandfather who fought a war against a power with ten times the area, a hundred times the men and a thousand times the resources, because all he believed was necessary to win a war was love of country and courage. Faulkner described a little mongrel dog that attacked a six hundred pound bear, knowing he would be killed in the attempt, because of duty, pride, courage, and honor.

"On Saturday, October 25, 1983, the funeral bell tolled for Patrick Celestine, but as it is stated in John Donne's seventh Meditation, 'No man is an island, entire of itself, every man is a piece of the continent, a part of the main.....any man's death diminishes me because I am involved in mankind, and therefore never send to know for whom the bell tolls; it tolls for thee.'

"Patrick Celestine was involved in mankind and a piece of all of us passes out of this world with him. He personified the

170

concepts of duty, honor, courage and pride, and we will miss him."
The article was signed by Lieutenant Miles McCullough,
Louisiana State Police, BOI Narcotics.

The agents read the column in the office. Hungry Harv
said, "I think the family will appreciate the article. It will be a nice
thing for D K's kids to have to remember him by. By the way, I
thought Simple Eddie told you not to have any contact with the
media."

"Roger that," Mac replied. "When he hears about the
article, he will be pissed. He will call the office before close of
business today. Loan me your recorder."

"Uh oh," said Hungry Harv, "I don't like where this is
going."

Mac took the mini recorder and plugged it into the phone
at his desk. He waited patiently for the call, knowing that it was
imminent. At precisely 4:15 p. m., the phone rang.

"Region II Narcotics, may I help you?" answered Mac
politely.

"This is Colonel Kazan, Lieutenant. I'll get right to the
point. I ordered you not to have any contact with the media, and
every damn paper I pick up has your name printed all over it."

"Yes sir," Mac said without emotion.

"You disobeyed a direct order and furthermore I don't like
the implication that Celestine was passed over because he was
black. The superintendent is pissed too."

Mac avoided answering Simple Eddie's accusation and
replied, "I don't remember seeing you at the funeral, Colonel. It
was a good one, and, as Patrick's highest ranking supervisor, I
thought you and your customs friend might show up." Mac knew
that mentioning his relationship with Agent O'Donnell would twist
him off.

"Let me tell you something, shithead, I did not know
Celestine personally, but as far as I'm concerned, he was just
another alcoholic nigger who had too many girlfriends and ended
up eating his gun."

"Yes sir."

"I'm going to the superintendent about you," Simple
Eddie was on a roll, "I will have your ass transferred if it's the last
thing I do."

"I don't doubt that you can and will," answered Mac, who placed the phone in its receiver.

Mac carefully removed the tape from the recorder and wrote the date and time on it before slipping it into his pocket.

Three days later, Mac found himself yet again reporting to the superintendent's office.

"Good morning." Mac smiled at Buck Carter's secretary, as he entered her office.

She ignored him.

"Mind if I have a cup of coffee while I wait for the superintendent?"

"Help yourself," she said bluntly and turned away.

Mac smiled, and said, "I know there are people in this building who don't like me, but I don't recall any situation where I may have insulted the superintendent's secretary," knowing that it would insult her to be called a secretary.

"I am not the superintendent's secretary; I am his administrative assistant," she vehemently corrected Mac.

"Still, it seems like an obsequious position to me." Mac was enjoying the verbal sport.

The door to the superintendent's office opened. "Please come into my office and have a seat, Lieutenant," said Buck Carter, dressed in the blue uniform of the state police with freshly polished eagles on his collar. Simple Eddie was sitting in a leather wingback chair dressed in a pink button-down shirt, starched khaki pants, blue blazer, and expensive Italian Gravatis shoes. Lower middle class wanting to be upper class, Mac thought. He was wearing enough gold chains around his neck to stop a forty-five caliber handgun, and the imitation gold Rolex he sported was spiked with garish fake diamonds.

"Nice watch, Colonel," Mac said.

"Have a seat Lieutenant," Buck Carter stated. "I'll get right to the point. I asked you to come in today because Lieutenant Colonel Kazan has brought to my attention some very serious allegations against you. We are going to give you an opportunity to clear this matter up, and possibly resign from the force without going through an Internal Affairs investigation that could become public record and embarrass you and the department."

Mac sat still, somewhat dumbfounded, trying to recall any behavior that was illegal or at least against company policy. He was at a loss, but he knew Simple Eddie was behind it, and it was possible that Buck Carter was assisting in the set-up.

Carter continued, with his best imitation of a grim face, "I've already had a discussion with Internal Affairs, and they suggested that I should have you sign a Garrity Warning form."

Mac was gathering his thoughts and looking for more information. "What if I refuse to sign it?"

"You can bend over and kiss your ass good-bye," retorted Simple Eddie.

"If you refuse to sign it, according to departmental policy, I can terminate your employment with the state police," said Buck Carter, flatly and without emotion.

Buck Carter leaned forward and reached down below his desk momentarily. Mac suspected that he was initiating a recording device.

"Okay," said Mac, who was now getting angry and wanted the upper hand. "I'll sign the form." He looked at Simple Eddie and back to Buck Carter, "According to Garrity, your questions must be specific and tailored directly to my job, not my personal life. Secondly, since you are threatening to terminate my employment with the state police, my answers to your questions, as well as the fruits of my answers, cannot be used against me in a criminal investigation."

Simple Eddie squirmed at Mac's determination and knowledge of Garrity, and clearly did not like the implication that criminal prosecution was being avoided.

"Now," said Mac, after signing the form. "What the hell criminal act do you think I have committed?"

Simple Eddie spoke first. He leaned forward in his chair, with a red face and bulging eyes, and said, "I have been contacted by a woman who has accused you of statutory rape."

It all came to Mac in a flash of light and he started laughing; not a chuckle or snigger, but uncontrollable belly laughter. He closed his mouth and bit his lips and clutched his stomach and tried to stop, but it only turned into something that sounded like a choking pigeon. Tears were running out of Mac's squinted eyes when he finally caught his breath.

"You think I raped someone?" Mac asked, when he caught his breath. He looked directly at Buck Carter. "At least now I know why your secretary treated me with disdain when I walked into her office. You told her I was a rapist."

"This is a serious matter," said Buck Carter.

"No it isn't," replied Mac who was beginning to laugh again. "I'll give you the short version. One of my agents is temporarily staying at my house. He met a woman in a bar, who followed him to my house at two o'clock in the morning. The agent passed out, and the woman wanted to get laid, so she woke me up. I tried to resist, but she wouldn't take no for an answer." Mac was standing now. "I've done a lot of stupid things in my life, most of which were driven by my misguided dick. No doubt Roscoe has been the root cause, no pun intended, of most of my problems. But I can't really blame this situation on Roscoe. I am well aware that Roscoe is morally disabled, but when you are single, sleeping alone in your own home, and a naked Gina Lollobrigida climbs into bed with you demanding to get laid, how much will power are you expected to have?"

"The allegation is statutory," said Buck Carter.

Mac was suddenly laughing again. He pointed at Simple Eddie, but said to Buck Carter, "You are obviously getting your information from this persona non grata, lieutenant colonel, whose thought processes are slower than humidity. Albeit the woman was mad as hell when she woke up, but it was not rape, and especially not statutory rape."

Mac was looking directly at Simple Eddie now. "Statutory is a legal term that is used to describe sexual activity where one participant is below the age required to legally consent to the behavior. In Louisiana, the age is sixteen or younger, but past the age of puberty, aka carnal knowledge. The woman at my house was over thirty years old." Now he looked back at Buck Carter and said, "You might want to explain to Lieutenant Colonel Kazan what the word 'statutory' means."

Simple Eddie was squirming. His anxiety was further increased because he did not know what 'persona non grata' meant, or that the age of sexual consent in Louisiana was seventeen. He had forgotten to ask the woman her age.

"No use wasting a trip to Baton Rouge," Mac continued. "I had just as soon go to Internal Affairs right now and get it over with. I never cease to be dumbfounded by the unbelievable shit that stupid people believe without investigating first. In fact, I want to go to Internal Affairs. The story will make me a folk hero."

"That won't be necessary," Buck Carter said. "Maybe we jumped to conclusions, but I was trying to do what is best for the department. You've been a productive agent, and a dedicated and loyal supervisor, but Colonel Kazan thinks you are a loose canon."

"Loose canon? Moi? Of course I'm a loose canon. How can you work narcotics and not be a loose canon? It's part of the damn job description. I've been a narc for ten years, and I've seen it all—dopers, thieves, hookers, child molesters, and even a party or two that got out of hand. For the most part I've just been doing the best job I could, with confidence and enthusiasm while at the same time trying to develop people skills and leadership ability, but I'll be damned if I can understand politically driven, state police supervisors."

"Your problem," interjected Simple Eddie, "is that you are dangerous to the stability and complacency of the department."

"My problem," said Mac, looking directly at Simple Eddie, "is that I talk too much, and tell the truth. I hope that my actions and work in behalf of the people we serve will win out over politics, but I'm naïve about such things."

Buck Carter rolled his eyes slightly, as Mac looked at Simple Eddie and said, "You are a mendacious person, Colonel." Mac knew that Simple Eddie would not know the meaning of the word, but would think it had something to do with being manly. "Let me ask y'all a question. Which is more important, your career pattern or the work we do for the people of Louisiana?"

"You are always quoting Bill Spencer," said Buck Carter, ignoring the question. "Did you ever hear him say that no one ever got fired from the state police for doing too little, but several got fired for doing too much?"

"Then in order to avoid making a mistake," responded Mac, "we should say nothing, do nothing, and be nothing."

"You better quit while you are ahead, Lieutenant," said Buck Carter, who, right or wrong, was not going to be lectured.

"Yes sir," said Mac, turning to leave. He looked at Simple Eddie and said, "By the way, the woman that called you: She was a squealing, lust-ridden, dirty-talking, closet treasure. You wouldn't happen to have her number would you?"

175

Roy W. Frusha

"Get out of my office," said Buck Carter.

CHAPTER 17
The Panamanian Connection

His full name was Manuel Antonio Noriega Moreno, and he was the military dictator of Panama in 1983. He was born in Panama City and educated in military science in Lima, Peru. In 1967 the CIA picked him for intelligence and counterintelligence training at the School of the Americas at the U.S. Army base at Fort Gulick in Panama. The School of the Americas was also known as the school of coups, and even better known as the school of assassins. At that time, Noriega was a lieutenant in the Panamanian Army. He had been actively involved in the 1968 overthrow of Arnulfo Arias and helped place Omar Torrijos into power. For his assistance, Torrijos promoted Noriega to lieutenant colonel and chief of military intelligence.

Noriega had been the Central Intelligence Agency's most famous snitch since the 1950s. It was perfect that he had been promoted to govern the intelligence division of Panama. For his dedicated service to President Torrijos, Noriega was later promoted to chief of staff, and finally commander of all military forces.

Throughout the 1970s, Noriega was able to use his connections with the CIA to manipulate himself into a position of absolute power in Panama. It was a serious foreign policy failure for the United States to turn a blind eye to his attempts to seize total power; regardless, the United States looked the other way. Finally, in 1983, Noriega promoted himself to full general and had the Panamanian Legislature declare him "Chief Executive Officer" of the government. He would also meet Leigh Starwood in the late 1970s, with whom he would establish a friendly and professional relationship. It would prove to be a mistake for Noriega.

By 1978, Leigh Ray Starwood and Vince Vargo were the largest marijuana and cocaine dealers in the history of the United States. Starwood dealt almost exclusively with the Nasser-David organization in Columbia, and Vargo had a distribution network that ranged from New Jersey to Texas. The cash was rolling in faster than they could spend it.

During the winters, Vargo often brought his girlfriends, many of them prostitutes, to Starwood's three million dollar villa in Georgetown, Grand Cayman, to escape the freezing temperatures of Ann Arbor, Michigan. The four bedroom, four-bath mansion was located on an acre of lush gardens and manicured lawn overlooking the pristine beach and beautiful Caribbean Sea. The beachfront property was a kaleidoscope of roses, wild banana orchids, and inkberries. Starwood went to great lengths to keep his property as beautiful as his rich neighbors. Nothing less, nothing more. He did not want to stand out either way. The concept was lost on Vargo, who enjoyed attention.

The beachside residence also included a boat slip where Starwood kept a forty-eight foot Sea Ray cruiser, which had three bedrooms, two baths, was fully air conditioned and had a double refrigerator stocked with wine and champagne. Vargo was often seen around the island on the boat with four or five naked women. He often joked that the Sea Ray made women's clothes fall off, and he once said to one of Starwood's island friends that, "The funny thing is that Leigh's boat always smells like fish, but we've never been fishing in it." The inappropriate comments made Starwood cringe.

"We need to talk a little private business," Starwood said to Vargo one day as they were sitting on the beach. "We are making more money than we ever dreamed, and we currently have some of it stashed in vaults and some in various banks in the U.S. and in Grand Cayman. It's risky to have a paper trail, and I think I can do better with our investments."

"I'm listening."

"When I was with the Army's Counter Drug Intelligence Section in Columbia, we spent a great deal of time and expense studying the Medellin Cartel and a Columbian drug lord named Pablo Escobar. I had several opportunities to meet with Escobar and arrange business deals with him, but I steered clear because of his propensity toward violence."

"We are doing fine with Nasser-David," replied Vargo. "What does Escobar have to do with anything?"

"Hear me out. We also collected a massive amount of intelligence on General Manuel Noriega, president and military dictator of Panama. Noriega is in the drug business with Pablo Escobar and is raking in millions. The U.S. Army, the CIA, FBI and Drug Enforcement Agency all know about Noriega, but here is the catch: The U.S. government has taken the moral low ground. They don't give a shit what Noriega does because he is a snitch for the CIA, and has been since the 1950s. I learned that in 1971, the Drug Enforcement Agency wanted to indict him, but the CIA stepped in and blocked it. He is protected by the United States Government, who has full knowledge of his drug dealing and is purposely allowing him to be the first, of what my supervisor used to call a 'narcokleptocracy.'"

"A what?"

"Narcokelptocracy," answered Starwood. "It is a society or country that is ruled by thieves. Military juntas, and the ruling class of the society, steal from the mass population by taking money out of public funds. In other words, the national treasury of a country is also the personal bank account of the rulers. In the case of Panama, the ruler is Manuel Noriega, and he is making a killing by authorizing the manufacture and distribution of marijuana and cocaine in Panama, so one of our Army intelligence guys started calling Panama a 'narcokelptocracy.'"

"Okay, I get it," said Vargo. "It's a government that exists expressly for the benefit of those who run it, but how does it relate to our business?"

"We've got millions in cash stockpiled all over the place," answered Starwood. "We need to consolidate the majority of it in a safe location where it can work for us, but not leave a paper trail that can be connected to us. The last thing we want is for the IRS to be on our ass. The IRS can be like shit; the smell is easy to get on you and hard to get off."

"I'm still listening," said Vargo.

"We learned that Noriega keeps his money in the BCCI, which stands for the Bank of Credit and Commerce International. The BCCI is located in over fifty countries and has over four hundred branches. They have assets in the countless billions. It is the biggest clandestine money network in the world, and it has essentially no regulatory oversight. It's a big shell game played with massive amounts of money. Noriega has placed twenty-five million in four secret accounts in the BCCI."

"You want to make your point before I miss happy hour with the girls," said Vargo, who was getting bored with the lecture on Noriega.

"Here's the bottom line. Noriega is like us, he understands our trade. He sees it as a business like we do. We buy and sell a product. If there were no demand, there would be no supply. I still have contacts in Columbia who can introduce me to Noriega. I believe we can expand our business into Panama and we can get into the Panamanian branch of the BCCI, where the IRS can't get to us."

"Okay, I'm in," said Vargo, who was suddenly interested.

"There is another, even better reason for doing business with Noriega," said Starwood, sitting up in his chair and looking directly into Vargo's eyes. "If we get busted, Noriega is our ace in the hole. We can trade up. We are not headlines except for a few local papers. Noriega is famous, and the feds love a big headline. If the shit hits the fan, we will go free, and Noriega will go to jail. Take my word for it."

One month later, in March 1978, Leigh Starwood flew over the Panama Canal and landed at Tocumen International airport near downtown Panama City, Panama. The temperature was ninety-five degrees and the ocean breeze caused the humid air to feel salty against his skin. He was dressed in a tan wool suit, but not one that was flashy or even noticeable. A cab took him to the quaint Hotel DeVille, near city center, where he had reserved a top floor suite with French doors leading to a large balcony overlooking a lush patio filled with ten-foot Panama roses and dove orchids. Water flowed over a brass Harpy Eagle into a concrete fountain where small birds bathed.

Starwood showered and dressed in a white linen shirt and lightweight, breathable cotton seersucker suit, perfect for the tropical climate of Panama. The outfit was completed with black and white saddle shoes and topped off with a white Borsalino Panamanian Fino hat with a black band. For the first time since had had become a smuggler, Starwood wanted to be noticed. He considered the suit not only protocol but in good taste. After checking himself carefully in the mirror, he picked up a black leather Tumi Portfolio briefcase, which contained three hundred thousand in cash.

It was a short walk to the Presidential Palace, which the locals called "Placiode las Grazas" after the African herons that walked the palace grounds. Starwood met his old friend from Columbia at the prearranged place near the fountain in the ancient patio of the palace.

"Como estas mi viejo," said the Columbian.

"Muy bien, gracias," answered Starwood, happy to practice his Spanish.

"Has the meeting been scheduled as planned?"

"Si, el president Noriega le espera."

"Good," said Starwood. "Let's not keep him waiting."

Fifteen minutes later, they were escorted into the office of the president and military ruler of Panama. Starwood had expected to be searched, or at least questioned, but there was neither. Apparently his old friend from Columbia was very well connected. He had also expected an ostentatious office, but it was simple and unassuming. There was some ornate polished wood bookcases and matching desk. Some military memorabilia adorned the walls with a few pictures of dignitaries, but otherwise it was not unlike an office of any executive you might visit in the United States.

Noriega, who was dressed in the uniform of a four star general, walked to the front of his desk and spoke to the Columbian first. The Columbian introduced him to Starwood, who answered Noriega in Spanish. Noriega was notably impressed and grinned widely at Starwood. He was surprised at how personable and approachable Noriega was. He would later describe him as courteous and pleasant. The first fifteen minutes, they discussed their educational and military backgrounds, and for the first time Starwood spoke openly and honestly of his experiences in the U.S. Army Counter Intelligence Section. Starwood did not believe that Noriega was a fool, and understood well that Noriega may have had detailed information about him. He would not get caught lying to him. The next fifteen minutes they spoke in general terms about doing international business that earned millions in cash and of Starwood's desire to invest some of his money in the BCCI in Panama.

"Your Spanish is very good," said Noriega, in English. "I would be interested to learn how you perfected our language. Also, regarding your business interests in Panama, I will help you

181

any way I can. Obtaining accounts with BCCI can be handled as early as tomorrow. You are always welcome in Panama City. I look forward to visiting with you again soon."

Starwood understood that the meeting was over. He shook hands with Noriega, smiled and bowed slightly. He then shook hands with the Columbian, thanked him, and left the office. The Columbian stayed in with Noriega, and Starwood knew that they would discuss details of his business ventures. It was part of the plan. He wondered how long it would take them to realize he had left the black leather briefcase in Noriega's office.

He walked slowly back to the Hotel DeVille taking in the sights surrounding the central business district, and heart of Panama's financial center. The area, which was surrounded by investment companies, restaurants, and art galleries, was a gathering place for traveling businessmen. He walked along Casco Viejo, the beautiful historic district of the old capitol city, down Beatriz Cabal Avenue along the charming narrow streets which were bordered by flower bedecked balconies of two and three-story buildings.

The Hotel DeVille was a step back in time. Starwood half expected Ferdinand de Lesseps to walk into the hotel bar with business associates and lay out his plans for the Panama Canal. Or even further back in time, see the pirate Henry Morgan come tearing down the street with his crew to loot the city, as he had done in 1671.

The lounge consisted of a twenty-foot bar, five or six round tables that had been imported from France and half a dozen antique ceiling fans, each turning at a speed barely fast enough to move the sultry air. French doors opened onto the patio. He chose a table shaded by old trees that allowed him a view of the street. He ordered shrimp ceviche and a bottle of Balboa beer, and waited.

One hour later a three-car motorcade screeched to a halt in front of the hotel. Four heavily armed Panamanian soldiers got out of the advance vehicle and entered the hotel. They saw Starwood in the lounge. One soldier approached him while the others cleared the bar of the five or six patrons that were drinking there. Soldiers from the other vehicle circled the hotel. Manuel Noriega and the Columbian entered the hotel lounge, walked up to Starwood's table and sat down.

"It seems you forgot a very special briefcase in my office," said Noriega.

"It was not a mistake," replied Starwood. "It was left as a small gesture of my appreciation for your time, Mr. President."

"Ah," said Noriega, smiling. "Do you mind if I join you for a beer?" They drank half a dozen beers each at the hotel bar, after which they walked out without paying the tab. Noriega invited Starwood to join him for a night on the town. They gambled at the Royal Casino, watched young girls dance at the Gugu Clubbing Cult, and picked up Cuban cigars and prostitutes at Habana's Bar. They brought the prostitutes to Noriega's three million dollar mansion at the upscale, ritzy neighborhood of Altos de Golf, where they listened to loud music, snorted cocaine, and had an orgy until daylight.

It had been a productive trip for Starwood. For the next five years he would vacation and party with Noriega on regular intervals. He shipped cocaine and marijuana to Panama and made huge deposits in the BCCI.

Starwood and Noreiga were visiting Paris to chase women when Noreiga received a call from Panama in which the caller said, "We have the rabid dog." Noriega's response was, "And what does one do with a dog that has rabies?" Starwood later learned that the dog was Hugo Spadafora, an outspoken critic of Noriega who accused him of drug trafficking. Spadafora's decapitated and tortured body was found wrapped in a United States Postal Service mailing bag.

The Panamanian connection would prove to serve Starwood and Vargo very well.

CHAPTER 18
When Cows Fly

Sunlight escaped through brackish clouds as the narcs sat on the front porch of Doc Frederick's cypress camp in Arnaudville drinking draft beer out of plastic cups and eating boudin and cracklings from brown paper towels. Mac had picked up the beer, and Hungry Harv had purchased the food from the nearby Poche Bridge store. A few large drops of rain sounded like distant gun shots as they hit the tin roof of the old Cajun structure. The autumn squall passed, but the air was still wet and salty. November in Louisiana can be one of the better months, and the cool front behind the rain was a welcome relief to the agents. Clouds were dispersing and the temperature had dropped ten degrees. Changes in Louisiana temperature were never subtle. They were having their monthly choir practice.

"Let's bring each other up to date on our investigations," instructed Mac. "Hungry Harv will go first."

Hungry Harv, stood and spit a mouth full of Red Man tobacco into a puddle near the porch. He was dressed in work boots, faded denim jeans, and a colorful short sleeve shirt that his wife had gotten him on a vacation in Destin, Florida. Hollywood was going to ask him if it was his Hawaiian wedding shirt but thought better of it.

"Just when you think you got it figured out, you're wrong again," Hungry Harv began. "I think we have a problem in state police. We've been looking at everybody except us."

"Kind of like Pogo," stated Bubba.

"Who?" Hungry Harv asked.

"He was a comic strip character...never mind, it's over your head," said Bubba.

"Like I was saying," continued Hungry Harv. "Everybody here knows Boogie Blanchard, our state police stock patrol guy. I drive by Boogie Blanchard's house every morning on the way to work. He was living in a rundown, leaky trailer, all patched up with plywood he stole up from construction sites. Now he has a new brick home down on Highway 343 near the Meaux community, and his wife is driving a new Crown Vic. I went though some records at the courthouse. Boogie put down forty grand on his house."

"Maybe he saved his money or sold some cows," Bubba said.

"Boogie never had a pot to piss in or a window to throw it out of," said Hungry Harv. "The only thing Boogie ever owned of any value is his horse. He and his wife spend their money faster than a democrat can spend your taxes."

"Got any probable cause?" asked Bubba.

"Don't need it with Boogie. He's scared of his shadow. If we confront him, he'll give it up."

"Okay," said Mac, moving on. "Hungry Harv and I will handle Boogie. What do you have scheduled, Bubba?"

"I have some info on a local oilfield salesman name of Blackie Cunningham. He likes to run with the big guys. He wears a fancy Rolex and drives a new Corvette. Good reputation with the ladies. They like cocaine, and he always has a supply. He sold some bad weed to a local dealer. The dealer got pissed, walked into the office, and offered to give him up."

"Sounds good," said Mac. "If the snitch will make the introduction, get Bert to wire you up and purchase ten pounds of weed. Let the money walk, and a week to ten days later, arrange for a second purchase of twenty pounds. Rooster can set up surveillance and an arrest team. The district attorney usually likes at least two purchases before he'll prosecute, but we are limited as to how much cash we can walk, so play it by ear.

"What about you, Hollywood? What are you and Tatou up to?" Mac continued.

"We have a good one for you, boss. A former Lafayette mayor's son is dealing weed, pills, and cocaine. His partner in crime is a good-looking, long-legged blond whose daddy owns the largest construction company in the area. The girl is kind of sloppy, and Tatou managed to buy a little weed from her. It's not much, but it's sufficient probable cause for a search warrant."

"Good," said Mac. "Let's shake some trees."

"One more item," said Hungry Harv. "An old Cajun called the office yesterday, and said he wanted to talk personally to a narcotics agent. He's coming in this afternoon."

Boogie Blanchard was thirty-five, married, and had two kids. He was short, thin, and nervous. His coffee-colored skin was darker than normal, even for a Cajun, from long days in the sun. He wore Wrangler jeans, Justin work boots, and striped cowboy shirts with pearl snaps. Born and raised in Vermilion Parish, Boogie had desperately wanted to be a real cowboy, a rodeo professional, but the talent wasn't there. He had made little more than minimum wage working for area ranchers since he was twelve years old, and even that was seasonal. He and his family lived in a small trailer behind a rancher's barn.

The only steady income Boogie had was from the Louisiana State Police, which provided him with a small salary, and a truck, and a cattle trailer. Boogie was on call for the patrol division, and his only duty was to be available to pick up livestock whenever they broke through a fence and meandered onto state highways. It was the kind of work Boogie enjoyed, but it did not put groceries on the table.

Boogie was sitting in a coffee shop on the side of a service station in Maurice when he was first approached by Freebase Freddy Patout and Peter Rochon, both of whom he had known since childhood.

"Comment les haricots?" Freddy said. It was a greeting common to Vermilion Parish Cajuns, literally meaning, "how are the green beans?" but figuratively, "how are things?"

"Ca peut faire," answered Boogie, meaning life was not great, but would do.

"How would you like to make some good, easy money?" Freddy asked.

"You know I need money, Fred. I'm so broke if it cost a quarter to shit, I'd have to throw up." Boogie squirmed in his booth and looked at his old friend suspiciously. "What do I have to do?"

"Do you know the bridge over the Vermilion Bayou near Forked Island?" Freddy asked.

"Of course."

"I have some property leased along the river bank just south of the bridge. I would like for you to put some of your cows on the property and be seen there occasionally feeding your cows, fixing the fence, and stuff like that."

"What else?" Boogie asked.

"Crew boats and fishing boats will occasionally dock there. I want you to take the contents from the boats and put them in your horse trailer and then drive them to a truck stop in Lafayette. You go inside the truck stop for coffee. When you come out, the contents will be gone."

"What will be in the trailer?" Boogie asked.

"You don't need to know all that," said Peter Rochon.

Boogie shook his head and said, "No thanks, I'm not going to jail for anyone." Boogie had heard rumors about Freebase Freddy and Peter Rochon smuggling dope into Vermilion Parish for years. They both had nice homes on the river and drove new trucks. It was commonly known that Patout had never been employed. Also, Peter had a small boat dealership, but it never seemed to do much business.

"I'll give you ten thousand dollars in cash for every load you drive," said Freddy.

Boogie could not believe the amount of money. It was half of a year's salary for a few minutes work. "All I have to do is drive a truck and trailer to Lafayette and walk away?" he asked.

Two or three times a month, one of Peter Rochon's offshore fishing boats would pull up to the leased land on Vermilion Bayou, and Boogie would load marijuana or cocaine into his cattle trailer and drive it to a truck stop in Lafayette. Sometimes Boogie would include a couple of cows to make it look good. One year later, Boogie Blanchard was living in a new brick home on five acres in North Vermilion Parish. His wife had a new car and he drove a new truck, pulling the state police cattle trailer. He also purchased over one hundred head of cattle which he ran on the leased property near the Forked Island Bridge.

While Boogie Blanchard was living the good life Hungry Harv and Mac had returned from choir practice to wait for the old Cajun. He arrived at four o'clock. The receptionist notified Mac, saying, "He barely speaks English, but I think he wants to talk to a narcotics agent about his cattle ranch."

Hungry Harv approached the old Cajun and asked, "Comment les affaires?" immediately connecting with him.

"Pas trop mauvais," meaning not too bad, said the old Cajun, relieved that someone spoke French.

"Come in and have some coffee with us; tell us how we can help you." Hungry Harv introduced the old man to Mac, and they sat around a conference table drinking coffee and making small talk.

"Well," said the old Cajun, "a few days ago, I called the Customs people here in Lafayette, and they told me to call the Drug Enforcement Agency in Baton Rouge, which I did, but none of them were interested in helping me. I think it is because my English is not so good as my French."

"Why were you calling drug enforcement people?" Hungry Harv asked.

"At my place in Arnaudville, I have two hundred acres of pasture land, and I raise pure bred Black Angus cattle. At any given time, I have more than one hundred head. All of my animals are allowed to roam freely; there are no feed lots on my place. Free range cattle produce a higher quality meat. I make a good living selling my beef to restaurants all over Louisiana."

"Why were you trying to get in touch with the feds?" Hungry Harv asked.

"I never went to school past the fifth grade, me, but I'm not stupid. Two foreigners came to my place and wanted to purchase ten cows."

"What kind of foreigners?" Hungry Harv was focused on the old man.

"They had dark skin and hair and spoke very little English. They spoke Spanish to each other, but they were not Mexicans. I've had Mexicans working at my place many times. I think they were from South America."

"What is so different about these people wanting to purchase your cows?" Mac inquired.

"They did not know the difference between a Black Angus and a Jack Russell Terrier. They didn't even want to see the cows. They just wanted me to have them ready to take to the airport, and they promised to pay me in cash.

Mac and Hungry Harv looked at each other. "Quel jour?" Hungry Harv asked the old man.

"Demain," he answered, "just before sunset."

188

"We'll be at your place by noon tomorrow and set up," Hungry Harv said. "We appreciate you contacting us. They are up to no good, and we'll find out what it is."

After the old Cajun left Region II, Mac looked at Hungry Harv and said, "Whatever these people are up to is obviously going out of state, and probably out of the country. Is there anyone at the FBI who can support us with this operation and take it federally?"

"They say Agent Paul St. Pierre was a real policeman down in New Orleans before joining the FBI. I'll give him a call and ask him to meet us early tomorrow morning," Hungry Harv replied.

Agent Paul St. Pierre was a stocky man, whose primary hobby was to work out. He had a prominent nose and a moustache Groucho Marx would have been proud of, except that it was more closely trimmed. St. Pierre grew up in an area of New Orleans locals call "The Irish Channel." Originally settled by Irish peasants before the Civil War, the old neighborhood between the Mississippi River on the south and Magazine Street to the north was a melting pot of bricklayers, butchers, construction and other lower income workers. By the 1960s, it had become majority African American, and his neighbors were mostly drug dealers, petty thieves, and prostitutes. He learned to mind his own business at an early age. He also learned to fight.

After graduating high school, St. Pierre attended Loyola University and earned a degree in Criminal Justice. He was six feet tall, muscular, with dark wavy hair, and sky blue eyes that seemed to penetrate a person's thoughts. He joined the New Orleans Police Department and was quickly promoted to detective. After two years with NOPD, he was selected to join the ranks of the Federal Bureau of Investigation and was sent to Miami where he kept tabs on the mafia for the next six years. He put in for a transfer back to New Orleans, but Lafayette had the only vacancy.

Bubba said, "He smokes cheap cigars, drinks good whisky, and appreciates subtle wit, so he can't be all bad."

"You ever worked a drug investigation?" Mac asked at the first meeting.

"I haven't seen any drugs since I moved out of the Irish Channel," St. Pierre responded. "But I'm a quick learner, and I can make things happen within the federal bureaucracy."

"We'll see," said Mac, whose experience with federal authorities made him cautious.

"Why me?" St. Pierre asked. "Why didn't you contact Customs?"

"The boss prefers the FBI," answered Hungry Harv. "Just let it go at that."

"I think I understand," St. Pierre said. "Let's do it."

At noon the next day, Mac, Hungry Harv, Agent St. Pierre, and a few others from Region II Narcotics set up in the woods, barn, and out buildings at the old Cajun's ranch in Arnaudville. Hungry Harv wore canvas Carhartt overalls, worn leather work boots, and a faded Stetson cowboy hat. He would stay with the old Cajun. Agent Bert DeBlanc wired Hungry Harv for sound so each agent could monitor the conversation.

Just before dusk, two men arrived in a rental car. Each was no more than five foot eight, and weighed less than one hundred sixty pounds. They had long, greasy dark hair and olive skin. They wore sandals, chino shorts, and short sleeve silk shirts.

Agent St. Pierre, who was looking at them through binoculars from one hundred feet away, said to Mac, "They are definitely South American, but I'm not sure which country. Maybe Colombia, or close to it. What do you think they are up to?"

"No good," Mac responded. "Probably drug smugglers, but I don't see the connection yet."

Hungry Harv and the old Cajun were in a corral near the hay barn, where they had placed ten young heifers for the foreigners to observe. The old Cajun waved for the foreigners to come to the corral.

"Are the cows ready?" One of them asked.

"Yes sir," said the old Cajun. "These are ten of the best heifers I have. Would you like to go in the corral and inspect them?"

"Not necessary," said the foreigner. "We trust your judgment that these are the best. Can you take them in your trailer to the airport in Lafayette five days from now and help load them on a plane for us? We'll pay you extra, in cash."

"We'll take them to the airport for you," Hungry Harv interjected. "Say, where are you all from, anyway?"

"Caracas, Venezuela," answered one of them.

"Y'all don't have cows in Venezuela?" Hungry Harv inquired. "I thought they had many large cattle ranches in your country."

"Si, we have many cows in Venezuela, but our boss wants to make his herd better with these black cows. Louisiana is a direct flight, and you have many good cows here."

"Whatever you say," answered Hungry Harv. "You can pay my boss now or at the airport in five days."

"What's next?" asked Agent St. Pierre, when they were alone.

"In five days, we'll set up at Lafayette Regional Airport and develop probable cause to search the airplane. Piece of cake," said Mac. Agent St. Pierre just looked at Mac, shook his head, and wondered if he was going to get into trouble for searching an international flight without just cause.

"Tomorrow I'll introduce you to our new federal prosecutor," Agent St. Pierre said. "She's only been in the Lafayette office for a few weeks, and she is looking for some cases. You'll like her. She's young, but she is competent and aggressive. Agents who worked with her in Texas call her the Black Widow."

Early the next morning, Mac drove to the Lafayette Federal Courthouse to meet Agent St. Pierre and federal prosecutor Allison Duvall. The incongruous marble and stone federal building covered an entire block. It was a monstrosity of a structure that reminded Mac of the Taj Mahal in Agra, India, except this building was not a symbol of eternal love. Rather, Mac said aloud, "This building is a monument to man's eternal arrogance and pride, never mind the cost to the taxpayers."

After entering the federal building, Mac approached a woman sitting behind what appeared to be a bank cage. He talked to her through a hole in a thick cut glass window.

"I'm Lieutenant McCullough with the state police, and I'm here to see Agent St. Pierre with the FBI."

"You will have to wear an identification badge and you can't carry firearms into the office," she said.

"No problem," replied Mac, who always wondered at the sense of self-importance of federal authorities. "I figured as much and left my weapon in my unit," he said, as he handed the woman his identification card.

In all his years as a cop, he had never known one of them to share a piece of information, though they had often claimed local investigations as their own. Mac recalled a time in Morgan City when he had caught one of the FBI's top ten wanted persons, and the FBI gave a carefully worded news release claiming the case as their own. Most of the federal prosecutors he had met kept to themselves and hoped to prosecute a local politician or even better, a local cop. It was a fast track to promote themselves to higher levels of the system to which they were indelibly tied. Regardless, he needed their assistance for certain crimes, and he hoped this experience would be better.

Agent St. Pierre greeted Mac, shook hands, and said, "Good morning, Mac. I would like you to meet Allison Duval, our new federal prosecutor." The effect on Mac was immediate. He quickly ascertained that black widow reference was not due to her tenacity as a prosecutor, but rather to her clothes. She wore a black short sleeve silk dress with an orange red scarf tied loosely at the waist. The dress hung naturally over a firm body with full breasts, which rose and fell with her breathing. Mac guessed she was in her mid thirties, stood about five-foot-four, and weighed no more than one hundred and twenty pounds. Her brown hair was in a ponytail tied almost at the top of her head. She could have passed for Barbara Eden in "I Dream of Jeannie," except for the dark hair. She had deep-set honey-colored eyes that sparkled in the light. High cheek bones and olive-colored skin gave her a Mediterranean look. She was smoking hot, and if she had dressed for effect, it worked.

"I'm Allison Duval," she said, with a raspy, north Texas accent. She extended her hand. "Please come in and sit down, Lieutenant." The handshake was firm. "Don't touch her," Mac thought to himself. "You might get burned."

Mac was somewhat caught off guard by the stunning looks of the prosecutor, and he looked quickly around the office, trying to compose himself. He glanced at Agent St. Pierre, who was smiling, clearly enjoying Mac's discomfort. The office was not overly large. The desk, chairs, and rug were clean and orderly. He noted her Juris Doctorate degree from Georgetown Law School nicely framed and hanging behind her desk. "Not a good thing." Mac thought, "Too liberal."

"It's nice to meet you, Miss Duval," said Mac, sitting down. "My friends call me Mac."

"Well, Mac, I hear you jump off bridges and save damsels in distress."

"Aw, that's nothing," said Mac, with a fake southern drawl. "I was also one of the flag raisers at Iwo Jima."

"Wasn't that in February 1945?" she responded, laughing. "You are a lot older than you look."

"Maybe I was confused; come to think of it, it was at the Battle of Hastings," answered Mac, enjoying the verbal judo.

"I believe the Battle of Hastings had to do with the Norman Conquest of England, and took place in 1066," she replied, with a coy smile.

"Actually, there was another Hastings. Specifically, it was called Operation Hastings, and it was in July 1966 at a place called Quang Tri Province," Mac said. "And it was just a small flag, and I planted it in some dirt around a fox hole I had dug. It wasn't as glamorous as Mount Suribachi."

"Vietnam," she said knowingly. "I appreciate your service."

"How is it you know so much about history?" Mac asked.

"I majored in History at Texas Tech. My father's last duty station was at Dyess Air Force Base, near Abilene, so my brothers and I attended Tech."

"Was your father an aviator?"

"No. He served in the Air Force Office of Special Investigations. He was career military police. Specifically, he worked with local authorities to identify and neutralize terrorist threats to Air Force personnel and equipment. He was successful because he worked with, and relied upon, local authorities."

Mac smiled and nodded, taking her point.

"Don't let the Georgetown credentials give you the wrong impression," she said, looking toward the certificate. "It's a great law school, and I'm privileged to have gone there on scholarship. But I come from conservative roots. My parents met when my father was stationed at Barksdale Air Force Base in Shreveport.

My mother was attending Centenary College, but she is originally from St. Martin Parish. I'm half Cajun."

Mac nodded, realizing that the St. Martin Parish connection explained the dark skin and deep set eyes. "Miss Duval, is the Toombs Bar still active in Georgetown?"

"Yes, it is still a very much a college hangout. How do you know the place?"

"It was a college hangout when I was in officer's candidate school, a long time ago."

"My friends call me Al," she said, with a confident smile. "When you grow up with four brothers, you become one of the guys."

"Mac has an interesting investigation working," Agent St. Pierre interjected. "Some Venezuelans are purchasing cattle from a local, and Mac thinks they are dirty. If they are smuggling drugs, it has to be a significant amount in order to justify the expense."

"We also have some other investigations that fit your parameters, but the Venezuelan thing is imminent. They will be here with a plane in three days."

"Do you have a name for the investigation?" Allison said, as she reached for a pen.

Mac thought for a few seconds before responding, then smiled and said, "When Cows Fly."

Just after daybreak on Friday morning, Mac, Paul St. Pierre, and several Region II agents were drinking coffee in a borrowed airplane hanger at the Lafayette Regional Airport when Hungry Harv arrived with the old Cajun pulling a dusty, beat up trailer containing ten Black Angus heifers. Mac and the others had been there since four o'clock in the morning, quietly watching an old military version of a Douglas DC-3, which was stationary in front of the hanger. Mac had recognized the old twin engine workhorse. In Vietnam, the old timers called it a "Gooney Bird." It could easily carry as much as twenty-five thousand pounds over long distances at a speed of one hundred fifty knots. The Venezuelans arrived shortly after eight o'clock with a pilot.

Mac advised the old Cajun to go inside the hanger, have some coffee, and wait, while he, Agent St. Pierre, Hollywood, and Hungry Harv approached the pilot and Venezuelans. Mac cut to the chase.

"I'm Lieutenant McCullough with state police narcotics," Mac informed the pilot, who appeared to be an American, about fifty years of age. He was wearing denim pants, a white tee shirt, a worn leather jacket and naval issue flight glasses. "Please take off your sunglasses," he instructed the pilot.

Hollywood and Hungry Harv frisked the Venezuelans, advising them it was for safety reasons. They were not carrying weapons. However, they quickly became nervous and spoke quietly to each other in Spanish.

"Hollywood," instructed Mac. "Take the South Americans over to the hanger and wait for us there."

"Do you mind if we ask you a few questions?" Mac turned to the pilot after the others were out of hearing range.

"Not at all," he responded, seemingly concerned, but not overly worried or nervous, thought Mac.

"What are you transporting?"

"It's pretty obvious that I'm flying cattle."

"Where to?" interjected Hungry Harv.

"The two men you have detained at the hanger are paying me good cash money to deliver cattle to Venezuela."

"How many trips have you made for them?"

"This is my fourth."

"The DC-3 is a great old war bird," said Mac. "Do you mind if we take a look inside?"

"Knock yourself out," said the pilot.

Hungry Harv entered the plane first. Door steps had been replaced by a portable ramp. All seating, except for the cockpit, had been ripped out and replaced by aluminum railing designed to stabilize and limit the movement of the cattle. Mac and Hungry Harv walked to the rear of the plane, where there were several bags of cattle feed stacked neatly against the bulkhead. Hungry Harv lifted a bag which he judged to weigh about sixty pounds.

"Look on the floor, in the back corner of the fuselage," said Mac, pointing to a heavy duty sewing machine. Hungry Harv turned it upright and looked at the tag. "This machine was purchased at Guidry's Hardware in Lafayette."

"Cut open one of the feed bags," said Mac.

Hungry Harv opened his Buck folding tactical knife and sliced open a bag. "Cocaine, and a lot of it," he said. He counted the bags. "Eight bags at fifty to sixty pounds each, and we have five hundred pounds of cocaine, more or less."

The pilot and Venezuelans were arrested, advised of their rights, and transported to the Region II office for interrogation. The pilot took a quick polygraph and passed, which indicated that as far as he knew, he was transporting cattle. He was released. Four hours later it was learned that the Venezuelans were nothing more than low level mules hired to move cattle around and deliver feed bags to the Holiday Inn in Houma.

"All I know," said one of the Venezuelans, "is that we rent a car, put the bags in the trunk, and drive it to the Holiday Inn motel in Houma. We get a room and wait. During the night a man meets us at the motel room. We give him our keys and he gives us his keys. The car we drive back to Lafayette always has suitcases full of money, which we put on the plane and deliver to Caracas."

"Do you have a name for the man in Houma?" Mac asked.

"Yes," said one of the suspects. "He is called Marcello, and I think he is from New Orleans."

Agent St. Pierre took a deep breath and let it out slowly. "I think it might be fun working with y'all."

"Beautiful, we didn't have enough to do." Mac looked at St. Pierre. "Now we are screwing with the mafia."

CHAPTER 19
The Task Force

The Venezuelans had been booked in the Lafayette Parish Correctional Facility where they would get three hot meals a day, and sleep in an air-conditioned room watching HBO until a local bondsman paid cash to bail them. They would never return to Lafayette for court. Mac had given a news release to the local paper and television stations, forcing the dopers to pose with the bags of cocaine in front of the Gooney Bird. Peter Piazza smiled as he took the pictures for the Daily Advertiser.

"Didn't Simple Eddie order you not to give news releases?" questioned Hungry Harv.

"Roger that," answered Mac, looking somewhat dejected. "I just don't give a fuck anymore."

The call came at noon the next day, shortly after Simple Eddie heard about the arrests.

"I ordered you not to give any more releases," he screamed into the phone.

"Couldn't be helped. No one else was here to handle it. I was in charge, and the media wanted to ask me the questions," Mac replied calmly. "An FBI agent was with us. Would you prefer that we turn the investigations over to them and let them give the releases?"

"It was an international case and I would have preferred that you let Customs handle it. We could have backed them up, if additional help had been required," said Simple Eddie.

"Actually, the case was given to Customs and DEA. Both agencies refused to deal with it."

"Why would they refuse a case involving five hundred pounds of cocaine?"

"Probably interfered with their golf game."

"Your day is coming soon, it's just that simple," said Simple Eddie, slamming the phone into its receiver.

At four o'clock in the afternoon, the Region II agents and St. Pierre were sitting at the concrete tables on the patio of Legend's when Allison Duval arrived. She was wearing jeans which were molded to legs and buttocks fit from years of training. A black silk blouse semi-revealed the curves of her breasts. The burnt orange scarf around her waist gave her the appearance of being gift-wrapped. A strong wind was out of the east, and the temperature had dropped ten degrees. The effect of the cool air on Allison was not lost on the agents.

"Bring us up to date on your investigations," said St. Pierre, moving the focus from Allison to the work at hand.

Mac and Hungry Harv briefed them on the Bulldog investigation, discussing possible roles of Freebase Freddy, Peter Rochon, and the Fontenot brothers. Bubba briefed them on written statements obtained and physical evidence seized from the rental houses.

"This could really be big," Allison said, smiling at the prospect.

"What would you do first?" asked St. Pierre.

"My first choice," said Mac, "is to bust Rochon and Patout. Get them to roll over on the Fontenot brothers. That may not be the best choice because it's personal between me and James Fontenot, but it would be a start. Another approach would be for you to use your FBI resources to collect information on the names of the out-of-state players we've identified from paperwork left in the houses we raided."

"The federal prosecutor's office is definitely interested in the Bulldog investigation, and it may want to prosecute the other cases, depending on the quantity of the drugs, or possibly the level of the dealer," Allison said. "The U. S. Attorney for the Western District covers forty-two parishes, from Shreveport to Lake Charles to Lafayette. We enforce federal drug law established by the Controlled Substances Act of 1970. Our very best tool is RICO, which stands for Racketeer Influenced and Corrupt Organizations Act. Any criminal act performed as part of an ongoing criminal enterprise fits into our criteria. It's very flexible."

"If three or four people discuss a criminal enterprise," interjected St. Pierre, "and one of them commits an act in furtherance of the enterprise, we arrest them all and let God sort them out."

"What do you suggest for the next step?" Hungry Harv asked.

"I'll talk to my supervisors, and St. Pierre can contact Customs and DEA. We'll form a federal task force and work together."

"We have the talent," said Mac, waving one hand toward the Region II agents, "to investigate a large scale operation, and local prosecution isn't too bad, but most of the big players in this operation are out of state, maybe even out of country. The state police would never let us run all over the country investigating people who don't live in Louisiana. A federally-led task force is the logical way to move forward, but my problem is that the feds are not known for sharing information. If we are going to be successful, we need to work together and share all information obtained."

"We have stringent regulations about the information we can give to local agencies, and your point is well taken," said St. Pierre. "However, if you will trust me, I will tell you everything I learn, but you cannot let the bureau find out that I'm giving you sensitive information."

"You work for a fucked up agency," replied Mac. "But at least you were a real police officer before joining the FBI."

There was a brief silence, while St. Pierre tried to work out whether he had been complimented or insulted.

"I will set up a meeting at my office and get back with y'all," said Allison, who left with Agent St. Pierre.

Kelly brought another round of drinks to the narcs as they watched the feds drive away.

"What is your impression of the federal prosecutor?" Bubba asked Mac, as he finished a margarita.

"I'm hoping she is a closet treasure, but the over-under on my chances look slim to none."

"You know what I mean," said Bubba. "Besides, she is not interested in you. I caught her glancing at Dee."

"My first impression is that she comes from good roots, military brat, very bright. She appears very aggressive and energetic, and she graduated law school at Georgetown and all that. I'm not sure about her experience level, but she is smart enough to see this for what it is."

"What's that?" Bubba inquired.

"It is a golden opportunity to become famous in law enforcement circles by prosecuting the largest drug importation case in the history of the United States."

"What is the next step?" inquired Bubba, while motioning for Kelly to bring him another margarita.

"She will work with St. Pierre to form a task force, made up primarily of FBI, DEA, and Customs agents. They will include us and whatever agents they can get from local and parish agencies. They will need experienced local agents in order to be successful. I've been involved with the feds before. It's not pretty. FBI will want to be the lead agency because it's a matter of pride with them. DEA will want to take the lead because it is a drug case, and they know that the FBI has not had a good record with drug investigations. Customs officials will do what they are told because they are limited and lazy and don't like to work past five o'clock. Miss Duval will find that it will prove difficult to keep all of her puppies in a box."

The first meeting of the FBI-led federal task force took place in the conference room of the federal courthouse in Lafayette. Mac and Hungry Harv were the only state agents present, and at that time, there were no city or parish agents involved. When she introduced Mac to the FBI SAC (special agent in charge) for the state of Louisiana, he refused to offer his hand, looked sternly at Allison Duval, and said, "I thought this was going to be strictly a federal task force. You know we have regulations governing sensitive information with respect to local authorities."

Mac waited calmly for the SAC to finish his sentence, and said, "You can take your task force and shove it up your pompous ass." Mac smiled at the agent, and continued, "Have a nice day." He then turned with Hungry Harv and started for the door.

The SAC stood still, with his mouth open, as Allison Duval grabbed him by the shoulder, "This is their investigation. They invited us, not us them. They have valuable evidence regarding the largest drug importation in the history of this country."

"Wait, wait, please wait," she yelled at Mac, as he reached the door.

"I will not work with a counterfeit, pretentious asshole," said Mac.

The SAC, who was gathering his thoughts, walked over to Mac, "I apologize; I thought this was all federal. I guess I misunderstood some of the details."

Mac ignored the SAC, but stayed in the room. An agent from DEA made a speech about not having any available agents at the time, and an underling Customs agent said Bill O'Donnell was out of town. St. Pierre was appointed to the task force full time. Allison Duval said additional agents would be brought in soon.

"It's not much of a task force," St. Pierre said, "but we can bring in agents from other departments as we need them. I've been briefed by the Region II agents on the evidence they've collected thus far. There are some leads in the Detroit area, and I can get Michigan agents working on them asap. In the meantime I'll start working on federal arrest warrants for Rochon and Patout."

Mac and Hungry Harv handed out copies of statements taken and pictures of evidence that had been seized. After the meeting adjourned, Mac and Hungry Harv were taken to the U.S. Marshall's office and sworn in as federal agents, which theoretically would allow federal agencies to share information with them.

At four o'clock the following afternoon Agent St. Pierre and Allison Duval arrived at the Region II office. "I have some interesting information," St. Pierre informed Mac and Hungry Harv while they sipped coffee. "I learned that the suspect you identified as 'Shine' Armstrong is really Clint Armstrong. For the past several years, he has worked for a large-scale drug organization in Michigan headed up by two suspects known as Leigh Ray Starwood and Michael 'Vince' Vargo. Armstrong is a four-time loser, and he is willing to talk if the government places him in a witness protection program. He knows most of the larger players in the Starwood organization. He was in Lafayette in June, when the tug and barge were off-loaded, and he has general knowledge of the amounts of marijuana and cocaine that came through the area."

"Excellent," said Mac. "Maybe we can coordinate the timing on the arrests between Louisiana and Michigan. I feel certain Rochon and Patout will give it up. I'm not sure about the Fontenot brothers."

"There's more," said St. Pierre. "Armstrong says Starwood has ties to General Manuel Noriega in Panama. If that is the case, decisions regarding arrests and prosecutions will come from Washington. Noriega is a high level government snitch. Other agencies, such as the CIA, will want to be involved, if not take over completely. Politicians, not cops, will be making all the big decisions. It's got the potential for becoming a Chinese fire drill."

"Shit," said Hungry Harv, "nothing is ever easy."

"One last thing," said St. Pierre, "and you better hold on to your chair for this one. I learned why your Customs agent, Bill O'Donnell, has not been around. It seems that when the tug and barge left Columbia for Louisiana, O'Donnell knew about it."

"How could that be?" Mac placed his coffee on a desk and stood up, disbelieving.

"It turns out that Julio Nasser-David is a super wealthy architect, real estate developer, and world class pot dealer. But he does not own tugs and barges," St. Pierre continued. "Nasser-David gets his boats from a Columbian who calls himself Joseph Montana. Montana had furnished boats to Nasser-David and Starwood in the past, and he was part of the conspiracy to deliver a barge load to Louisiana. Nasser-David had promised Montana between five hundred thousand and one million dollars for the tug and boat. However, he was mad at Montana because of some previous dealings, and he paid Montana only thirty or forty thousand. A very pissed off Montana called U. S. Customs."

"So O'Donnell knew when and where the tug was to dock in Louisiana?" Hungry Harv observed.

"Not exactly," St. Pierre continued. "He knew the load was coming to Louisiana, but Starwood never gave up the location, which was very smart on his part."

"O'Donnell knew hundreds of thousands of pounds of marijuana and cocaine were coming to Louisiana, and he never informed the state police, a single sheriff's office, DEA, or the FBI. He wanted all the glory for himself," retorted Mac.

A white flash exploded in Mac's head; the revelation struck him like a bolt of lightening. He walked a short distance, turned, and looked at St. Pierre. "O'Donnell and Lieutenant Colonel Kazan are best friends, maybe even queer for each other. Simple Eddie knew about the operation and promised O'Donnell that the state police would stay out of it so O'Donnell could be a hero."

"This is the worst case of incompetency I've ever witnessed," Hungry Harv said. "Just when you think you've got it figured out, some shit happens that makes you figure it out all over again."

"What is the problem with your supervisor?" St. Pierre inquired.

"He is a self-righteous bastard who has a deep abiding distrust, if not hatred, for troopers who are more educated and successful than him. In his twisted mind, he thinks it makes him look bad."

"It's worse than you think," said St. Pierre. "You better sit down for this one."

"O'Donnell had customs agents spread out along the coast, checking every shipyard they had on file. An out-of-state agent was assigned Broussard Brothers and Fontenot's shipyard. He checked Broussard's first and found nothing unusual. He arrived at Fontenot's shortly after the barge was docked. He physically walked on the barge while it was still loaded with weed, but didn't make the connection. He left the yard thinking nothing was out of order."

"They had two chances at busting the load and failed miserably both times," Hungry Harv said, to no one in particular. "The next time that Irish pimp comes to this office I'm going to kick his ass so hard he'll land in Dublin."

"I don't think that will be happening," said St. Pierre. "The customs higher-ups think he will serve them better in Alaska, in a remote outpost. He's gone."

Mac waited patiently in his unit behind Troop I for Bugger Red to arrive in his blue and white state police helicopter. Fifteen minutes later, Bugger Red hovered and sat the copter down.   Bugger Red, whose mother had long ago had him diagnosed as being ADHD, literally jogged to Mac's unit, getting in while the chopper blades were still turning. He was exuberant and impulsive and had consistently refused the Adderall and Ritalin that had been advised when he was younger.

"Great to see you Mac, what's going on in coonass country?"

"We were having a little choir practice at Legend's this evening and thought you might want to join us. You will like the bartenders. While we are there, we can talk a little about finding some marijuana patches in the basin. Hungry Harv has some information, and I thought we could schedule some flights." It was never difficult to talk Bugger Red in to an evening of drinking and chasing women. Finding marijuana fields was secondary, but Bugger Red was all over it.

The sun had gone down and a brief rain had passed. Pools of water at various depths surrounded the covered patio of the bar. Mac, Bugger Red, and the other agents were drinking beer and eyeing Jared's bartenders while agent Bert DeBlanc, expert at all things technical, crawled into the backseat of Bugger Red's helicopter. It took less than twenty minutes to install miniature cameras that could be activated on demand. He had not asked Mac why. He did not want to know.

Early the next morning, Mac called the superintendent's secretary and requested an audience.

"He has a busy schedule today; what is the reason for the request?"

"I want to talk to him about Lieutenant Colonel Kazan."

"Please hold," she said.

Two minutes later she said, "He is busy today, how about next week?"

"Tell him I'm coming to see him today, and if I don't see him, I will be seeing the media."

At ten o'clock in the morning, Mac walked past the superintendent's secretary, knocked on Buck Carter's door, and let himself in. He did not sit down, knowing he could think better and faster while standing.

"This had better be good," said Carter, spinning around in his oversized custom leather chair.

"I'm requesting an Internal Affairs investigation that involves Lieutenant Colonel Kazan, and I wanted to inform you about it personally prior to my contact with them." Mac began.

Buck Carter leaned forward and placed his hands on his elbows on the antique oak desk. "Based on what, Lieutenant?"

"Customs agent Bill O'Donnell knew the barge load of marijuana and cocaine was coming to the Louisiana coast, and he knew the approximate location and time frame. Yet he did not relate that information to a single agency. Not the FBI, not DEA or state police or sheriff's office."

"What's your point, Mac?"

"O'Donnell and Kazan are best friends, if not more, and I have reason to believe that Kazan knew about the load and purposely did not pass the information along to our section so that his buddy could be a hero."

Carter let out a sigh, looked up at Mac, and said, "There is not going to be an investigation."

"Why not?"

"Lieutenant, you were in the military, you know how it works. A sergeant fucks up, the company commander takes the hit. A lieutenant commander on a ship fails in his duty, the ship's captain takes the hit. I appointed Kazan to his current position; if he is placed in a bad light, it is a reflection on my judgment. I can't allow that."

"What about the people we serve?" Mac asked. "Do you have any idea what the consequences are from a barge load of marijuana and cocaine coming into this country? The contents of that load have negative ramifications for the whole damn country." Mac was spitting worse than a Baptist preacher. "Not just families will be ruined, but whole communities may be devastated by this. Murders, thefts, corruption, and rapes across the country will occur because of our incompetence. Eighty-five percent of the crimes committed in this country have a connection to the drug trade. In case you haven't read the papers lately, it's become obvious that we are losing the so-called war on drugs. It's enough to fight the bad guys, but it's a real pain in the ass to have state police supervisors fuck things up."

Buck Carter sat quietly.

"Do you read your scripture, Colonel?"

"I go to church on regular basis, what is your point?"

"My point," said Mac, still standing in front of the massive desk, "can be found in Matthew, Chapter Sixteen. What good is it for a man to gain the whole world if he forfeits his soul?"

"I will not be lectured by a womanizing alcoholic narcotics agent. I've made my decision. There is a difference between incompetence and corruption. I'm ordering you not to go to Internal Affairs with this. Furthermore, if it leaks to the media I will personally have you walking a levee in Lake Providence with a muzzle loader. Am I clear?"

Mac looked Buck Carter in the eyes for a full fifteen seconds. Neither person blinked. Mac left the office without speaking, walking past the secretary, who tilted her head slightly, and rolled her eyes.

Mac smiled at her and said, "Your boss thinks hypocrisy is a leadership quality."

He had known nothing would be done but felt it was important to have Buck Carter know about Simple Eddie's incompetence. He also knew that a price had to be paid for his attitude.

"Fuck it," Mac said, as he walked toward his unit. "At least I can take my integrity to the grave with me."

Bert was waiting for Mac at the Region II office. "The helicopter is wired for sound and visual. What next?"

"Take Dee with you to the state police hanger in Baton Rouge. Stay there for a couple of days. The superintendent and his girlfriend go somewhere in the copter almost every day. All I want is one surveillance video, which you will give directly to me, and promptly forget that it was ever made."

"You are one crazy redneck," replied Bert, shaking his head.

CHAPTER 20
What To Do About the Swamp

During the drive to the narcotics office, Boogie Blanchard was sweating like a whore in church. He drove the old rusty diesel truck that belonged to the state police, not wanting to bring attention to himself by driving his new one. His cheeks were thin and perspiration glistened on his brown, leathery face. He inhaled deeply on a hand-rolled cigarette. He had put on a starched white shirt with blue snaps on the pockets. It was wet under the arms. He did not know why Sergeant Gaspard had called him in, but he knew it was not a good situation. "I wish I had listened to Freebase Freddy," he said out loud. "Freddy told me to wait. I shouldn't have bought a new house, or new cars. I should have waited."

"Hello Sarge. What can I do for you, sir?" Boogie said to Hungry Harv, as he entered the Region II conference room, where Mac, Agent St. Pierre, and the Troop I commander were sitting.

"The lieutenant wants to ask you a couple of questions," said Hungry Harv.

"Does it have something to do with horses, or maybe cows?" asked Boogie. "I don't know much about anything else." He watched Hungry Harv shut the door to the room. Mac noted that Boogie was fidgety and apprehensive.

"Sit down," ordered Hungry Harv. "I'll cut to the chase. We could have done this the hard way, involving your wife and kids, but we didn't want to embarrass you in front of them, nor at this point in time do we want to involve your wife in criminal activity, but we can if necessary. It depends on you, Boogie."

"What do you mean, sir?" Boogie asked, looking around, first at the Troop I commander, and then at Mac.

"Arrest you, is what we mean," said Mac. "But first I have to read you your rights." Mac looked at the form in front of him, and began, "You have the right to remain silent. I want you to

207

understand that anything you say can be used against you in a court of law. You have the right to an attorney, and if you cannot afford one, the court will appoint one for you at no charge. Do you understand your rights, Boogie?"

Boogie Blanchard, as predicted by Hungry Harv, placed his head in his hands and began to weep.

Mac quickly glanced at Hungry Harv and continued, "Boogie, we know that you are involved in smuggling activity, but at a low level. Sergeant Gaspard told me you have a nice wife and two wonderful little children. We don't really want to put you in jail, but the law is the law, and somebody has to take the fall. Of course, if you cooperate with us, we might be able to help you. I don't think a cowboy like you would do well in captivity." Mac chose his words to be simple and meaningful.

"I'll answer all your questions," said Boogie, openly crying. "I wasn't made to be locked up. I'd go crazy in a jail cell."

"Okay," said Mac. "Tell us how you bought the new house and cars."

"Freddy Patout gave me the money," Boogie stammered. "Him, Peter Rochon, and Boo Boo Delcambre. They asked me to drive some trucks from Abbeville to Lafayette. The first few times I drove for Freddy and Peter and they gave me as much as fifty thousand dollars. I drove more times for Boo Boo, but he paid me well, too. I didn't know there was that much money in the world. All I had was a broken down trailer, and my wife wanted a nice house for the kids."

While Boogie Blanchard was baring his soul Mac glanced at Hungry Harv and whispered, "Who the fuck is Boo Boo Delcambre?"

"Did you drive a tractor-trailer rig full of marijuana from Fontenot's shipyard?" asked Hungry Harv.

"Yes sir," Boogie replied. "It was full, but it wasn't the only one. There must have been a dozen of them pulling out of the yard. I didn't look at the other drivers. It was dark, and I didn't want to know who they were, but we all went to the same place. We left the trucks, with the keys in them, at the Union 76 truck stop in Lafayette."

"When did Freddy Patout pay you?" Mac questioned.

"Two weeks later. The money was in a brown paper bag."

Mac handed Boogie Blanchard a sheet of paper and instructed him to write down all the details he could remember. It took him over an hour. "We are not going to arrest you today, but you will be arrested. Sergeant Gaspard and I will do all we can to keep you out of jail, but your continued cooperation will be expected. Do you understand?"

"Yes sir," Boogie answered. He looked up at Mac, who was standing. "Uh, do you think this will cause me to lose my job with the state police?"

That same afternoon, the agents met again at Legend's to brainstorm the next step for the smuggling investigation and discuss plans for pending local investigations. Agent St. Pierre and Allison Duval came later. The sky was clear and the temperature cooler than normal. Most of the agents were gathered around the inside bar, near the drive-through window where they could eyeball leggy bartenders leaning over the beer box.

They were on the second round of margaritas when Hungry Harv spoke. "Why is Simple Eddie on our ass all the time?"

"Besides the fact that he is dysfunctional, inflexible, uneducated, and egotistical?" Mac responded. "Actually, there is a lot wrong with him. First, he has a grandiose sense of his own self-importance. He is always in a three-piece pin-striped suit. He has his fingernails polished like a woman. He gets a haircut twice a week. Even worse, he loves the feds," Mac glanced at St. Pierre and smiled.

"He may also have some gender problems," Mac continued. "And O'Donnell may have been more than a good friend. He thinks that he is special and entitled because he was promoted to lieutenant colonel. He is incompetent, but doesn't realize it. His personality is such that he can only feel good about himself when he causes other people to suffer. When people below him do well and are recognized for their works he feels harmed and threatened. He can't cope with it; in a perverted way, he thinks other people's success makes him look weak. He thrives on being an asshole. When he screws with subordinates it gives him a sense of power."

"He is a throwback to the old days of politics in Louisiana," interjected Bubba. "He considers arrogance and intimidation to be leadership qualities."

"The difference between a groove and a rut is the depth," said Hollywood. "Sounds like Simple Eddie is in a rut. Is there anything we can do about him?"

"Unfortunately, not right now," replied Mac. "However, the crown jewels don't stay in one family forever. His day will come. In the meantime, he will continue to do what he can to prevent us from being successful, and that's a shame because the state police and the people of Acadiana are the ones who suffer for it."

"What about Buck Carter," asked Hungry Harv. "Why doesn't he put Simple Eddie someplace where he can't do mischief?"

"It's a puzzle to me," said Mac, motioning for another cocktail. "For the life of me, I cannot see the connection. The word around headquarters is that Carter keeps himself locked up with his secretary. Maybe he doesn't realize Rome is burning."

Hollywood looked at the closest bartender, and said, "Hi, my name is Bob and I'm an alcoholic. Could you pour us another round of ritas?"

"What's next?" Hungry Harv said, referring to a plan of action for pending cases, and ready to get the agents back on track.

"First," said Mac, "I want us to forget about the pricks in Baton Rouge, and concentrate on having a good time being cops. Never lose your sense of humor. We work insane hours, for which we don't get credit, and our work is the most dangerous type of cop work. We do it for the challenge and the adrenaline rush and because we are making a difference. Most people live dull lives selling insurance or cars, and never know if they made a difference or not. Narcs don't have that problem. We have some good cases pending. How do y'all want to handle them?"

Hungry Harv spoke first. "I've got a track on Boo Boo Delcambre. He runs the livestock barn down in Abbeville. He has a kid in medical school. When we confront him with the information we obtained from Boogie, I'll tell him we believe his wife and son may be involved. It could ruin his son's career. If he loves his son he will give up the information rather than take that chance."

Hollywood was next. "Tatou and I will concentrate on the Mayor's son."

"Rooster and I can take a look at Blackie Cunningham, the playboy dude who is selling bad weed to his customers," said Bubba.

"There is a lot to do," agreed Mac. "But we'll get there; just don't forget to have fun along the way."

"No problem," said the cousins, smiling.

Monday morning, the cousins entered the back door of the Region II office, approached Mac's desk, and sat down.

"Remember Tee-Boy Batiste and Sharkey Senegal?" Hollywood spoke first.

"The entrepreneurs?" Mac responded.

"Ten-four," Hollywood continued, "We have them on the snitch payroll, and this weekend they walked us into a small house in the Saints Streets, where we purchased some coke and weed from the former mayor's son and his girlfriend. We did a warrant on the house and seized a pound of coke, five pounds of weed, some pills, and a handgun. The handgun was with the dope, which ups the ante. The district attorney will have to prosecute this one."

"Maybe, and maybe not," interjected Tatou.

"Have you booked them into LPCC?" asked Mac.

"Not yet," answered Hollywood. "They are locals, and neither one is a flight risk. The girl is from a local rich family. She lawyered up, wanted to call her daddy. The dude wants to trade up."

"Okay," said Mac, waiting for Tatou to get to the point.

"It gets better," said Tatou, clearly having a good time with the information. "He is willing to give up his source of drugs and his clientele. He even offered to let us wire him up and arrest his customers after purchasing his drugs. I asked him to meet me yesterday at a local hotel to go over his customer base. He told me to pack a lunch and bring lots of paper. It was an extensive list, but most were small-time users, mainly college students. However, he has one customer you may be interested in."

"Who?"

"A district judge from Vermilion Parish," said Tatou, grinning.

211

"Shit, why me?" said Mac. He let out a slow breath, sighed, and finally asked, "What's your plan?"

"The dude said the judge just buys personal use marijuana, usually a few ounces per week. He charges him three hundred dollars, which is a break-even price for him. I asked him why he sold it so cheaply, and he laughed at the irony of the situation, and said, 'You never know when you might need a judge.'"

Mac sat still, thinking about the situation. A rich girl, just as guilty as the dude she lives with, will likely not be prosecuted because her father has connections. A dealer, who is the son of a former mayor, whose father is friendly with a former governor, can probably get the charges dropped as quickly as the girl. And it's just as doubtful that the district attorney will prosecute a judge from the same judicial district.

"Nothing good can come from this," Mac looked at the cousins.

They waited.

"What the hell? A judge should know better. I'll contact the feds and see if they want a pearl like the judge. In the meantime, don't discuss this with anyone. Let's keep it close."

First thing Tuesday morning, Mac walked into Allison Duval's office where she and Agent St. Pierre were waiting. Mac explained the situation about the mayor's son selling marijuana to a local judge. "Our district attorney might find the situation awkward dealing with this, would the U.S. Attorney's Office be interested?"

"You bet," Allison said, knowing the arrest would make headlines and place her in the spotlight. "Let's move on it as soon as possible. Keep me informed on your progress and let me know how I can help. Also, I would like to be present at the arrest, and if you don't mind, I would like to handle the press release."

"No problem," said Mac. "I'll be in touch."

The following afternoon, Mac, the cousins, and the dude met in an interview room at the Region II office. A secure phone, registered to a fictitious name, was wired to a tape recorder. The dude called the district judge at his office in Abbeville.

"Hey Judge, it's me, Billy. I just scored some of the best weed I've ever had, and I wanted to ask you if you wanted some before it's all gone."

"I don't know who you are, or what you are talking about," answered a nervous judge, "and don't ever call my office again." The line went dead.

Hollywood and Mac looked at each other, and then at the dude. "What the hell was that all about?" Mac questioned.

"Somebody tipped him off," said Tatou, looking at the dude.

"Hey, it wasn't me," the dude said. "This is my ass we are talking about. I swear I never told a soul, not even my girlfriend."

Later that afternoon Mac called Allison and briefed her on the situation. "Meet me and the guys for a beer after work; let's talk about it."

"Why?"

"Something went wrong. Let's find out what it was so we don't make the same mistake again."

The sun was setting when Allison walked into the bar with Agent St. Pierre. She was wearing black pants with a matching black silk shirt that hung loosely over her breasts. A burnt orange broach was pinned over one breast. The black widow was consistent, imposingly tall with heels, and also breathtakingly beautiful.

"I think she may cause my eyes to bleed," Mac said to Hollywood.

She walked over to an old wooden booth in the corner of the bar and sat down with Mac and the cousins. Mac ordered drinks and got to the point.

"Allison, did you tell anyone, anyone at all, about the judge?"

There was no answer for several seconds, while she thought about her response. "I was excited about the prospect of prosecuting a district judge, but I felt I had to inform my boss. I confronted him shortly before coming here. He admitted to informing the district attorney to clear the way for federal prosecution. He said his conversation with the district attorney was confidential. Busting a judge would have been huge. Did I screw it up?"

"No," answered Mac, "but your boss did. It's not complicated. Your boss called the D A to give him a heads up on

Roy W. Frusha

the investigation. It's the professional thing to do. However, this is Louisiana. It's different than Texas, or just about any other state, for that matter. The district attorney, or more likely, one of his assistants, called the judge and warned him, stopping the investigation dead in the water."

"Why would he do that?"

"Who knows? Maybe they were friends, or maybe he just didn't want the fifteenth judicial district to get a black eye. Maybe it's just politics. The judge owes him now, and will have to openly support him in the next election."

"We try to objectively and thoroughly analyze our investigations, "said Bubba, who was becoming inebriated. "In our type of law enforcement, we have to anticipate problems and find answers to the problems, sometimes before the crime is actually committed. However, when you are up to your ass in alligators, it's hard to remind yourself that your initial objective was to drain the swamp. God, I hate politics."

"Jolie Blonde," by Rod Bernard, was playing on the jukebox, when Mac nodded at the bartender and another round appeared. Two hours later Mac was visibly weaving as he attempted to walk Allison across the parking lot to her car. He noted that she seemed perfectly sober.

"Need a ride home, Mac?"

"No, my house isn't far. I'm fine."

Just before getting into her car, she smiled at Mac and said, "Sorry about the mistake at work. It won't happen again. And thanks for the drinks. I'm also sorry the night didn't go exactly like you hoped, but don't give up, there may be other opportunities. By the way, I noticed that the bartender was giving you singles and me doubles. Nice try."

"It's going to be easier for you to find Jimmy Hoffa than get into her pants," Hollywood said, as Mac stumbled toward his car.

"The last time I had a meaningful sexual experience," Mac retorted, "was my last visit to the proctologist."

CHAPTER 21
The Round Up

Christmas had come and gone with little fanfare. Traditionally, it was a slow time for the agents, but not because dopers stopped dealing drugs during the holidays. Drugs were just as prevalent in December as any other month, if not more so, but most of the agents were married, had kids, and it had become a tradition to burn some of the hundreds of hours of compensatory time that had been acquired during the year. It was family time for those agents with a family, and party time for those agents without families. For Mac and Bubba and the other agents who were veterans, it was a reminder of R and R, as they had called it during the war. It was typically a wet month, and the heavy rains reminded Mac of the Vietnam monsoons, which lasted from October to April. He had experienced better holidays.

A short period of Rest and Recuperation during the Vietnam War meant as little as three days in a "camp town" that had been established close to an area of operations. It was cheap girls and hot beer, but it was better than being in the bush. A week off meant a trip to Bac My An, also known as China Beach, near Da Nang, where the girls were prettier and the beer was cold, and penicillin was in high demand. Two weeks of annual leave meant going to an exotic destination. A few of the grunts went to Hong Kong, but most went to Bangkok. One Marine had written his mother that he was going to "Bang Cock," Thailand, to rest.

Mac's personal favorite had been Taipei, which was safe and clean. Chiang Kai-shek was still alive and the country seemed to be governed by a rule of discipline. Unlike America, Taiwan had little tolerance for illicit drugs and petty criminals. Regardless of the destination, young men fresh from the killing grounds of Vietnam pursued the same source of R and R. They sought stinking brothels with live music, twenty-five cent beer, and young girls who called themselves Trixi or Super Sexy Sandy, or some similar trick name. It was five dollars for thirty minutes, but it never took that long. When they returned to their regular units, they were more exhausted than when they left. It didn't matter; when you are a nineteen-year-old killer, you are bulletproof and invisible.

While Mac was in Taipei, Bugger Red had taken his R and R to Hawaii to meet his wife. Bugger Red had been married only six months before he was deployed to Vietnam. He had sent her the money for the plane trip to the exotic island and had waited for her patiently at the airport. She never arrived. He later said to Mac, "That's what you call a clue."

The last investigation of the year came in late December, when Hungry Harv and Agent St. Pierre had confronted Boo Boo Delcambre at his residence in Maurice. Delcambre seemed almost relieved that he had been caught. He gave statements regarding as many as twenty loads he had done with various organizations. The only thing he asked was to keep his son out of it. "I'll go to prison, if I have to," he said, "but please don't arrest my son. He has only one year left in medical school." Most of the loads Delcambre moved involved Freebase Freddy Patout and Peter Rochon. "There were so many boats of marijuana going up Vermilion Bayou," Delcambre explained, "that one night two boats from two separate operations ran into each other in the dark. One of the loads was Freddy's, so he pulled out his AR-15 and ripped off the other boat. He put all of the marijuana into a motor home, and drove it to Lafayette."

Boo Boo Delcambre was fully cooperative, and seemed glad that his smuggling career was over. He and Hungry Harv had clicked, and Delcambre gave him a detailed list of the many loads he had done, some of which were for Freebase Freddy, and some of which he had organized. He showed Hungry Harv solid gold belt buckles he had purchased with the smuggling proceeds, along with receipts from renting private jets for Vegas trips. For the past few years, Boo Boo Delcambre had lived the good life. Hungry Harv thanked him for his cooperation, and informed him he would be booked at a later date.

Weather in Louisiana is extreme, and the second week in January was bitter cold. The sky had cleared after the December rains, but the east wind was up and the humidity excessive, even for coastal Louisiana, which is heavily affected by continental and marine influences. The sky was clear, but the temperature had dropped to below forty degrees. Hungry Harv, who hated cold weather, said to Ruby Rae, "It's colder than a polar bear's ass out there."

The meeting between state and federal agents to organize the "round-up," as they called it, took place at the federal building in Lafayette. Mac had borrowed agents from around the state, and had called in Bugger Red and his people for air surveillance. All state evidence regarding the tug and barge had been turned over to the U. S. Attorney, and Allison Duval had obtained warrants for James and Jude Fontenot, Freebase Freddy Patout, Peter Rochon, Boo Boo Delcambre and Boogie Blanchard. Most defendants would be charged with at least two counts of engaging in a continuing criminal enterprise, five counts of conspiracy to import marijuana, and at least one count of conspiracy to possess with intent to distribute cocaine, and five substantive counts of drug importation and distribution. Everyone in the room was aware that these arrests would lead to other arrests, as defendants gave evidence and "traded up" in order to avoid jail time. Future arrests, across the country, and maybe out of country, would be forthcoming. State agents would assist in serving the federal warrants, and at the same time complete the investigation on the mayor's son and Blackie Cunningham.

Mac began the meeting with a discussion of the Operations Plan, using the SMEAC (situation, mission, execution, administration, and command and communications) structure that he knew would be universally understood. SMEAC is the five paragraph military order that was used by Marines in Vietnam, and every other war, to organize infantry action. It was simple and could be utilized and adapted easily into raid tactics. Mac explained the situation first, detailing the sequence of evidence and events leading to the meeting, explaining cautionary actions, and detailing the duties of all supporting agencies. Each defendant was discussed, giving detailed physical descriptions, locations, background information, tendencies toward violence, addresses, hangouts, and associates. Specific duties of each agency and team were detailed in the mission statement, including air support by Bugger Red. Rules of engagement, contingency planning, coordinating instructions, time schedules, order of movement and rendezvous locations were covered in the execution stage. Administration included information about where the defendants would be transported and who would interrogate them. It also covered evidence procedures and weapons and ammunition to be used. Command and communications was last, and Mac covered the chain of command, equipment to be used, radio frequencies, call signs, and the location of a centralized mobile command post. By ten o'clock in the morning, the agents were rolling.

The cousins, Tatou Breaux and Hollywood Bourdelle, met with Bert DeBlanc at a northside motel and wired a confidential informant for sound. Bugger Red was circling overhead in a state police helicopter.

The informant was a small-time Lafayette dealer who regularly purchased his marijuana from Blackie Cunningham. The weed had been splashed with saltwater when being transported from a mother ship to a fishing boat in Vermilion Bay, and the informant was out five grand. Cunningham had refused to refund the informant's money or replace the marijuana, and the informant was pissed. He had simply walked into the Region II office and offered up Cunningham on a silver platter.

"Am I going to be prosecuted if I help you make a case on Blackie?" The informant asked.

"Absolutely not," said Hollywood, "though it will be apparent to Cunningham that you gave him up."

"I was planning on moving to New Orleans, anyway," replied the informant. "Fuck him; payback is a bitch."

"What goes around comes around," agreed Bert. "How are you going to you set this up?"

"Blackie is greedy. He has a good job selling oilfield supplies, but he likes cocaine and ladies. He trades it for sex, and he likes to set up his clients with coke and women. He supports his expensive habits by selling large quantities of marijuana. I don't know where he gets it, but he always has a supply."

"Will he be armed?" Bert inquired.

"No way, Blackie wouldn't dirty his hands. Besides, he thinks he can get out of anything."

"What does he expect from us today?" Tatou inquired.

"I said I had a couple of guys with some money who didn't want to go through a middle man. The deal is set for a first-time purchase of ten pounds for twenty thousand cash. I made it plain you'd want more later on. Money is so important to him, he's become careless. Plus, like I said, he thinks he is invisible to the law, that he can't be touched."

The meeting was set for noon in the parking lot on the north side of Blackham Coliseum, between the arena and the cattle barn, almost in dead center of Lafayette. The coliseum had been replaced by the Cajundome, and was seldom used except for an occasional rodeo or Cajun music festival. The parking lot was grass and shell, and there would be nothing unusual about a few cars parked in the lot. The cousins waited in Hollywood's unit with the informant. Bert was parked on the south side of the coliseum monitoring the conversation from a hand-held radio. Blackie Cunningham arrived alone in a late model Ford pickup five minutes after noon. He was of average height and weight, and Hollywood noted the metallic, wavy hair over his ears, but short of his shoulders. His face was pale with high cheek bones, and a red, lumpy nose from too much cocaine. Behind tinted glasses, transparent eyes showed no expression. He wiped a runny nose with a white handkerchief as he approached the cousins.

Introductions were made and Hollywood gave Cunningham twenty grand in one hundred dollar bills which had been marked and copied for court proceedings. Tatou took possession of ten pounds of marijuana which had been tightly wrapped in duct tape in one pound quantities. They watched as Cunningham drove north on Johnston Street. Bert pulled out behind Cunningham, listening carefully to Bugger Red, who was following Cunningham at eight hundred feet overhead. The cousins followed behind Bert. Cunningham turned east on Pinhook Road, and continued another four miles, until, just prior to reaching Broussard, he pulled into T-Boy's Store N Lock. Bert and the cousins parked at a nearby gas station, and waited for Bugger Red to give them instructions.

Once Cunningham had opened a storage bin, Bugger Red gave the cousins a signal and they moved in. They screeched to a stop on each side of a stunned Cunningham, but he had already locked the storage bin. The cousins pulled weapons and pointed them at Cunningham, screaming, "State police, get down on the ground." A pat down revealed no weapons, just a greasy comb.

Bert read Cunningham his Miranda rights, after which Tatou said, "We would like to search your bin, will you give us permission?"

"I know my rights; I want a lawyer," was all Cunningham said. Hollywood couldn't decide if he was just an empty headed dumb fuck, or just confident that he was not in trouble.

"I'll call for a dog and some lock cutters," said Bert.

Tatou cuffed Cunningham and placed him in the backseat of his unit. "I want to call my lawyer," he said.

"I'd like to take a bubble bath with Bridgette Bardot," Tatou replied, "but it's probably not going to happen."

Thirty minutes later, a member of the criminal patrol unit arrived with a Labrador retriever. The handler started four doors down from Cunningham's storage bin. When he reached Cunningham's bin, the lab scratched furiously at the door. Hollywood quickly wrote out a search warrant and drove the short distance to the Lafayette Courthouse for a judge's signature. Once the paper was signed, Bert cut the lock and Tatou located eight bales of marijuana in the back of the bin. A truck was called for and the agents loaded three hundred eighty-six pounds of weed into the back for transfer to the Troop I vault. Hollywood sat on the bales and waved at the bums and dopers hanging around the streets as they passed through the "Four Corners" area of town. They whistled, waved, and shouted, "Throw me some, mister."

At the same time Hollywood was waving at the dopers hanging around "Four Corners," Agent Bubba Green simply phoned the mayor's son and his girlfriend and requested that they meet him at the jail so they could be formally booked. Bubba allowed them to prepare bond in advance, so they would not have to spend the night locked down.

After booking the mayor's son, Bubba drove south to Maurice and knocked on the door of Boogie Blanchard's new house. Boogie answered the door and immediately started bawling. "I can't stay in jail," he said, "I'll go crazy."

"I know," said Bubba, "that's why we arranged for you to be released on your own recognizance."

Boogie stood still, but stopped crying.

"You look like a monkey staring at a wrist watch," Bubba said.

"I don't know what recognizance means," Boogie answered.

"It means that a bond has already been entered before the federal magistrate, promising you will appear when called and give your testimony at a later date. We are just going to do some paperwork, and then you will be released."

Bubba placed Boogie Blanchard in the front seat of his unit for transport to LPCC. He saw no reason to cuff him.

While Bubba was picking up Boogie Blanchard, Rooster Milam was on the outskirts of Maurice arresting Boo Boo Delcambre. "I knew you was coming, sooner or later, officer. Sergeant Gaspard had told me to be ready, so here I am. Just please don't cuff me in front of my wife or kid."

"I see no reason to cuff you at all," said Rooster, and they departed for LPCC.

Two hours later, that same afternoon, Paul St. Pierre, and other agents from the FBI, drove to the Vermilion Bayou home of Freebase Freddy Patout.

"We have a federal arrest warrant for you, Mr. Patout," Agent St. Pierre said.

Freebase Freddy Patout hesitated, started to say something, but only tightened his jaw, and then sighed. He did not ask any questions, nor did he ask for a lawyer. He was patted down for weapons, cuffed, and escorted to St. Pierre's unit. He did not say one word during the trip to the Lafayette jail. Mac assumed he wanted to think about the situation and talk it over with Peter Rochon prior to making any statements. It was a smart move.

At almost the same time Freebase Freddy was being arrested, Buzzy Bonin and some federal agents arrived at the Abbeville home of Peter Rochon. "I have a federal warrant for your arrest," said Buzzy. Rochon only shook his head dejectly.

"I knew this day was coming," Rochon said, quietly and passively. He seemed withdrawn and a little sad. "I've been praying about it."

Mac had specifically requested that he and Hungry Harv be allowed to serve the warrants on James and Jude Fontenot. They were quiet as Mac drove along state Highway 696 in Vermilion Parish toward James Fontenot's dilapidated residence.

Hungry Harv watched a swamp rabbit step nervously out of a briar thicket on the levee. "Those are good in a brown gravy," he said.

"I don't know about Jude Fontenot, but James will resist arrest violently," Mac said, looking over at Hungry Harv.

"Maybe if we go in with guns out," replied Hungry Harv.

"No, you don't understand my meaning. James Fontenot will resist, but I don't want to have to take him to the hospital before we book him," Mac spoke with more emphasis.

"Ooh," responded Hungry Harv, with sudden recognition. He smiled, "I understand."

They drove slowly down the potholed shell driveway to Fontenot's house, almost into the front yard, parking between the chained pit bull and the front door of the neglected old house.

James Fontenot, wearing the same work boots, torn jeans and dirty tee shirt opened the door, and threw his head back when he recognized Mac. "What the fuck do you want?" he screamed at Mac and walked menacingly toward him.

Fontenot did not see the blow coming; he only saw white light and felt something large and powerful stop his heart, and take all of the air from his lungs. Hungry Harv had bent his legs slightly, came from a crouch, and landed a giant fist into Fontenot's solar plexus. Fontenot did not know he could feel that much pain. His eyes bulged, and he fell to the ground, wanting to puke, but could not get enough air even for that. He was in the fetal position with his mouth open when Mac stepped over him, pulled his arms behind his back, and cuffed him.

"You have the right to remain silent, and all that other shit," said Mac.

They picked up Fontenot, and Hungry Harv held him while Mac opened the door to his unit. "You hit him so hard you knocked his dick into his watch pocket. I think he pissed his pants."

The last arrest of the day occurred in Detroit, Michigan, when federal agents picked up Clint "Shine" Armstrong. Probable cause for the warrant was based on evidence that Mac and Hungry Harv had found when searching the Ridge Road residence back in June. It was flimsy, but enough. Armstrong was a loser and wanted no more of prison. He was offered the federal witness protection program, and he gladly took it. He would give the feds whatever they wanted.

It seemed like the snowstorm would last weeks, and Vince Vargo was contemplating a trip to Grand Cayman to visit Starwood when Detroit FBI agents knocked on the door of his Barton Hills mansion in Ann Arbor Township. "Oh well," he said soberly, when he was shown the warrant. "What the hell!"

Within six hours of Vargo's arrest, a team of international agents, led by the FBI, showed up at Starwood's beachside residence in Grand Cayman. Starwood was good natured; as one agent later said, "He was very likable, but not talkative. He wanted time to think about his situation." Their arrests would be front page news in the Detroit Free Press, the seventh largest newspaper in the nation, for three days in a row. Additionally, the Press flew an investigative reporter to Lafayette to interview Mac and Hungry Harv for specific details regarding the state police narcotics section's role in the investigation.

While Mac and the other agents were celebrating a successful "round up," Simple Eddie Kazan was in Buck Carter's office.

"That bunch of cowboys in the Region II Office arrested the sons of the number one Mason in the state," said Simple Eddie. "If that's not bad enough, they arrested a former mayor's son, and the mayor is good friends with former governor Edwards, who, by the way, still has powerful friends in the legislature."

"How does that affect us?" Carter asked.

"It was in the paper that the mayor's son was dealing mostly to college kids. Now the vice president of the university is calling the governor's office complaining because the article makes it look like there are drugs on his campus, and he doesn't like the bad publicity. And if that's not enough, the pricks gave interviews to the Detroit Free Press. The whole damn country will be reading about them."

"What do you suggest I do about it, Colonel?" Buck Carter was tired of hearing about Region II narcotics agents. "We can't fire Lieutenant McCullough for doing his job."

"Nobody has ever been fired from state police for doing too little," Simple Eddie retorted, "but several troopers have been fired for doing too much. I want to transfer that fucker to the road. In fact, I want to transfer the lot of them. I can replace them with personnel from the troop."

"Okay," said Buck Carter, looking out of his window, toward the capitol. "Go to Human Resources and make it happen, but keep it as quiet as possible."

Smoke-colored clouds splashed with traces of sunlight were coming in from the Gulf on Monday morning. The moisture in the air was almost tangible. As Mac began walking toward Region II office, he looked up at two crows that were cawing from the top of a nearby pecan tree. Not one leaf was left on the old tree.

When he walked into his office, the troop commander was sitting across from his desk sipping on a cup of coffee.

"Sit down, Mac," was all he said.

"What's up, Captain?" Mac said, though he suspected the reason for the visit and somber face.

"I have some bad news for you Mac," he started. "A shake-up is in the works. Most of your agents are being transferred. Some will go to work at the troop, and some are going to the gaming division. Their transfers will be coming in writing later this week. For whatever reason, they will not put your transfer in writing, but, effective immediately, you are transferred to the Troop. Look, you have a college education and considerable leadership experience; I need a good man to be my executive officer. It will be straight days with weekends off."

Mac said nothing, attempting to show as little emotion as possible.

"You okay?" the troop commander asked.

"Sure, happy as a puppy with two dicks," Mac said, in a derisive tone.

"What?"

"I said I'm as happy as a Mexican that has a truck that runs. Who is taking over the narcotics section?"

"One of my shift lieutenants."

"Does he have any investigative experience?" Mac asked.

"None," said the captain. "I think the general idea is that if he doesn't know how to run narcotics investigations, there won't be any investigations. Therefore, there will be no controversy; it's state police leadership at its best."

"I don't know whether to scratch my watch or wind my ass," Mac replied.

The captain looked at Mac for a moment. "You may have a contemptuous attitude, but at least you have a sense of humor. Come with me and I'll show you your new office."

"What the hell?" said Mac. "At least I'll be working for someone that has a vocabulary with multi-syllable words." He stood to follow the troop commander, saying, "Louie, this could be the beginning of a beautiful relationship," quoting a line from "Casablanca."

The captain turned and smiled. "Don't call me Louie, and you ain't Humphrey Bogart."

EPILOGUE

Hungry **Harv Gaspard** was transferred to Troop I as a desk sergeant. It was the first time in nine years that he had to put on the blue uniform of the Louisiana State Police patrol division. The troop commander sent him to the barbershop three times before he would obtain a regulation haircut. The cousins knew that Hungry Harv would eat a large lunch because he was depressed. They watched and waited quietly from the squad room, until Hungry Harv walked down the hall and into the men's room. They gave him precisely enough time to enter a stall and sit down, after which they threw a three foot corn snake under the stall, and turned the bathroom lights off. Damage to the men's room was extensive.

****

The **cousins** were separated for the first time since they had joined the state police. Anthony "Hollywood" Bourdelle was sent to protective services in Baton Rouge. He received a temporary promotion to sergeant and was assigned to protect the governor's wife. They traveled extensively together. If the governor had known Hollywood, he would not have allowed the transfer. Eventually, the cameras overlooking the mansion swimming pool had to be disconnected, lest some tapes fell into the wrong hands.

****

Bennett **"Tatou" Breaux** returned to shift work at Troop I. Always the hard worker, he was promoted to sergeant within a year and lieutenant in another two years. Against all odds, he would eventually become a high ranking state police supervisor.

****

Bertrand **"Bert" DeBlanc** was transferred to a local drug task force, and continued working along the same lines as he had with

Region II Narcotics. Bert's father was too well connected for Simple Eddie to do him any real harm.

****

Grady **"Rooster" Milam** stayed in the narcotics arena, but was relocated to a newly created Morgan City field office. It turned out to be a good gig, and Rooster completed his career working at that location.

****

Buzzy **Bonin** was transferred to the state police gaming division, where he was allowed to continue developing his investigative skills. He was eventually promoted to sergeant.

****

Otis **Ray Coody**, who was never totally comfortable as an undercover agent, requested a transfer to Troop D in Lake Charles, which allowed him to move back to his hometown of DeRidder, Louisiana. He immersed himself in his hobbies of hunting and fishing. He supplemented his state police income by peddling moonshine to the tourists who fished at Bundick Lake.

****

Duane **"Dee" Pellerin** had kept a low profile, avoiding all things political. He would remain in the narcotics section, and become attached to the federal task force that that had been created to investigate smuggling activities in coastal Louisiana.

****

The only agent to create a stir was **D**arrell **"Bubba" Green**. Bubba quit the state police, but he did it in a way that would be remembered and discussed for generations. Bubba had been at his new job with Troop I for less than a week when he drove his marked unit to headquarters in Baton Rouge. He walked into Buck Carter's office unannounced, and standing before a stunned superintendent, and without muttering a word, Bubba removed his gun, shirt, car keys, pants and boots, dropping them on the floor in front of the massive oak desk. He walked out of Carter's office in a v-neck tee shirt and white boxer shorts, winking at Carter's secretary on the way out. No one ever learned how he returned to Lafayette.

****

Marcelle Stevens was dumped by her married boyfriend. She became a traveling nurse, and eventually moved to California. Mac never heard from her again.

****

Allison Duval, aka La Contessa Negra (the Black Widow), worked diligently on the smuggling case for almost five years. The Bulldog investigation led to the Masterblaster load, the Lady Mauricette load, the Bobby M load, the Shreveport load, the Seamaid load, and the Dallas conspiracy. Investigative areas moved from Louisiana to North Carolina to Michigan to Florida to Columbia and finally to Panama. The continuing criminal enterprise became a massive bureaucractic quagmire of egos, trials and appeals. She wanted judicial stardom but was denied the opportunity to prosecute Noriega. After five frustrating years, Allison quit her federal job rather than be transferred out of state. She became a Lafayette prosecutor and married Agent Duane "Dee" Pellerin.

****

One month after Mac was transferred to the Troop, the governor's office received an anonymous package from the Lafayette post office. An aid informed the governor that he should take a look at the short film clip and pictures that were enclosed. An incredulous governor watched Buck Carter having sex with his secretary while circling over Baton Rouge in the back of a clearly marked state police helicopter. Shortly thereafter, the superintendent's secretary was terminated by the Director of the Division of Administration. Buck Carter was allowed to retire. He left his wife and three kids, married his secretary, and moved to Florida where he obtained a job teaching at a local university.

****

Colonel Buck Carter's replacement was an African American state police major from North Louisiana. Mac arranged for an appointment with the new superintendent. It took less than a minute to hand him a copy of a tape recording. The new superintendent listened without emotion to Lieutenant Colonel Edward "Simple Eddie" Kazan using the "n" word to demean the deceased Trooper Patrick "D K" Celestine, and the Negro race in general. Mac left the office without further discussion. Simple Eddie resigned from the state police rather than be demoted.

****

Miles "Mac" McCullough had been the Troop I Executive Officer for almost two years when his replacement in the narcotics section developed nervous tics and became irritable and prone to sudden mood swings. He had also lost considerable weight. Mac had paid no attention to the differences, until the replacement complained to the troop commander that people were following him, that his office phone was tapped, and that people could be heard talking in the attic above his office. At this time, Mac called Internal Affairs in Baton Rouge and calmly suggested that the Region II Narcotics Section vault be audited. It was discovered that many of the inventory records were missing or incomplete, but eventually it was determined that between fifty and one hundred pounds of cocaine were missing, along with over two hundred thousand in cash. The new narcotics commander was subsequently arrested and convicted, spending one year in the Lafayette Parish Correctional Center as a trustee.

One week after the replacement was arrested Mac McCullough was asked to return to his old position as the Region II narcotics commander. "On one condition," Mac said, "only if Hungry Harv comes with me as a second in command."

****

Leigh Ray Starwood transported massive amounts of marijuana and cocaine into the United States from South America. In the summer of 1983, over three hundred thousand pounds of marijuana and cocaine were successfully off-loaded in Banker, Louisiana into waiting tractor-trailer rigs. He testified that he had been introduced to Louisiana smuggler Alfred Patout while in Florida visiting a former LSU track star who was a friend and associate. He also said that Fontenot's shipyard "was the best offload site he had ever used." Drugs from the barge were transported to Michigan and Ohio for distribution throughout the northeast. The load had a street value well in excess of seven hundred million dollars. He was arrested at his mansion in Grand Cayman Island. He was later convicted of two counts of continuing criminal enterprise, six counts of conspiracy to possess marijuana with intent to distribute, three counts of conspiracy to possess with intent to distribute cocaine, and five counts of importation and distribution. He admitted to making three hundred fifty thousand dollars per month in interest on the money he had put in Panamanian banks with the help of General Noriega. He explained, "That will at least pay for your champagne and women." He had lived the lifestyle of the rich and famous. He had millions in the bank, mansions, boats, a Mercedes in his garage, and a Lear jet in his hanger. He had been partying with a ruler of a country, and for a while, had been relatively free from apprehension by U. S. authorities. He was also quoted as having stated, "I actually believe that I can reconcile my problems at some future point through my work in Panama." And he did. He gave testimony against his partying buddy, General Manuel Noriega. He gave detailed explanations to the authorities about how Noriega provided airport and dock access, armored trucks, armed bodyguards, limousines, and exclusive bank accounts. He spent less than four years in prison, and he was allowed to keep twenty million dollars in drug proceeds in return for his testimony against General Noriega and others. He currently lives in a waterfront mansion in Florida.

****

In **1989**, the United States invaded Panama and General Manuel Antonio Noriega Moreno was overthrown and arrested in Operation Nifty Package. He was initially held as a prisoner of war and then transported to the United States for criminal prosecution. He was tried in 1992 in Florida, and was convicted of eight counts of drug trafficking, money laundering, and racketeering. He was sentenced to forty years in prison.

****

Michael "Vince" Vargo rode the coattails of his associate, Leigh Starwood, and served less than five years in a federal prison. He retired and currently lives in a prestigious, gated neighborhood in Michigan. He drives a new porche every year. As Vargo predicted when he was in high school, he would never work a day in his life.

****

Julio Ceasar Nasser-David and his ex-wife, Sheila Nasser Arana, admitted to sending more than thirty loads of cocaine and marijuana into the United States. In 1998 U. S. authorities seized 180 million in Swiss bank accounts from the couple. It was the "biggest-ever cash criminal forfeiture in U. S. history." Attorney General Janet Reno split the money with Switzerland. Nasser-David was sentenced to prison in Colombia. He died of natural causes shortly after being released.

****

Clint **"Shine" Armstrong** was placed into the federal witness program. No one knows his whereabouts.

****

Sherry **Cox** was indicted, but never prosecuted.

****

James **Fontenot** was never formally indicted in the Bulldog investigation. However, in the mid- 1990s, he was charged with conspiracy to possess, with the intent to distribute, in excess of one thousand pounds of marijuana. He was sentenced to one year in prison and two years probation. He was out in less than a year. None of the million dollars he received for his participation in the Bulldog smuggling venture was recovered.

****

Jude **Fontenot** was charged with simple possession of marijuana. The charge was refused. His only convictions were DWI and reckless operation of a vehicle. He quit the family business and moved to New Orleans. Like his brother, James, he was allowed to keep his million dollars.

****

Boo **Boo Delcambre** cooperated fully with federal and state authorities, giving detailed written and verbal information leading to the arrests and convictions of Alfred Patout, Peter Rochon, and others. He admitted he was guilty and would not accept the services of a lawyer. His only request was to give a statement to the federal judge before sentencing. In his statement, he spoke of committing offenses against his country, his community, and his family. It was a heartfelt emotional appeal for understanding rather than compassion. When he was finished, the normally intransigent Allison Duval had tears in her eyes. At Duval's request, the judge sentenced Delcambre to five years probation.

Delcambre returned to Vermilion Parish and his old job at the cattle barn.

****

Blackie Cunningham smiled throughout his ordeal. Charges of distribution and possession with intent to distribute were dropped. It was later learned that his sister was dating the assistant district attorney for prosecution of drug cases in Lafayette Parish. Mac was quoted as saying, "At least the state police did not have to return the almost four hundred pounds of pot they seized from him."

****

Peter Rochon gave investigators a detailed account of how Starwood instructed him and Alfred Patout to fly to Detroit and check into a motel, after which an unknown person knocked on their door and gave them the keys to a rented Lincoln Town Car located in the motel parking lot near their room. Less than ten words were said between them. They drove the Lincoln south toward Louisiana for one hundred miles before stopping at a rest area and looking in the trunk. It contained a suitcase with four million dollars in cash, one million each for Rochon, Patout, and the Fontenot brothers. Before being sentenced to seven years in a federal prison, Rochon experienced a religious conversion. He said, "I'm going to preach the gospel of Jesus Christ, whether in jail or out." He was true to his word, but died of natural causes less than two years after becoming a free man.

****

Freebase Freddy Patout was sentenced to seven years in a federal prison. He claimed he buried the million in cash he received from Starwood. He and agent St. Pierre dug up half the property around Patout's residence in Maurice. The money was

233

never located. He currently lives in his old residence on the Vermilion Bayou which he had purchased with drug proceeds.

****

Before the investigation was over, there would be one hundred eighty-seven indictments. Forty-two would plead guilty. Only twenty-three were eventually tried. After the dust settled, only a handful of suspects were actually convicted. As quoted in the United States v. Ellender-AtlLaw, "The low ratio of convictions to the number of defendants tried, plus the very small sentences against those convicted, best demonstrate the flaw in the government's apparent assumption that 'bigger is better' in this type of proceeding."

****

The Baton Rouge Morning Advocate stated, "The trial was a public failure, a flogging for government attorneys."

****

News releases subsequent to the Bulldog investigation issued by the U. S. Attorney's office in Lafayette made no mention of the participation of the Louisiana State Police Narcotics Section. Assets seized as a result of the investigation included in excess of two million, two hundred thirty-five thousand dollars in cash, a three hundred fifty thousand dollar boat, one hundred twenty-eight thousand dollars in gold, hundreds of guns, Porsches, Ferraris, and other vehicles and property.

****

None of the assets were shared with the Louisiana State Police.

About the Author

Roy Frusha is a former Marine officer, Vietnam veteran, and high school English teacher. He served 24 years in the Louisiana State Police, during which time he completed DEA Basic and Advanced, Police Management from Northwestern University in Evanston, IL, and the prestigious FBI National Academy in Quantico, VA.

He is the recipient of numerous awards, including the LSP Meritorious Service Award, Sons of the American Revolution Commendation Medal, and the Veterans of Foreign Wars Life Saving Medal. Frusha and his wife of 30 years reside in Lafayette, LA.

Visit Roy Frusha online at http://www.royfrusha.com

Bales of marijuana discovered inside the barge.

Another view of the marijuana LSP discovered in the barge.

The smaller boat is Louisiana State Police

From left to right: Hal Hutchins, Chris Owens, Harvey Duplantis, Buzzy Trahan, William "Bill" Stout, Brad Breaux, Grady Thibodeaux, Kenneth Bailey, Roy Frusha, Bryan Zerangue, Tommy "Hollywood" Romero, Bert Berry, Suzanne Chaillot (Air National Guard), Unknown (Air National Guard)